NOTHIN

REMAINS

A Clara Reynolds Thriller

Colin Anthony

Table of Contents

Chapter 1

Clara Reynolds surfaced in a tangle of sweat and sheets, her pulse still jacked high and tight from the dream. She clawed at consciousness, groping for the last shrieked syllable of her brother's voice before it slipped beneath the surface. Lost, like him. Her skin was clammy and her hands shook.

For a moment she believed she was at her apartment in Omaha, then the ceiling of Emma Hinton's guest bedroom met her with the same cottage-white blandness it had last night. She listened to the pulse in her ear until it faded.

She sat up, untwisting the duvet. The digital clock on the nightstand declared 7:13 AM. Her phone was facedown next to it, charging from a wall adapter she'd borrowed from Emma's husband, Russ. There were no missed texts or calls. The Bureau had gone radio silent since her forced leave, which in its own way was more disconcerting than the bureaucratic whirlwind that came before.

She drew her knees to her chest. Her brother's scream echoed in the hollow behind her ribs. Alex, who'd been dead almost fifteen years now, was never more alive than when she slept.

1

Clara pushed herself out of bed and stood a moment, barefoot on the chill slats. The house was a ranch style from the late seventies, nothing but cheap carpet and wood paneling, but Emma had dressed the spare room with the unassuming care that suggested both tact and defeat. On the dresser, next to a ceramic lamp, sat a hand-me-down photo frame containing an image of Emma and Clara, both seventeen, both holding Solo cups and grinning with the practiced ferocity of girls who had something to prove.

From below: "Clara?" Emma's voice, filtered through the floorboards. "You up?"

Clara made for the closet and located her jeans and hoodie, which she'd draped over a hanger in an attempt to keep up appearances. She dressed quickly and scrubbed her face at the vanity, where a basket of scented lotions loomed like an accusation. She regarded herself in the mirror, not liking what she saw. The look of defeat.

Emma was in the kitchen, pajama pants tucked into wool socks, a thermal shirt stretched tight across her back. She poured black coffee into a mug, then nudged the ceramic creamer closer to the rim as if it might tempt Clara. The kitchen was clean in the way of households run by people who'd given up on chaos: no toys on the floor, no sticky fingerprints on the fridge, not even a stray crumb on the counter. Clara recognized the discipline and respected it.

"You want eggs?" Emma asked, voice low. The Hinton marriage had not yet produced children, but Emma cooked as if it might at any moment.

"Just coffee." Clara tried to make her voice neutral, but it came out rough and sleep-burned.

Emma hesitated, one hand on the French press, then poured a second mug and slid it across the counter. "You okay?"

Clara nodded, then shook her head.

"The harvest festival," Emma said, "are you sure you won't change your mind?"

Clara's lips barely moved. "Probably not," she answered, her voice flat and certain.

"You always loved these kinds of activities," Emma continued, undeterred. "I really thought you'd want to come."

Her voice had the same warmth Clara remembered from childhood, softening the edges of what might otherwise have felt like a nudge or a push. Clara tried to make a convincing excuse, but her mind remained bogged down by thoughts she couldn't let go of, and she said nothing. This time, Emma's smile almost faltered.

"Still," she persisted, "I'll save you a ticket just in case."

"Like I said," Clara repeated. She wasn't trying to be harsh but knew she probably sounded that way. Emma's eyes studied her from across the table, full of concern. A small silence settled between them, the tick of the kitchen clock becoming suddenly audible, an unwelcome metronome counting down the awkward seconds.

"You probably know better than me," Emma said with a bite to her tone. She reached for her mug of coffee, watching Clara from across the table. "But maybe a distraction would do you some good."

Maybe, Clara thought, if distractions ever did any good. She stabbed another piece of cantaloupe and gave Emma the best version of a reassuring nod that she could manage.

"Hey," Emma tried again. "About the case. I know you don't want to talk, but…"

Clara put the fork down, clenched. "But what?"

"Did it have anything to do with Alex?" The question came out softer than Emma likely intended, floating across the table with cautionary warmth.

Clara felt it burn anyway. "How? How could it possibly have anything to do with Alex?" Her chair scraped as she stood, a shriek that broke the quiet.

"Clara." Emma stayed seated, hands drawn to her lap, tentative and still. "I don't mean to pry, but you won't talk to me."

"And how is it your business?" Her voice rose sharper than she meant, and she exhaled to cover it. "I came to get away from this. From questions."

Emma looked at her, gentle and steady. "I don't mean to be pushy. I'm worried, is all."

"I can't do this," Clara snapped. Her pulse picked up, somewhere between anger and escape. She headed for the door.

———

She should never have come to Cedar Hollow, she told herself. What had she expected? The streets were always misted over. The people were as unfamiliar as the never-ending trees to Clara, who had lived the entirety of her life in the wide-open expanses of Texas and Nebraska and found the forests of Oregon to be uncomfortably claustrophobic.

She was already hauling a duffel bag out of the closet when she heard Emma behind her.

"You're really leaving, just like that?" Emma sounded bewildered, then more pleading than Clara had ever heard from her.

"What, you thought I'd stick around for an interrogation?" Clara spun around. She already knew she was being unfair.

5

"You haven't talked about leaving until now," Emma said, careful but still hurt. "We've been friends for—"

"I came for peace and quiet. I didn't come here to make you my therapist." Clara pulled a sweater from the bag, let it drop to the floor. "You don't get it. You don't have to deal with this."

Emma folded her arms, a rare show of steel in her frame. "Maybe not. But I do have to deal with you not talking to me. I thought the whole reason you were here was to reconnect."

Clara slumped onto the bed. The corners of her eyes burned. "You think I like it like this?" She heard the break in her voice and hated it. "Emma, I can't do this right now. Really."

Emma's stance softened, though a line stayed creased in her brow. "Maybe I don't know what's going on, but that's why you're here, isn't it? To figure it out?"

Clara's resolve cracked. She knew Emma was right. When she'd arrived two weeks ago, it had seemed like a refuge from her troubles, a chance to lick her wounds and figure herself out. Now she wasn't sure she could put in that work.

Friends since they were children growing up in the middle of Texas, the two women had grown quite different. Tall with an athletic build perfect for an FBI agent, the recent dark circles under her eyes

6

and tension in her shoulders nevertheless made Clara appear older than her thirty-one years. Even away from the job she hadn't let go of her brusque, focused intensity. Emma, meanwhile, had filled out ever so slightly as she'd fully settled into the stability of the small-town wife with the part-time bookkeeping job for years now.

They stared each other down, as if waiting to see who would concede first. Emma spoke. "You need more time."

Clara shook her head. "I don't know what I need."

"I'd say," Emma sighed, sitting next to her, "but you're not listening anyway." She reached over, gave Clara's hand a brief squeeze, one that tried too hard to reassure.

"Like I said, I'm worried about you."

Clara shifted on the bed, uncomfortable with how much warmth it almost let in. "You always have been."

"You always confided in me," Emma said. "I used to feel like you needed me that way, that you'd fall apart otherwise. You know, the only hesitation I had about moving here was losing touch with you. And that's exactly what happened. I was so glad when you reached out. I'm sorry about the circumstances, but I'm not sorry that you're here. I

7

just wish I could help. I shouldn't have brought up Alex."

Clara flinched. "In a way everything is always about him. I still think about him every single day. But…"

"Then stay until you're ready to open up," Emma said.

"I told you," Clara began, already feeling herself retreat.

"Or at least until you really feel ready to go back," Emma interrupted.

Silence settled, broken only by Clara's thoughts warring with each other. She stood again, more slowly this time. "I just need to take a walk," she said.

Clara zipped the bag shut, leaving the contents inside.

———

Clara shouldered her way outside, fog weaving through the leaves and into her skin. The town was a hush of shadows and echoes. Every footstep fell softer than she expected, deadened by distance and damp. There was no escape from the endless trees, and they felt more suffocating every day.

She had been wrong to come to Cedar Hollow, to think that hiding away here was going to help her come to terms with the mess she'd made of herself. Her whole career had been wrong, maybe, but she'd wanted it so much she'd convinced herself otherwise. How could something she wanted so much feel like such a trap?

Emma's question about Alex stuck with her like burrs on her skin. The case had nothing to do with him, of course, but she knew her failure was wound tight around his name. The word that got at the center of it—the knot of her own mistakes.

If she was no good at this, she was no good at anything, she told herself. Every time she closed her eyes she saw the disappointment etched on Bryant's face when he'd suggested she take some time away. She should make this leave permanent and quit the FBI. That was probably what he wanted anyway—only he preferred her to reach that conclusion on her own.

Start fresh. Do something else. But what else was there?

———

The morning seemed darker than it should, the thick air suffocating sound and smothering light. As she moved, her breath joined the mist that curled across the ground. She imagined herself folding into it, disappearing.

9

She reached the trailhead, its sign slick and unreadable with damp. The gravel crackled underfoot. The woods seemed to menace her, each Douglas fir standing sentry against her intrusion. Clara was halfway up the hill, unsure how long she'd been walking. She was emptying herself, maybe. Making room for decisions. Leave the Bureau? Stay?

Time bled into itself here, more so than in the office where days passed unnoticed and lost. Where she forgot what it was to leave work behind. If this was what free time felt like, maybe she'd been better off before.

She found a weathered bench, drenched in a thick, opaque air that clung to everything it touched. She sat, enveloped in the shroud, until the cold seeped into her very core, leaving her unable to focus on anything but her own heavy breathing. Her legs throbbed with a dull ache, and her hands grew numb as she rubbed her temples with a growing sense of frustration and futility. The chill air bit at her cheeks, leaving them tinged with a rosy hue, as the dampening gloom wrapped around her like an ethereal cloak.

She stood and began walking again, feeling the gravity of her choices in the mud that slowed her progress. The trail bent away from the main loop, narrowing and twisting like a scar. This wasn't how her career was supposed to go. It was the hardest part to admit—that she was never really cut out for the

FBI in the first place. Just because you want something bad enough doesn't mean you'll be good at it.

It was supposed to be simple: you take a leave of absence, you go home, you let the world recede as you get your bearings, then you go back. She couldn't face going back to her parents' house, so she'd looked up her old friend and jumped at the chance to disappear in the trees of the Pacific Northwest. So different from the monotonous landscape she was used to.

The official Bureau line was that she was welcome to return, but that was just a euphemism for invisible ink. She knew she'd been written out already. Her badge—an artifact now, tucked in her suitcase with its cheap laminate sheen—felt lighter each week she was away, as if the authority it imparted had always been an illusion.

She walked, each step a negotiation with rocks and mud that would delight in tripping her up should she lose herself too much in her thoughts. The sound her feet made was muffled, and the trail itself—a vein of churned leaf litter and half-buried gravel— meandered deeper than she would have imagined.

It was a strange thing to be haunted by a life that, from the outside, seemed so successful. Right now, each bend in the trail felt like the next stage of some exercise in humiliation: here's where you ignored the obvious clue, here's where you told the victim's mother you'd find answers, here's where you said "trust me" and meant it.

She wasn't even angry, not really. It was more like resignation, a reluctant acceptance of her own mediocrity. The Bureau made you think everything could be forgotten, that every failed case was just paperwork to file. Then you started over on the next one unscathed. But she knew the difference. Some things were permanent. Some things you couldn't bury.

She wasn't sure how long she walked—ten minutes, half an hour, more—but eventually the trees thinned and the ground leveled off. She paused, listening. In the distance, maybe a hundred yards ahead, she heard the faintest echo of a voice, or maybe just the suggestion of one—the woods flexing their old habit of making you believe in ghosts.

Her thighs were burning now, the cold sinking through her jeans, and she shoved her hands deeper into her pockets, feeling the outline of her old Bureau lanyard pressed against her hip. She wondered if Emma knew—really knew—how broken she was, or if Emma just needed to believe in someone else's salvation.

She kicked at a stone, sending it skittering off the trail. It felt good, that tiny pointless act. The kind of thing she used to do as a kid. She closed her eyes and tried to summon up some resolve, some idea of purpose. Nothing came.

And still, she couldn't bring herself to walk back to Emma's. Not yet.

————

Clara saw the body immediately—a shape slumped against the world in a way only the dead could be. She found herself hoping against hope that her eyes were playing tricks on her. Her feet were moving before her mind caught up, the years of training propelling her forward, but it was her own voice she heard screaming: stop, stop, stop. A young girl, seventeen or eighteen most likely. Clara knelt, her own pulse ringing as the small wrist confirmed what she already knew. Her gaze traveled upward, halted at the tree, at the strange markings. She shivered.

The young face was frozen, eyes empty of everything but mist and dread. A scarf was wrapped around her neck, the edges worn and dirty. Clara's stomach twisted as she noticed the fabric was tightly knotted, digging into skin, and it took all her will to examine the rest. Shoes scuffed and caked with mud. Thin jacket, not enough for the weather. The body was cold and stiff—likely dead since the previous evening.

Clara sat back on her heels. A sound escaped her throat, something between a gasp and a sob.

————

She stood slowly, her entire body protesting. Her head pounded with the familiar questions. Who? Why? How? A bad case and a leave of absence, yet here she was, right back in the middle of it. She circled the scene, her instincts taking over despite her own resistance. The scarf and how it was wrapped. The girl. Young, white. Local? Runaway? Abduction?

Clara couldn't make herself leave, so she stayed by the body and stared at the tree, at the symbols cut into the bark. They were sharp, geometric, almost mathematical in their precision. There was nothing organic about them—no wild slashing or frenzied hieroglyphics, just a sequence of angles within a circle, so deliberate it was nearly bureaucratic. She'd heard mention of the old ruins outside of town with strange markings—were these the same?

The low moan of the wind moving through the branches added to the desolation of the scene. Her skin prickled with the sense that she was not alone, that something else lingered here—something more than what she could see. She tried to imagine the girl's final moments. Did she cry out? Did anyone hear? Or had the grey shroud swallowed the sound whole, like everything else in this town?

She looked away, up through the clotted branches toward the sliver of gray sky. If she timed it right, she could get back to Emma's before the clouds broke into rain—before the town woke up and someone stumbled over the body and contaminated the perimeter.

Forcing herself to move, she started back down the trail, each step adding to the growing weight in her chest. Was she running away from this? Running toward it? There was nothing that made sense anymore.

She paused at the split trail. There was a moment, a brief hesitation, where she contemplated turning left and veering off to the overlook, never telling anyone what she saw. Just let the process work as it was supposed to. But already her phone was in her hand. Her thumb hovered over the call icon. She hesitated, suddenly aware of her own breath fogging the phone's screen. She didn't want to be the one to report it, didn't want to be pulled back into the undertow. But the alternative was worse.

She dialed.

The act of reporting it did not bring relief. Instead, it was as if a timeline had forked, and Clara was forced to walk both paths at once. One version of her returned to Emma's, drank tea, pretended to be a civilian. The other was already reconstructing the last hours of the girl's life, replaying every mistake, every missed sign. She couldn't remember the last time she was able to stop thinking about a case, even if that case wasn't hers.

She pressed on down the path, a desperate need for distance mixed with an insistent pull to return. It wouldn't leave her alone. Cedar Hollow, the girl, Alex—the whole damn mess she thought she'd left behind. All one thing. She told herself again she wasn't going to get involved. It had nothing to do with her.

She wished she could believe it.

Chapter 2

A shadow of coffee sloshed in Clara's mug. It was as stale as the air inside the small-town station, but she drank it down anyway. She sat across from the local sheriff, Luke Fisher, recounting the same facts she'd repeated three times: Girl, late teens. Found on the trail. Scarf. Markings on the tree. His pad collected notes; his eyes collected Clara.

"Special Agent Clara Reynolds, FBI, then?" She nodded. "You're leaving it to us, though?" She knew she should. She should leave Cedar Hollow altogether.

"Yes," she said. Her voice was a half measure. "It's not my business. Anyway, I'm on leave."

"We'll do our best, but a case like this..." The sheriff let it hang in the air, something unspoken between them.

She watched him. No flash of a badge, no mention of jurisdiction, just the bare facts. "We don't see things like this around here, not for a while. Town's grown some but..." he trailed off. "We could use someone with your expertise," he said, scribbling on the pad.

She laughed, harsh and too loud. "Expertise?"

"Someone like you on this, we might stand a chance. Help us," he urged. "Unofficially."

It sat there, gnawing at her resolve, tugging her closer to where she shouldn't be.

"You're a long way from Omaha," he mentioned. She was tired of this line of questions too.

Clara shifted in her seat, a flare of tension across her shoulders. It felt too much like it used to, before the Bureau pulled her from the field. The sheriff had a presence to him, calm and unshakeable, his eyes pinning her in place without ever seeming forceful. It was disarming, a soft-spoken insistence that she wasn't ready for. Her own gaze flitted to the wall, to the closed door, to anywhere else.

The sheriff sat across from her in a posture that managed both patience and subtle pressure. He was shaped like every other small-town lifer, with a wind-burned face, iron-grey stubble, and a uniform shirt that couldn't decide if it fit. But it was the way he held still, unmoving except for the occasional dip of his pen, that set him apart from the cops she usually dealt with. He didn't use silence as a weapon, just let it roll, gentle but persistent.

The door was only a meter away, but the office was cramped, the walls all crowded with decades of jurisdictional pride: small plaques for community service, a shelf of battered trophies, a blown-up aerial photograph of Cedar Hollow from the seventies—a town frozen in time, barely changed.

"Wasn't expecting this when I came here," she said. Her voice sounded small in the drab office.

He gestured with his chin toward the file on the desk. "You know, we used to have a saying out here. Nothing beneath the pines but secrets and shadows. I always figured it was townie nonsense. But that girl, what happened... It's like the past is trying to claw its way back in."

Clara looked up. She saw something raw there, something she'd learned to spot in others but never in herself: the palpable, unvarnished uncertainty of being in over your head. It was oddly comforting.

It took Clara a moment to find words. She tried to convince herself she could forget what she saw. The markings on the tree floated back into her mind. "You sure you have the resources?" she asked.

"Resources?" His eyes crinkled, amused. "The state police'll send a couple of detectives out, but they'll bolt as quickly as they can. Best we can hope for is keeping the locals from tearing each other apart. Like I said, a case like this..."

They fell silent, the weight of expectation between them. She should have refused, walked away, but instead she imagined the girl's face, eyes still and glassy. How was it that one body on a cold forest trail seemed to matter so much?

"I'm sorry," she said. She wanted to mean it.

The sheriff leaned back in his chair, still watching her. "I don't believe you. It's too hard to just walk away, isn't it?"

A pause. A war within herself. She already knew which side won. "Yes," she finally admitted. "But I can't promise anything."

He smiled. It was an honest smile, one that expected nothing more than what she'd already offered. "Thank you. Truly."

Clara shifted again. There was no relief in this, no comfort, only a pull that dragged her deeper into a place she was supposed to be hiding from. What did she expect? She should've known better. Of course it would follow her here. Her failure.

"You must be curious about who she is," Fisher's voice cut into her thoughts.

"Local girl?"

"Name was Lila Hays." His expression turned grim. "Only seventeen."

"Seventeen," Clara echoed. Her stomach twisted.

"Coroner says she was killed between 8 p.m. and 12 a.m. We didn't even know she was missing." The sheriff looked pained as he said it. "Not until you..."

She closed her eyes, the image of the young face already burned there. A sense of the inevitable tugged at her.

"Parents say she wasn't into anything bad. She wasn't seeing anyone. Best as they knew, she worked her shift at the café and didn't come home." He watched Clara's reaction.

"I should have just filed the report and left," Clara muttered to herself. She felt the edges of her resolve fraying.

"Maybe," Fisher said gently. "But it's better this way."

For a moment she wanted to believe it.

The clock ticked its hollow echo. Her silence stretched into something she might've called acceptance. The ghost of her mistakes didn't feel so far away anymore. She stood. "You have my number."

Fisher gave her a knowing nod. "And I know where you're staying."

She almost smiled, but it's too thin, too brittle. As she stepped into the haze outside, her mind returned to Lila Hays. And Alex. It always came back to him.

———

The next day Clara is was approaching the front steps of the police station when Fisher found her. He moved like a man carrying a heavy thing, careful and urgent at once.

"A girl's come forward," he said, trying to keep pace with Clara's refusal to look back. It slowed her to a stop.

"How? We just made the announcement," she said.

"Cecilia Day. Lila's best friend."

"Probably knows something, then." Clara's mind shifted to what this meant for the investigation. It was too fast, but she's seen stranger things.

"She said it was John Mills," Fisher told her as they enter the station.

"Boyfriend?" Clara asked.

"Rumors, maybe. The parents said it was news to them."

"What do you think?" Clara's curiosity rose with the first crack in the case.

"Cecilia's sure it's him. It's a solid lead." He nodded at the interview room. "Should we?"

She met his gaze, one last pretense of hesitation. It vanished as they walked into the room. Cecilia sat fidgeting with the hem of her shirt. She was small, like she wanted to be unnoticed. The moment Clara and Fisher entered, she looked up, defiant.

There was a sour, nervous energy in the room. Cecilia's sneaker tapped a metronome against the tile, relentless. Clara noticed the crusted red at the girl's cuticles, the old bruises up the forearm—nothing suspicious, just the catalogue of adolescence—yet it lingered in her mind.

"You know who killed Lila?" Clara opened, choosing her words carefully.

"Yeah," Cecilia replied. "I do."

Fisher took a seat, nodded for Clara to join. "John Mills," he said.

Cecilia's eyes darted between them. "It was him," she insisted, though her voice trembled.

Clara read the reluctance in Cecilia's eyes, the doubt in her voice. It reminded her of all the shaky witnesses she'd ever interviewed. The stories that never added up.

"How do you know?" Clara asked, measuring every inflection.

Cecilia's chin jutted forward. "I just know."

Clara felt a familiar rush, the thrill of being back on a case. But suspicion tempered it. "Why would he do it?"

"They were dating. He's crazy," Cecilia said, her words more emotional than factual.

"We need specifics," Fisher said.

"I...I..." The girl seemed panicked, unsure of herself. "I just thought I'd point you in the right direction."

Clara exchanged a glance with Fisher. He knows the look. They'd both seen enough false leads. Clara doesn't want to get excited over something flimsy. But they'll check it out.

"What are you thinking?" Clara asked as they stepped out.

"Girl knows more than she's saying." Fisher rubbed his chin. "Thinks it's her fault somehow. The way she talks. We should follow up."

Clara nodded. She'd only been away from this world a few weeks and she felt the rhythm coming back. "John Mills?"

"Nineteen," Fisher confirmed. "Just graduated last year. Works at Kane Construction with his dad, he'll be a lifer there. Best get back to it."

"You're eager." Clara's teasing masked her own eagerness.

"I like having you around, FBI or not." Fisher smiled.

Cecilia waited in the room, eyes narrowed as Clara and Fisher reenter. "Thought you didn't believe me," she accused.

"We're listening," Fisher assured her.

She doesn't look convinced but leaned forward, eager to speak.

"You said John's the one. But her family says she wasn't dating anyone." Clara's voice was steady, probing.

"She was," Cecilia snapped. "But he was bad news."

Fisher glanced at Clara, a look that says this is worth hearing out. "You think he'd hurt her?" he asked.

Cecilia paused, uncertainty creeping in. She recovered quickly. "He did hurt her," she insisted. "He killed her."

"You seem pretty sure," Clara said, pushing just enough to see if Cecilia breaks. "Did Lila tell you something? Did you see something?"

The girl hesitated, her fidgeting more pronounced. "I don't know. Maybe. I heard them fighting."

"What did they fight about?" Clara pressed, leaning in.

"He wanted her to quit school. Didn't want her going off to college next year."

Clara nodded slowly, pieces falling together, though they're still jumbled and incomplete.

"Where did you hear them?" Fisher asked.

Cecilia hesitates again. "At her house. He'd sneak over when her parents were asleep." Her voice drops, suddenly small. "I told her he was bad for her. I told her to end it."

Clara studied the girl, sees her struggle, the weight she places on herself. Her instinct said that Cecilia believes she's right, whether she actually is or not.

"We'll talk to him," Fisher said, standing. "See what he has to say."

Cecilia nodded, showing some relief. "You'll see," she told them. "He did it. I know he did."

Outside the room, Clara exhaled sharply. "What do you think?" she asked.

"Not a complete story," Fisher admitted. "But enough there to push on."

"More than I expected this early," Clara conceded. "Let's do it."

Fisher nodded. "I'll make some calls."

She felt her old instincts kicking in, sharper than they've been in months. "When do we start?"

"As soon as you're ready," Fisher said, heading for the phone.

"Already was," Clara muttered to herself. But there was no denying that she was fully back into it now. Cecilia's words, fragile as they seem, have drawn her all the way in.

———

John Mills looked Clara in the eyes. A challenge or an honest gesture. She wasn't sure yet. "Did you know?" she asked. "About Lila?"

John hung his head low and face was raw and unreadable.

"Not until I heard the neighbors talking." His face betrayed a disbelief at the situation. "I didn't hurt her," he added.

Clara listened for the note of guilt or fear. She's learned that the innocent sound just like the guilty. She'd learned not to trust what she hears.

"Were you two together?" Fisher jumped in. John's head lifted. Clara waited for the denial.

"We were." John didn't flinch.

"She hid it from her family," Clara said.

He breathed out slowly. "They wouldn't have understood."

Fisher kept a steady gaze. "And why is that?"

"We were serious." John sounded like he's trying to convince himself as much as them. "I loved her."

"So what happened?" Clara pressed.

"She wanted to slow things down until she went to college." He was earnest, almost too earnest. "Said we'd make it work."

Clara felt the holes in his story. "But you wanted something else. You wanted her to stay."

He swallowed, nodded. "But not like that." John looked her straight in the eyes again. "I didn't see her that night."

"The night she died," Clara pointed out. "You expect us to believe that?"

"She was working, I was working." His voice broke a little. "Said we'd talk this weekend."

"We have a witness," Fisher prodded. "Says you killed her."

Clara watched his reaction, searching for the crack.

His surprise seemed genuine, but she couldn't be sure.

He shouted. "The fuck? Someone's trying to set me up."

Clara sensed a shift, a change in his demeanor. "You said you were working," she said, moving the conversation forward.

"Yes." John latched on to the topic, relieved to leave Cecilia behind. "At the new church site. Four to eleven. You can ask my boss."

"We will," Fisher assured him.

"Seems late," Clara pointed out.

"Overtime," he shrugged. "Kane wants it done yesterday; he's buddy-buddy with the priest."

———

John's father was the first to show. A weary-looking man, brow furrowed with either worry or mistrust, Clara wasn't sure which.

"Kid's been pulling long shifts all week," Trevor Mills told them. "Picked him up late Wednesday. Worked til eleven, maybe later. Went straight home and he passed out immediately. I'd a heard if he made a sound."

"Who else can verify that?" Clara asked, withholding doubt.

"The whole crew," Trevor said.

29

"Get us some names." Clara pushed, though her instincts told her the alibi will hold. Her instincts have failed her before.

"We'll talk to them," Fisher said, scribbling down the info. He caught Clara's eye. "I think we're good here."

John fit the part, big guy, tough-looking, but Clara knew better than to trust appearances. She knew she should still walk away, knew she wouldn't.

————————

A few more questions, a few more probing looks, and they had everything they need. Names, numbers, statements that they'll confirm soon enough. "You're free to go, John," Fisher told him.

John stood, relief in his posture, though his face is clouded with confusion and grief. Trevor gave him a reassuring clap on the shoulder, a gesture of solidarity, and they left together.

"Think he's telling the truth?" Fisher asked once they're gone.

Clara crossed her arms, deep in thought. "Don't know yet."

"Pretty solid story," Fisher said.

"He could have left the house again that night. Dad could be covering for him."

"Maybe, but Lila was done work at seven and didn't go home. What was she doing for over four hours before he shows up?"

"I don't like dropping him so fast," Clara admitted. "But it doesn't add up. What do you make of John? Is he capable of something like this?"

"He is known as something of a hot head. Would it be the biggest surprise in the world? Probably not, but that doesn't mean anything." Fisher placed a hand on her shoulder, the weight of it heavier than he intends. "We'll see what shakes out."

She knew he was right. "It's always the husband or boyfriend. If not him," Clara asks, "then who?"

"We'll figure it out," Fisher replied. But his words did little to comfort Clara, who knew she shouldn't be involved in this in the first place. The FBI wouldn't be happy if they found out what she was doing. That she couldn't help herself wasn't an acceptable excuse and this really would be the end of her career. As they leave the station, the mist wraps around her like doubt, clinging and inescapable.

Chapter 3

The fog was thick this far from town, chewing away what little resolve Clara had left. She hadn't planned on going to the old ruins while in town. She had no real interest in that kind of stuff. Now she had no choice but to see what all the fuss was about. She had to admit the markings on the tree above Lila's body creeped her out, even as her instincts told her it was probably a misdirection meant to distract the investigation.

She felt Fisher's anticipation more than she saw it, an unspoken challenge to see how deep she'd let herself get. He led her through trees with the practiced steps of someone who had walked this way countless times. As she walked Clara kept thinking how strange it felt not to have her gun at her hip.

The path narrowed, the woods thick with damp and shadows. Clara hadn't said a word since the station. Fisher kept quiet as well, as if testing how long her silence would last. "Curious, aren't you?" he finally asked as they arrived. His voice was easy, not the push she expected.

"Can't help myself," Clara said. She saw through his approach, the same subtle insistence he'd used before. It made her want to push back, but the pull of the symbols was stronger.

He halted at the boundary of a clearing, where jagged rocks jutted from the earth in eerie, almost unnatural formations. The surfaces of these stones were etched with the same cryptic symbols that Clara had noticed earlier on the bark of a tree. Her heart began to race at the sight, a mix of excitement and trepidation coursing through her veins.

She scanned the marks. "Same as what I saw on the tree. Some of them."

"Ornate. Deliberate. But never decoded." His words lingered between them, almost like a dare. "We've got a few theories."

Clara kneeled to examine the carvings more closely, her curiosity slipping past her resistance. "These other symbols," she pointed to a cluster on another stone. "I didn't see these on the tree. How old is this anyway?"

"A couple hundred years, maybe. That's what some people say. Suppose to be completely unique, not seen anywhere else."

"You'd think it'd be more well known then," Clara said. "Outside the town, I mean."

"Some folks get interested from time to time. Then they usually declare it a hoax and leave. Because they can't make heads or tails of it, some of the locals say."

"What do you think?"

"Always thought it'd be funny if it was just the doodling of a bored teenager. They must have had those back then too. All I know is it's a touchy subject around here. Most don't really care but those that do won't let it die." Fisher's voice had a forced casualness to it, like he was making sure Clara understood the significance without stating it outright.

"Touchy, how?" she asked. She moved among the stones, her unease growing.

"Some of them think we've got our own special little occult reputation, but of course it's no fun to them if it's just long dead history. It can provide an excuse for some people to criticize others they dislike. Especially some of the more prominent members in town. The Harringtons have had run-ins with people accusing them of all kinds of things."

Clara listened, wondering how much of the Sheriff's judgment she could trust.

"Town's been lucky for a while, no new outsiders barging in, nothing boiling over," Fisher said, a shadow crossing his face. "But if this story breaks..." Clara caught the note of desperation he was trying to hide.

"The Harringtons, who are they?"

"Wealthiest family here, have been forever. Own a few of the businesses, a lot of the land. Not as numerous as they once were though. Nowadays it's only Liam who lives at the estate. The others went off to Europe or something like that."

Clara looked away, back to the symbols, back to the lines and curves she couldn't ignore.

"The markings," she asked, breaking the silence she tried to maintain. "Have they ever been associated with a crime scene before?"

Fisher nodded after a while. "You could say that."

Clara furrowed her brow. "Keeping me in suspense?"

"Almost forty years ago. Teenage girl stabbed repeatedly and left by a tree freshly carved with new markings."

"Damn. You could have mentioned this earlier."

He shrugged. "Don't worry, you'll hear all about it. Let's head to the construction site."

———

Fisher was called back to the station, so Clara found herself alone at the new church site. It was much larger than the old church down the street. The foundations marked the edges of power and progress, new concrete at odds with the quiet town around it.

The scent was different here: not the mineral rot of deep forest, but the sharp tang of lime, wet stone, industrial glue. Despite herself, she felt a flicker of admiration. Someone had decided this town needed a cathedral, and somehow—by sheer will or money or both—they were getting one. That was one kind of power.

Father Callahan met her at the site, a man in his mid-sixties with carefully maintained clerical attire that shows signs of age. His smile was more genuine than she trusted. He seemed too eager to show her every detail, too eager to answer questions she hadn't yet asked. Construction dust hung in the air, covering her certainty like a layer she couldn't shake off.

"Agent Reynolds, you found us," he said, wiping his palm on his stole before offering it for a handshake.

Her eyes moved over the skeleton of the new building. A crane loomed like an oversized cross, construction material stacked in precise and pious rows. "Quite an operation." She glanced back at him.

Callahan must have sensed her ambiguity, because his smile faded for a beat. "I know what you're thinking. The old church is barely half full on Sundays. A building three times the size, what sense does it make? I ask myself that every day." He let that hang, waiting to see if she'd bite.

She didn't.

"What brings you here then?" His voice said he knew. His gaze settled on Clara with a curious intensity.

"A girl was killed. We're looking into it." Clara kept her voice neutral, watching for a crack in the priest's composure.

Father Callahan nodded. "Lila Hays. Tragic." He sighed with dramatic flourish, leading her past stacks of rebar and bags of concrete. "I heard you found her."

"You hear a lot then," Clara said.

"A town this size, you know." He let the implication hang. She wondered if his willingness to talk was strategic or naive. Maybe both.

"Lila's boyfriend works here. Was he on shift that night?" Clara scanned the site for anyone matching John's description.

"Trevor's boy, John? I believe so. They're working long hours, pushing to finish." He looked pleased with the construction's pace. "But you'd know more about his schedule than me."

Clara noted his evasiveness. It didn't seem hostile, but there was more to the priest than she first thought. If he knew John was Lila's boyfriend, then he really did know a lot about what's happening in Cedar Hollow.

"Rumors," Father Callahan continued, dropping his voice as if sharing a secret, "spread faster than the gospel around here. Much to my chagrin, mind you."

Clara fixed him with a look.

His eyes twinkled with something she couldn't pinpoint. "Not much gets past me." They walked toward the emerging frame of the altar, each step unsettling Clara's attempts to appear aloof.

He pointed out details in the architecture, how it would reflect both the town's history and its future. "The older families," he said, voice lowering, "don't take well to change."

"Families like the Harringtons?" Clara prodded.

Father Callahan chuckled. "Yes, they prefer to preserve the past." There was a hint of satisfaction in his tone. "It seems the past has a way of catching up to them."

"Meaning?"

"Oh nothing. They used to be very involved with the church." He spoke with the care of a man who knew when to stop talking. Clara suspected he meant to imply something more.

"I imagine you have theories about those symbols on the ruins?" she asked. Her thoughts returned to the symbols she saw earlier, her curiosity mounting.

The priest adjusted his collar again. "Pagan stuff, certainly," he said, his voice slipping into a more guarded tone.

"I've heard people associate the site with the Harrington family, but I can't quite make out why."

"Ah, yes. Well, there was the whole business with that cult a while back. In the 80s, it was." The priest paused and let out a small chuckle. "Back when I was a young man."

"Tell me about it," Clara prodded.

"A group of outsiders, always hanging around the site. Acting peculiar. Suspicious, more like. No one knew anything about them. People started saying they were a cult who had uncovered the secrets of the ruins."

"Your thoughts?" Clara kept her skepticism visible, an invitation for him to prove her wrong.

Father Callahan spread his hands. "Depends on who you ask. Hard to separate fact from fiction. But as I heard it, the symbols were part of their..." he paused, searching for the right word, "rituals."

"Was there a ritual crime?" Clara asked.

"There was that poor girl, Margaret. Brutally murdered. I'd rather not talk about it if you don't mind. The disturbing thing…" he trailed off.

"The symbols showing up again now," Clara filled in the blanks. "Could they be connected?"

"Hard to say," he told her, though his expression indicated he thought otherwise. "That was a long time ago. But people remember. Some never thought that this cult ever went away." His enthusiasm was unsettling.

"And what does the cult have to do with the Harrington family?" She'd almost forgotten what led them to this topic.

"Rumors, everything rumors. People need someone to blame. Pardon me for being vague but as I said, I don't want to talk about that incident. But it's accurate to say the Harringtons don't get the benefit of the doubt around here."

"Why is that exactly?"

The priest seemed momentarily puzzled, as if he'd never really considered the question before.

"I wonder if I can adequately explain it to you. If you grow up here you're bound to hear people talking. Someone was fired by the Harringtons, someone was denied a loan by the Harringtons, someone's kid was teased by their kids. You never hear of anyone having gained anything by their association with the Harringtons."

"They breed resentment around here."

"Yes, that's exactly it! There are not many people around here who wouldn't be happy to see that family get some comeuppance."

"Perhaps that explains the markings on the tree then?" Clara wondered.

"How so?"

"Let's say someone commits a crime of passion. They realize they will be the prime suspect and start to panic, until they realize how easy it is to use the local boogeyman to shift the focus away from themselves."

She watched his expression shift; he clearly found the notion farfetched.

"They would have had to be very familiar with the symbols," he said.

"Do you think this cult from the past could still be active," she said.

He didn't miss a beat. "It's possible. Something like that leaves a mark that's hard to scrub away. I've heard things, but I didn't want to believe them."

"You hear a lot," Clara said, echoing her earlier sentiment.

41

"Not as much as you think," he sighed deeply. "People aren't as involved in the church as they used to be." He pointed at the construction around them. "But I hope the new church will show them we're not a relic."

"Thank you for your time, Father," Clara said, made to leave.

"May I ask what brings you to Cedar Hollow in the first place?" he asked with a little too much force.

"Visiting an old friend," she said.

"I've learned to tell when people are lying," he stared at her. "Much like you can."

She met his eyes but gave no indication he'd hit a mark.

"I don't mean to press," he continued. "But I've found it's easier to let the truth out than keep it in. You're welcome to come back for confession if you'd like."

Clara absorbed his words with a mixture of suspicion and intrigue. She knew the type, but she couldn't quite read him yet.

"I may be back," she replied vaguely.

"You'll find," he said as they returned to where they started, "people are eager to unearth the past, especially when it was never buried properly."

Clara left the site, his words ringing in her ears. The priest had given her more than she expected, but it was less than the whole story. The mention of a cult, the Harringtons, and the rumors all spun around her mind. It seemed to all tie into the death of another girl. She needed the details but it was too late to go back to the police station right now.

The path back to Emma's seemed longer than before, and every step weighed heavier. She couldn't shake the feeling that the priest had let her go too easily, that she was walking into something bigger than she knew.

———

Clara returned to Emma's, her thoughts frayed by the day's discoveries. It felt too easy to sink into a soft chair and lose herself in the oppressive vapor that refused to let her go. She found Emma and Russ at the table, quiet and steady, their comfort almost unnerving.

Russ looked up with a gentle smile, but Clara couldn't manage more than a thin reply. "Heard anything about cults lately?" she asked. Emma's surprised laugh echoed through the room.

"That's an odd way to say hello," Emma said, pouring Clara a cup of coffee.

Russ shifted, unsure whether to join the conversation or wait.

Clara stirred her coffee, watching the dark swirl as if it might reveal something. "I was at the new church ground. Father Callahan mentioned some... interesting things."

Emma hesitated. Russ looked at her, curious but waiting for her to speak first. "Go on," Emma said, sounding as if she might regret asking.

"You already know." Clara leaned in, feeling the distance between her world and theirs grow as she said it. Emma's expression was guarded.

Russ rubbed his chin. "Folks have stories, but..." He trailed off as Emma picked up the thread.

"People love to talk," Emma replied, evasive. "It's a small town. Rumors are our biggest export." She tried to sound dismissive, but Clara saw the tension.

"Lila's death." Clara's persistence sharpened. "It's similar to something that happened forty years ago?"

Emma seemed taken aback by the directness, but she shouldn't have been. She knew Clara well enough. "There was a murder a while back, before any of us were born. But if you live in this town long enough you can't escape it."

Clara's interest piqued. "Same story?" She felt a familiar thrill, the kind she used to live for.

Russ nodded. "Margaret Dooley. She was William Harrington's girlfriend. He was the heir to the family. Liam's uncle. Her body was found next to a tree carved with symbols."

Clara's mind raced, connecting the pieces.

"They blamed some cult back then," Emma said. "But who knows."

Clara leaned back, pondering. "People think the Harringtons were connected to the cult?"

"Nobody knows for sure." Russ looked to Emma for guidance. "But a lot of people thought so."

"They never proved it," Emma interjected.

Clara stared into her cup. It was all too similar. She knew it could be simple misdirection, but forty years is a long time ago even if the town hadn't forgotten. It could be some kind of message.

"William?" she asked. "What happened to him?"

"Disappeared," Emma said. "Soon after."

"Convenient." Clara sat in thought. "Russ, you grew up here. Do you think the Harringtons are an evil, cult leader, murderous family?"

"Well, hmm, when you put it like that, I mean…" Russ seemed unsure how to answer.

"Just give me your honest opinion."

"OK fine. I don't really know about the cult thing, that was before my time. But growing up I was always warned by my parents and grandparents to keep a wide berth of the Harringtons. If one of them were to talk to me, I wasn't supposed to say anything. My grandmother especially seemed really spooked by them."

"Any reason?" Clara asked.

"I asked my father once, when I was older. He told me that my grandmother's next-door neighbor when she was a child, a boy around her age, disappeared one day. They found him a few weeks later, deep in the woods, looking like he'd been mauled by some kind of animal. Except that's not what most people believed happened. They thought the Harringtons had taken him and done something terrible to him in the woods. Kind of a crazy conclusion to jump to when you think about it." Russ paused, lost in thought.

"Clara," Emma said suddenly. "Why are you involved? I thought you wanted to get away from police work." Her voice was shaky, frustration blending with concern.

"I know," Clara replied. "But this might be my chance."

"Your chance?" Emma looked incredulous. "At what?"

"Redemption," Clara whispered, more to herself than to them. The word hung in the air, raw and telling. She hated the vulnerability of it.

Russ cleared his throat, a steadying presence amidst the tension. "We're here to help," he said simply.

It was meant to be reassuring, but it pressed harder on Clara's uncertainty. She felt herself splitting between the need to prove she wasn't a failure and the need to keep from losing more than she already had.

The talk turned softer, more cautious. They walked on eggshells around her, knowing she was already pulling away again. Clara heard their voices, but her mind was already on the case, on the clues that haunted her thoughts. They didn't understand. They couldn't.

Chapter 4

Clara's rental car barely settled on the gravel drive when the Harrington estate loomed up to meet her with an imposing stare, as if every malicious thing said about the family was barely scratching the surface. Two stories of hand-chiseled granite, a roofline jagged with gables and spires, and a front façade so aggressively symmetrical it recalled the bleached jaws of a predator. The mansion stood like a monument to the family's dominion over Cedar Hollow. Even parked and silent, it radiated hostility— a kind of static charge. She took it in, uneasy in the shadow of so much history.

A pair of columns boxed in the main entrance, each engraved with a different stylized sigil. She'd expected something like the family crest (three stag heads, Latin motto), but these were older, weirder, their curves and angles echoing the strange ruins with the original symbol markings. Clara made a mental note: the Harringtons wanted guests to be unsettled before they even reached the doorbell. She supposed it was working.

This place had its own gravity, pulling at her sense of resolve, unmaking it bit by bit. Her steps were hushed and hesitant as she approached, and the brass bell clanged with a violence that almost startled her into leaving. Almost. She pressed forward instead, guided by the wary eyes of an old housekeeper.

The interior echoed the threatening exterior. Antique furniture and family portraits lined the hallways like sentinels. Subtle displays of wealth peeked through every detail, challenging her presence with quiet confidence. She felt the eyes of the long-dead Harringtons as she passed beneath chandeliers that looked like they belonged in a palace.

The housekeeper led her without a word, a silent judge in this court of opulence. Clara couldn't shake the feeling that this house had seen more than any one person could tell, that it carried secrets as heavy as its ornate architecture.

She tried to keep her breathing steady. The last time she'd been inside a house this expensive, it had been to dust for prints after a murder-suicide. Money didn't buy happiness; maybe it just bought thicker doors to keep the unhappiness in.

Her guide halted at a large oak door, rapped sharply, then turned and left. Clara opened the door herself when she heard the voice from inside calling her in.

The room, like the rest of the house, was a testament to old money's unyielding grip. Liam Harrington sat behind a desk that seemed built for the sole purpose of keeping people at a distance. Probably about mid-forties, she guessed. Tall, broad shoulders, careful tan, with hair gone just gray enough at the temples to project inevitability. The classic picture of old money refinement. His posture was rigid, his expression one of thinly veiled impatience. He did not rise to greet her.

She discerned the practiced impatience of a man who'd built an entire personality around never waiting for anything. He let the silence stretch long enough for her to notice the absence of chairs on her side of the desk. Clara was left to stand, and she did, resisting the urge to fidget.

"You must be Miss Reynolds." His words sounded as routine and impersonal as signing a check, with no courtesy or real interest.

She clocked the way his gaze flicked to her hands and shoes, already tallying up her threat level and finding it, presumably, wanting. "Thank you for meeting with me, Mr. Harrington," she said, her tone measured and free of deference. The man had spent decades as the gravitational center of local rumor, scandal, and wealth; she understood the game well enough to refuse the obvious invitations to intimidation. There were photographs of him at various charity events with governors and senators in the local paper archives, always with that same tense smile affixed to his face like a surgical mask. Present, but not exactly presentable.

He made a show of checking his watch, then steepled his fingers and let out a long, silent breath. "I trust you'll make this brief. I'm quite busy."

Clara suppressed an urge to roll her eyes. She'd interrogated corporate fixers and family patriarchs alike, and this wasn't even in the top ten for choreographed condescension. "I'll get right to the point, then," she replied. "I'm assisting the sheriff's office in their investigation. The Hays murder." She watched the effect: a flicker of muscle beneath his left eye, the smallest hesitation in his practiced, leisurely blink.

"My understanding is that you're not on the case in an official capacity." He said it almost gently, but the barb was there, sheathed in velvet.

"I'm consulting," Clara shot back, letting the word hang in the air. She returned his stare, unblinking. This was the part where most people fumbled or tried to ingratiate. Instead, she watched the subtle shifts in his demeanor—the imperceptible straightening of posture, the recalculation behind the eyes.

"Tell the sheriff I appreciate his tact, not drawing attention by coming here himself. But I don't see how I can help you," Liam said, voice clipped.

"Information," she said. "About Lila Hays, about your family's connection to the ruins, and about certain rumors that have persisted for decades." Clara

51

watched for a reaction and got one: a teeth-on-edge grimace, almost too quick to read.

"I don't know where you're getting your information," Liam said, voice losing some of its measured warmth, "but these stories have been dogging our family since before I was born. Every time something strange happens in Cedar Hollow, people manage to twist it into another Harrington drama." He leaned forward now, as if the desk itself might shield him from the contagion of scandal. "I would have thought a federal agent would be above entertaining small-town gossip."

"Sometimes," Clara replied, "gossip points to the truth." She'd said it before in the course of interviews like these. It sounded like a cliché, but truth did have a tendency to nest in the places people were most eager to overlook.

He regarded her with impatience. "Let me make it clear, Miss Reynolds. We have no involvement with whatever sordid affair this town has decided to place at our door this time."

"But the last time?" Clara asked, testing the limits of his composure.

Liam's irritation surfaced fully now, abandoning his earlier attempt at aloofness. "Tangentially, granted. But the rest is nothing but the overactive imagination of people with nothing better to do."

She didn't let up. "It's hard to sustain forty years of talk on pure conjecture."

His response was quick, rehearsed. "Every few years, someone decides to resurrect these tales. I've learned to ignore them."

"As I understand it there are a lot of similarities between the murder of Margaret Dooley and that of Lila Hays." Clara met his gaze, unblinking.

"I don't know anything about that." Liam's voice held a mix of resignation and anger. "If so it would only suggest William was never the killer to begin with."

"Can I speak with William?" Clara pushed, noting how his posture changed at the name.

His eyes narrowed, and for a brief moment, Clara saw a crack in his defenses. "My uncle left town forty years ago."

"I've heard he went to Europe. Why did he leave?"

"Does it matter?" Liam's irritation flared again. "He didn't want to live under the weight of this town's accusations. Something I can sympathize with."

Clara watched him, the smallest details revealing what words did not. She had touched a nerve. "It would help if you'd cooperate."

Liam shook his head, regaining his cold composure. "The truth is I don't keep in regular contact with the Harringtons over there. We've had certain…disagreements over the years. Do what you must but don't expect me to make it easier for you."

She noted his persistent avoidance of specifics. It was enough to fuel her suspicions, enough to keep her from backing down.

"Let's focus on the present then. I'm an outsider, rumors are all I have to go on right now. You deny them, fine. Perhaps you can point me in another direction. You must know everything that happens in Cedar Hollow."

"I know everything that happens in Cedar Hollow as it relates to business, but my expertise doesn't extend to the goings on of every teenager in town," his impatience flared back up. "Now if you'll excuse me…"

"Maybe not every teenager, but Lila Hays? Do you have any connection to her?"

"No, I'm not familiar with the Hays family. You're wasting your time."

"What about John Mills? There's been an accusation laid against him."

It was quick but Liam's demeanor cracked, spilling curiosity and concern.

"I believe I've met his father a time or two. That family has been here for quite a while. At one time they were pretty well to do I believe." His gaze demanded her to elaborate.

"Lila's boyfriend. Secret boyfriend, actually, it would seem."

"You've already spoken with him, presumably?" he asked, the sharpness in his voice breaking through the cold indifference of moments ago. The name of John Mills had altered his composure, and his expression carried the weight of something more than expectation.

Clara explained about John's alibi, watching as Liam visibly relaxed. His fingers loosened on the armrest, and he eased back into his seat. She'd already seen the opening, though, and it left her with more questions than answers.

The atmosphere of the meeting shifted. Where Liam had been guarded and dismissive, now there was a lingering trace of anxiety, barely masked by his attempt to regain control. Clara noted how quickly he tried to return to his earlier aloofness, but the reaction was there. Clear as the cold tone he'd first greeted her with.

"The alibi looks solid," Clara repeated. "But we're checking it."

"Yes, of course." Liam's voice was careful, strained between relief and irritation. He was again the very image of composure, but Clara saw that he knew he'd given something away.

His earlier dismissiveness wavered, replaced by a flicker of vulnerability that made Clara even more suspicious. She held his gaze, watched the way he struggled to maintain his cold exterior.

"Anything else, then?" He'd unconsciously ceded some deference to her.

Clara stood, the tension in the room hanging like a question unanswered. She turned to leave, not ready to push her luck at this stage.

Liam walked her to the door with a formality that felt more ceremonial than polite, as if completing an ancient rite to keep the wolves beyond the threshold. His voice, when it came, was sanded smooth and cold. "I'd appreciate if you'd leave my family out of your investigation unless you have actual evidence."

He paused, and the closing words hung in the vestibule with the weight of something unspoken—an expectation, a warning, or perhaps the hope that Clara was as easy to dismiss as the others who had come before her. The stare he gave her was more than polite courtesy; it was a calculated threat, one sharpened by a century of embattled family legacy.

On the drive, the air was thicker, the silence of the estate suddenly amplified by the muted closing of the Harrington door behind her. For a moment she stood on the stoop, waiting for the sound of retreating footsteps, but none followed. She closed the collar of her coat against the sudden chill; even the fog seemed to hesitate at the border of Harrington property, uncertain whether it was welcome.

She found herself retracing the entire interview: the initial impatience, the carefully measured responses, the practiced irritation at "small-town gossip" that snapped instantly into a controlled panic at the mention of the Mills family. There had been a beat—just a beat—where his guard had dropped, and the calculation was laid bare. He wasn't afraid of her, not exactly; he was afraid of something else. Something that Clara now suspected ran deeper than public image or inheritance. She'd seen the look before in men who'd spent years managing crisis: a flicker of prey beneath the predator.

From the main house, she could still feel the aura of surveillance. The windows were eyes and the hedges ears, and though she saw no one watching, she was sure that her every movement was being cataloged and fed to some hidden ledger. The Harringtons had spent generations learning how to make people doubt their own instincts, how to deflect and misdirect and turn every simple question into a labyrinth with no center. She'd been warned that the family specialized in obfuscation, but the reality was even thornier than she'd imagined.

Near the end of the gravel drive, she risked a glance back. The house, framed in haze and ancient rhododendrons, seemed even larger in her absence, as though it expanded to fill the space she'd vacated. She had the sense of being escorted off holy ground rather than a family estate, and the thought made her skin crawl in a new way.

Clara got into her car and sat for a moment, pen poised over her notebook but unable to write. The windshield fogged up from her breath, turning the distant hollies and stone pillars into a watercolor blur. Harrington should have been pleased that they already had a suspect in John Mills, but his reaction was more complicated. Perhaps there was a connection between them.

When she passed the iron gates and finally hit asphalt, Clara rolled the window down and let the wet air sting her face. A single light flicked on in the upper floor of the Harrington house, and she caught a glimpse of a silhouette at the window. She couldn't say for certain, but she suspected it was Liam, still keeping watch, still tallying her as part of the day's threats. The house and its owner cast long shadows, and Clara sensed she wouldn't escape them soon.

Chapter 5

Clara could still hear the echo of the Harrington Estate as she sat in the sheriff's office, each tick of the clock biting at her with renewed insistence. The investigation had ground to a halt. Her phone sat stubborn and silent, mirroring Fisher's stare.

"Where are we at?" Clara asked, knowing the answer. She didn't expect the burst of movement as Deputy Jones crashed through the door, urgency breaking the air.

"Kane's making a statement," he panted. Clara's pulse spiked. "Town hall," Jones added, as they rushed out.

———

The town hall was a roiling hive of bodies and voices, every inch of the battered hardwood floor roped off by tripods and the hungry eyes of local press. Even before she shouldered through the vestibule, Clara could taste the sour air. It was as if the entire population of Cedar Hollow had compressed itself to fit within these four walls, all of them vibrating at the same jittery, anticipatory frequency. The percussive whine of an AV tech testing microphones ricocheted off the wood-paneled ceiling, drowning out whispered speculation and the low thrum of civic unrest.

Up front, at the dais, Robert Kane stood alone, flanked by a pair of local business leaders who looked more like nervous groomsmen than civic dignitaries. Kane wore a pressed work shirt with the sleeves meticulously rolled—casual enough to telegraph blue-collar roots, but crisp and branded with the Kane Construction logo, block-lettered across the chest. Even his stubble looked deliberate, cut short enough to signal masculinity, not sloth. Kane's steel-gray hair was combed with the kind of precision Clara associated with the military or high-priced attorneys; his face had an unsettling, movie-villain symmetry.

He set both hands on the lip of the podium, aligning his fingers with the edge as if measuring a cut. He didn't speak immediately. Instead, he let the frisson of expectation build, looking from face to face with a faint, tight-lipped smile. The room seemed to shrink under his attention.

Clara watched his eyes sweep over the audience, making a subtle inventory of potential allies and adversaries. She felt his gaze pass over her, assessing. At her side, Fisher briefly tensed, then resumed his default stoicism. She wondered if he, too, recognized the power play unfolding: this was less a town hall and more an audition for the role of next kingpin.

The press was first to break the silence. The Herald's senior correspondent, a stoop-shouldered man named Bledsoe, angled forward. "Mr. Kane, do you have any comment on the status of the investigation into Lila Hays?"

Kane gestured at the crowd with open palms, inviting them to share his concern. "If only I did," he replied, voice low and melodic, meant to soothe but with a bare edge of threat. "We're all here tonight because we're frightened. We're angry. And frankly, we want answers."

The cameras rolled, their blinking red eyes feeding the tension to a wider audience. Clara heard the whispers rising in the snippets of gossip, the old accusations about the Harringtons, and innuendo about cults and cover-ups. Kane let the murmuring build, then shushed it with a single, measured tap on the microphone. The feedback whined, then stilled.

"I did not know Lila Hays personally," he continued, "but I know what it's like to lose someone to senseless violence. This town is my home. My children's home. I won't stand by as Cedar Hollow is made a punchline on the evening news." He paused, giving the statement time to percolate. Several heads nodded.

Kane continued, "There are those who say we should be patient, let the authorities do their work." The jab was not lost on anyone. "But how many days must we wait for even a single suspect?" He looked directly at Fisher, then at Clara, and the crowd's gaze pinwheeled to follow.

Fisher's lips pressed into a pale line, but he said nothing.

"We will not be bullied into silence," Kane said, voice rising in a controlled crescendo. "We will not let anyone, no matter how wealthy or powerful, intimidate us. Justice for Lila. Justice for all."

The room exploded into applause—raw, unpracticed, but quickly contagious—then subsided to the frantic scribbling of reporters and the hum of a town unsettled. Kane stepped back, allowing the momentum to crest.

It was only as the applause faded that Kane, with a showman's precision, announced, "Effective immediately, I am offering a $50,000 reward for information leading to the arrest of Lila Hays's killer." This set off a fresh eruption of flashbulbs and urgent voices. Clara could feel the heat of attention turn to her, to Fisher, to the entire law enforcement apparatus, which now sat squarely on the defensive.

The effect was instant and powerful, setting the stage for what Clara feared most. She and Fisher exchanged grim looks, knowing exactly what this meant for the investigation. As they left the hall, she glanced back at Kane, his figure towering like a force she couldn't yet reckon with.

———

The police station was loaded with noise and suspicion. The battered linoleum floor had never seen such traffic: boots caked in dirt and splintered with sawdust, scuffed heels of business casual, and the quiet hum of elderly slippers. All converged on the front desk, where the thin veneer of order threatened to buckle under the weight of the day's hysteria.

Clara stood at the threshold of the lobby, trying to make sense of the deluge. She watched as a toddler in a raincoat screamed at the sight of a half-uniformed deputy, while his mother, voice pitchfork-sharp, tried to thrust a hastily written note toward the overwhelmed receptionist. An older man, face inflamed with both weather and outrage, thumped a fist on the counter insisting his neighbor was "a known Satanist."

Every ring of the phone seemed to escalate the tension: civilian lines, local press, and the newly commissioned "tipline" that Kane had set up through his own construction office. The latter was answered by an off-site operator—an ex-barmaid, Clara later learned—who now funneled the worst of the tips straight to the sheriff's inbox with zero vetting. The result was an endless ticker tape of voice messages, some indignant, many incoherent, all demanding instant resolution.

For all the noise, the leads went nowhere. Clara felt it in the marrow: rumors recycled from the last scandal, sightings contaminated by opportunism or plain boredom, whispers about the Harringtons given just enough oxygen to become actionable. She saw Deputy Jones hunched over his phone, brow knitted, transcribing something so feverish she could almost hear the speaker through the line.

At the eye of this storm, Sheriff Fisher moved with weary precision. His shirt was unbuttoned at the collar, the day's exhaustion bleeding out as he moved from desk to desk, wordlessly reviewing notes before issuing a brisk, quiet directive.

"Run down the ones that seem credible," Fisher said to a fresh-faced deputy, barely audible over the din. "Prioritize the ones with names attached. Any mention of threats, even offhand, flag it red." The young officer, barely out of high school, nodded with a gulp, knuckles whitening around his pen.

"And keep the press out," Fisher added, eyeing the doors, where a local news crew had found its way inside and was now interviewing a parent whose main qualification appeared to be proximity to the vending machine. The parent gestured animatedly and, as the camera panned, Clara recognized herself in the background, hunched and hollow-eyed. She ducked into the nearest office, careful to keep out of the line of fire.

"Jesus," she muttered, closing the door behind her. She needed air, or at least a moment to piece together the narrative. The last twenty-four hours had rewritten the entire town's sense of reality, and Clara could see how Kane's reward—offered in public, with the full weight of expectation behind it—had turned a slow-burning investigation into a street brawl.

She found Fisher alone, briefly, in the incident review room. He'd commandeered a rolling whiteboard and was using it to diagram the town's gossip topography: Kane's statements at the center, Harringtons radiating out in thick, accusatory lines, tangents branching toward "Cult Activity" and "Lost Teens." He rubbed at the center of his forehead as if trying to erase a headache.

"You see it too?" Clara asked.

"What? Kane running the show now?" Fisher grunted, dropping the marker.

"He's not interested in solving the case," Clara said, more to herself than him. "He's interested in a spectacle. A scapegoat."

Fisher let the silence linger, then replied, "Doesn't change the facts. If there's a lead, we follow it."

Clara almost admired his resolve. She gestured at the whiteboard, where "Liam Harrington" now appeared three times in different handwriting. "And if it's just noise?"

"We wade through it." He tried to smile, but the lines at his mouth deepened into something like defeat. "That's the job."

She sighed and went back to sorting the statements, her mind running through scenarios she didn't want to consider. This wasn't how she'd planned her leave. It was supposed to be quiet. Instead, the chaos around her grew louder. She felt the weight of every rumor and knew they were only starting to build.

As she shifted a stack of papers, her gaze fell on Cecilia Day, seated and alone, her small figure almost swallowed by the commotion. Clara knew this was important. Without waiting for the dust to settle, she moved to the waiting area and gestured for Cecilia to follow.

"Come on," Clara said gently, her voice lost to most of the clamor. "Let's talk."

Cecilia's eyes were wide and unsure, but she nodded and stood, the movement quick and uncertain. Clara led her to an interview room, bare and echoing with simplicity, a sharp contrast to the noise outside. It was stark, with nothing but a table and two chairs. Cecilia seemed small and overwhelmed in the space, her fidgeting more pronounced than before.

———

Clara settled across from Cecilia, watching the way she chewed her lip and glanced everywhere but at her. The silence between them was charged, and Clara let it stretch, waiting for Cecilia to find her words.

"Okay," Clara said, keeping her tone soft but urgent. "Why did you come back?"

Cecilia hesitated, her hands wrapping tightly around her phone. Clara could see the struggle in the girl's expression, the weight of what she wanted to say. But this time Clara wouldn't let her off easy.

"Look, Cecilia," Clara pressed, "if you've got something to add, now's the time."

The girl's eyes flicked to Clara's, then away again. "I think maybe..." Her voice wavered, unsure. "I think Lila was having an affair with Liam Harrington." She spat the name out, like it was the hardest part to say.

Clara sat back. This would explain Harrington's connection to John and why he had reacted strangely when she'd brought him up as a suspect. But she'd heard Cecilia's version of the truth before and something about this felt a bit too easy. She let the pause linger, watching Cecilia's face.

"Are you sure?" Clara asked. "This is big. I need you to be clear."

"I'm not completely sure," Cecilia admitted, her words stumbling over each other. "But I... I think it's true."

Clara studied the girl, assessing the hesitance, the rush of emotion. "Why do you think that?"

Cecilia's fingers twisted nervously. "She was always getting new things. Disappearing for hours," she said, voice rising with the swell of each sentence. "I think I know who she was with. Kane's speech made me realize."

"But you never saw them together." Clara pushed for the detail that could change everything, a kernel of truth among the doubt.

Cecilia shook her head, her uncertainty palpable. "No."

Clara heard the echo of Kane's words in Cecilia's, the reward fueling more than just the tips at the front desk. "Why didn't you say anything before?" Clara asked, holding Cecilia's gaze, trying to see past the fear.

Cecilia fumbled with her phone, dropping it and picking it up with shaking hands. "I didn't know for sure," she said, voice thin. "Not until today."

Clara watched the girl's every move, every hesitation. It was fragile, like the other leads, but the chance it was real kept Clara from dismissing it outright. She couldn't afford to let this go, not if there was a possibility it was true.

The statement hung in the air, heavy and uncertain, just like the case. Just like Clara's own doubts. She saw both Cecilia's fear and hope that this revelation might relieve the burden of guilt she carried.

"Okay," Clara said finally, more to herself than to Cecilia. "We'll look into it." But she knew it wasn't as simple as that. Not in Cedar Hollow. Not with the Harringtons.

Cecilia's tension seemed to release slightly, the promise of follow-up enough to calm her frayed nerves. Clara watched the girl slip out of the station, a mixture of expectation and dread in her hurried steps.

Clara stayed behind, surrounded by the chaos of Kane's making while Cecilia's claim swirled in her mind, impossible to dismiss and impossible to fully trust. Like everything else, it could be the key or another locked door.

Chapter 6

Rain has a way of battering a house's defenses, leaching its warmth through old glass and brittle trim. Clara felt the chill before she even knocked. The Hays' front door opened on the second attempt, hinges shrieking their disrepair, and Mrs. Hays stood framed in the gap, a ghost in slippers and a bathrobe faded to the color of watered milk.

They were led through a tight, linoleum-floored corridor into a living room with a low, sagging sofa that seemed as exhausted as its owner. The window frames were streaked with chipped paint, the color gone vague and chalky where the moisture has bullied it for years. On the sill, an arrangement of dusty ceramic birds faces inward, as if refusing to acknowledge the drizzle streaking the glass.

Clara didn't bother to take off her coat. The air inside was barely warmer than out, and the rain's percussion seemed to drown out all thought. Fisher stood in the corner, looking like a man being punished, which is exactly how Clara felt.

Mrs. Hays motioned for them to sit, but she herself remained anchored by the entryway, arms knotted tight beneath her ribs. If she shivered, it wasn't from the cold. The veins on her hands, pressed against faded terry cloth, were pronounced and restless, as if mapping a terrain of constant unrest. She didn't sit and didn't invite them to be comfortable; it's more of a challenge than a courtesy.

Fisher edged onto the sofa, careful not to disturb the threadbare fabric, while Clara claimed the armchair opposite, forcing herself to ignore the dust from the cushion as she settles in. The space between them is dense with the heavy smell of mildew and lemon-scented polish, like the living room belongs to another decade that refuses to die.

Mrs. Hays appraised them both with indifferent but sharp eyes. She didn't bother feigning hospitality. Instead, she settled for a position by the window, arms and back rigid, the reflection of her silhouette warped against the rain-ribbed glass. She glanced over her shoulder as if expecting to see someone, and for a moment Clara wondered if she's waiting for her husband or just hoping for a better audience.

"Thank you for seeing us," Clara said, her voice measured.

The courtesy hung in the air, weightless, until Mrs. Hays torqued her mouth into a brief crescent and then set it straight. The gesture was a dismissal, not an answer.

"My husband should be back any minute," she said, voice flat. She spoke as if reminding herself, as if her husband's presence is required for the world to function properly.

Clara cut a glance at Fisher, who offered only the faintest purse of his lips. He was content to play background for now, the good cop in a silent act.

She leaned forward, elbows indexing knees, hands clasped, notepad balanced over thigh. The posture is calculated to make her seem more like a therapist, less like an interrogator. "We're following up on a few things. I know this is a difficult time for you and your family. I won't take more time than necessary."

Mrs. Hays pulled her robe tighter by the waist, eyes narrowing. Clara sensed the math behind those eyes; every word weighed, every question anticipated.

"Lila was a good student," Clara began. "We know she was active at the library, had close friends. There's some confusion about which circles she moved through. We're hoping you can help us get a better picture."

Mrs. Hays let out a sharp, involuntary laugh that slices the room. "What is there to say?" The words were scalding. "She did what was expected. Kept up her grades. Stayed out of trouble." She let the sentence trail, as if trouble were a physical thing lurking just beyond the door.

"Was she ever late coming home?" Clara asked, softening her tone. She could feel Fisher's gaze on her, shadowing each word, ready to interject if need be.

"Not unless she was helping clean up at the diner. We had rules." Mrs. Hays leaned back against the sideboard, the motion unsettling a stack of clipped coupons and unopened mail.

Clara nodded, scribbled something meaningless in her notebook, and modulated her voice to an almost-conspiratorial hush. "Mrs. Hays, have you ever known Lila to visit places you'd find unusual, or to spend time with people you might not expect?"

Mrs. Hays didn't hesitate. "She was friends with girls from her classes. Sometimes a few boys from the AP program. That's it." She delivered every line as a verdict, not a recollection. "She didn't have time for distractions."

"I know it was something of a surprise when you heard she was seeing John Mills," Fisher observed.

A flicker of irritation, then a scowl. "That was new to us. She never brought him home. Never even mentioned his name before." Mrs. Hays looked at Clara, as if expecting her to contest the point.

Clara paced herself. She's observed that silence is more revealing than any direct question; in it, people either fill the void with truth or with tells. Mrs. Hays didn't fidget, didn't flinch, just stared. This was a woman for whom grief was already a second skin.

"We're also following up on..." Clara paused, the words resisting her. If she said it outright, it will sound absurd, but she can't afford to appear credulous.

73

"There's chatter, and I know it's probably ridiculous, but did Lila ever mention Liam Harrington to you?"

Mrs. Hays's lips drew back and her eyes sharpened. "No." The word snapped in the air. "But I know it was him. He did it." Her conviction was so absolute, it wasn't even anger.

The rain outside slackened, as if even the weather is cowed by the certainty in her voice.

"You think so?" Clara said.

Mrs. Hays shook her head, not in denial but in disbelief at the stupidity of the world. "I know so. You might be from out of town, but people here know what's what." She spat the words through clenched teeth, a litany rehearsed in the sleepless hours since Lila's murder. "Harringtons get away with everything. Always have."

Fisher, sensing the wound open, probed: "Did Lila ever talk about them? The Harringtons?"

Another negative, this one laced with scorn. "No. She wouldn't. She had better sense."

Clara made a note of the pointedness in her voice, the way Mrs. Hays clung to the idea that only the inferior are drawn into the Harringtons' gravity. "What about the night Lila was found? Did she say where she was going or who she was with?"

The muscles in Mrs. Hays's jaw rippled as she grinds the memory down. "She said she was going to meet friends after work. I made her promise she'd be back before ten. She didn't show. Called her phone again and again, but it kept going to voicemail." She punctuated with a glare, daring them to find something suspicious in her pain.

Clara glanced at the window. The rain has slowed to an anemic patter, beads crawling down the glass in awkward rivulets. She wondered what it's like to spend every day in a room so saturated with absence.

Mrs. Hays, still standing, gestured at a side table. A single porcelain teacup sat on a coaster, a paltry wisp of steam. She lifted it with both hands, and they trembled, though whether from cold or from the force of long-hoarded emotion, Clara couldn't tell.

"She's all we had," Mrs. Hays muttered, knuckles whitening as she cups the mug. "I told her to keep away from people like that. I told her…"

The cup clinked as she set it back on the saucer, the sound as brittle as her voice.

"Do you know what it's like, Agent Reynolds? To lose a child in a town this small?" Mrs. Hays's voice thinned into something raw and private, an intimacy forced by circumstance. "Everyone sees you, every day. No one says anything. But they know." The emphasis on the final word left no room for misinterpretation.

"I'm sorry," Clara said, and she meant it. She meant it in a way that made her want to flee the room, run from the intimacy of this suffering. She had to force her own memories down as they threatened to bubble up to the surface again.

"Are you?" Mrs. Hays asked, tone knife-edged. "Liam Harrington killed my daughter. Maybe not with his own hands, but he did it. And you can sit here for hours and pretend you're listening, but nothing will bring her back. Not your questions. Not your notebook. Not the parade of useless men you send through that door."

Fisher sat up, voice low. "We're not here to make things harder."

Mrs. Hays cut him off. "You already have."

She stood even straighter, the full height of her indignation pressed the rest of the room down. "You must arrest him and rid us of the Harringtons for good."

Her face contorted as tears finally break through, tracking down her cheeks in uneven streaks. She swiped them away with the heel of her hand, furious at the betrayal of her own body.

There was a moment when Clara thinks Mrs. Hays might collapse, might shatter into glassy pieces right there on the rug. Instead, she spun on her heel, stormed down the corridor, and left them staring at the little disaster of upturned tea spreading toward the carpet.

The room sagged in her absence. The rain picked up, drumming against the window with frantic insistence. Clara studied the abandoned cup, the handprints on the wood, and wondered how long it will take for the echo of that accusation to fade.

She looked at Fisher. He shook his head, a subtle admission of what they both know: This is as much as they'll ever get from the Hays woman.

As they were heading out the door they saw Mr. Hays' car pulling up the driveway. He stared at them blankly as he parked the car.

"Give me a minute," he told them.

————

The kitchen was a snapshot from a catalog two decades out of date. The appliances were yellowed, the red-and-white checkered cloth was washed to a faint, ghostly pink. The only modern intrusion was a battered Keurig, its blue light blinking steadily beside a rack of mismatched mugs.

Mr. Hays was already at the table when Clara entered, Fisher close behind. The man was lean, prematurely shrunken by grief, his plaid shirt buttoned to the top and tucked with almost military precision. He didn't look up. His arms were crossed and welded to his chest, the fingers biting into his biceps like he was anchoring himself against the undertow.

77

On the table, a single mug rested in front of him, half-full and cooling. Clara recognized the logo, but its message was obscured by a thumbprint smudge.

Fisher took a seat across, settling with deliberate care. Clara hesitated, then pulled out the other chair, the legs scraping a small protest from the old linoleum.

For a minute or more, nobody spoke. The air vibrated with the kind of silence that felt thick and granular, as though the unsaid words had weight and mass, a dust that choked the collective breath. Fisher stared at the patterns on the table, gently tracing the cracks in the laminate. Clara watched Mr. Hays' hands. His thumbnail was chewed to the quick.

It was Mr. Hays who finally breaks the silence, lifting his gaze as if surfacing from an underwater trench. He didn't look directly at them, but somewhere off to the right.

"I suppose my wife has told you her theory," he said, and the phrase lands with the air of a preamble often rehearsed but never improved. His voice was flat but thick around the edges, as if every word must squeeze through a clot half-formed in his throat.

Fisher gave a small, almost reverential bow of the head. "We're gathering every possibility," he said. Clara can tell he's chosen his words for gentleness. They've both seen how parents can turn against anyone and everyone in the face of grief, how the impulse to assign blame overtakes all other rational considerations.

But Mr. Hays just shrugged, the gesture half-formed, shoulders never quite settling back into place. "She's hated the Harringtons since her older brother disappeared as a teenager." He said it as if reading from a police report, not lived experience. "Her parents convinced themselves the Harringtons had taken him, drove themselves mad imagining he was being tortured in the basement of their estate." He paused, the disbelief apparent on his face. "That family… they make people go a little crazy, you know?"

Clara nodded, careful to keep her own skepticism invisible. She sensed that for Mr. Hays, this personal history has soured his relationship with his wife over the years, that her persistent belief has gradually worn him down and driven him away.

He rotated the mug on the table, aligning its handle with his right thumb, and sighed.

"Truth is, her brother ran away. Tired of this town probably." He dragged a fingernail around the rim of the mug, orbiting the memory. "Couple years later they found out he'd joined the Army and died in combat." The recitation of facts was almost parodic in its impersonality, like he was reading off a casualty list from the public record. "Didn't matter. She never let it go. Still blamed the Harringtons for everything, even after the letter came. Maybe especially then."

Clara and Fisher sat in the hush that followed, not risking the introduction of sympathy or judgment. Clara knew the type of person that Mr. Hays was describing, those who fed themselves on resentment until their appetite became hereditary.

She shifted tactics. "Did Lila ever ask about any of that? Did she leave any notes, or mention those old rumors?" Her voice was deliberately clinical, but she tried for a kind of warmth in the question, an invitation to share rather than confess.

Mr. Hays shook his head, slow and deliberate. "If she did, she never brought it to me." He glanced at his reflection in the mug's surface, then back up to the bright clock face on the wall, which, Clara noted, is still stuck on half past six. "I'm not sure we even talked, the last year or two. Not really."

He said it without self-pity, just a dry record of the silent drift that had separated them. Clara wondered how many houses in Cedar Hollow are filled with parents and children living in parallel universes, oblivious to one another.

Fisher waited, then leaned forward a fraction, as if letting his own weight tip the conversation down a particular slope. "We've heard Lila may have been close with Liam Harrington. Anything you can tell us about that?"

Mr. Hays's eyes tightened. For a moment his whole face flickered, like an old slide being swapped out in a projector. "I don't know," he said, and Clara believed him. Not because he seemed incapable of lying, but because the lie would have required more conviction. "I didn't even know about John. She kept things private. Always had."

Clara took a slow breath, gathering a memory from Lila's file. "Was there anything unusual you noticed recently? Maybe something you didn't think twice of at the time."

Mr. Hays was still for a long moment, then picked at the tape on his thumb. "Maybe," he said finally. "One night a few weeks ago, she was dropped off by an old pickup truck I didn't recognize."

Clara lifted her pen, but let Fisher take the lead.

"Did you ask her who the driver was?" Fisher asked.

"No," Mr. Hays said, and there was a sigh folded inside the word. "I assumed it was maybe Mr. Tasker from the diner giving her a ride home. She might have gotten stuck late at work. She was always helping them clean up the kitchen." There was a flat resignation in his voice, as if he's compiling a list of plausible deniability for his own benefit as much as for theirs.

"What about the color?" Fisher prompted, making a show of writing it down.

Mr. Hays seemed to think about it seriously for the first time, scrolling back through his memory with the visible effort of a man straining to recall a dream that is already dissolving. "I didn't really notice in the dark. Maybe black or silver, I think the color was pretty well faded." He looked at Fisher, then at Clara, as if trying to gauge whether this tidbit meant anything at all.

Clara leant back. She read the man in the small movements: the way his gaze rested just past them, how his shoulders drew in with every question. This was a man who had built a fortress out of not knowing, and now he lives inside it, room by room.

Fisher stood, smoothing his shirt in a silent signal that the interview is over. Clara followed suit.

Mr. Hays didn't rise. He kept his eyes on the table, a man waiting out a storm he knows won't pass.

"Thank you for your time," Clara offered, but it felt redundant. She glanced at the faded photograph of Lila stuck to the fridge with a chipped souvenir magnet; a smiling girl caught in the amber of better years.

The kitchen had the hush of a place where time had stopped, except for the drip of the faucet and the steady, muffled rhythm of Mrs. Hays pacing in the room beyond. Clara followed Fisher to the front door. Neither spoke until the chill outside bites at their faces.

Only then did Fisher say, "This town never changes. It just gets better at hiding what's broken."

Clara didn't argue. She took one last look at the light in the kitchen window and wondered how anyone survives this place at all.

———

The sheriff's cruiser was a time capsule of bad habits and worse upholstery. Cracked vinyl weeps gray foam along every seam. The faint, resinous sting of pine air freshener does nothing to mask the undercurrent of mildew and old coffee. Rain needles the windshield, each drop smearing the world into a monochrome blur.

"Half the town drives a truck like that," Fisher muttered under his breath.

Clara rode shotgun, hands cradling a travel mug that's given up any pretense of warmth. The contents tasted like the aftermath of a house fire. She sipped anyway, because it was something to do, because it was better than talking.

Fisher guided the car through rows of dripping pines. Streetlights hang at intervals, their pale glow smeared by water running in arterial ribbons down the glass. Every few yards, the tires spattered through a standing puddle. The wipers flailed against the deluge, barely keeping pace. The only sound, apart from the engine and the weather, is the damp shuffle of Fisher's coat as he adjusts his grip on the wheel.

Clara glanced over. The blue-white dashboard light sharpened the lines on his face, turning him into a study in weariness. She weighed the question in her head, lets it tumble around with the coffee until the silence becomes more oppressive than the answer could ever be.

"You weren't kidding about the Harrington mystique around here. How exactly did it get so pervasive?" she asked, not expecting insight, just wanting to hear the words spoken aloud.

Fisher didn't answer immediately. He thumbed at the turn signal, slowing for an intersection where no car has passed in an hour. He looked like he's measuring the question against something only he can see.

"They've been the scapegoat since before my grandfather's time," he said. "The Harringtons built half of Cedar Hollow. Owned the rest. Every time something bad happened, people would whisper that maybe it's them, maybe it's their fault. It's easier to blame the old ghosts than face what's really wrong."

Clara snorted, the sound more bitter than the coffee. "So facts don't stand a chance here."

"Facts get buried under fear. Every time," Fisher said. He drummed his fingers on the wheel, tapping out a beat that's a little too steady, a little too rehearsed.

"You're always pretty neutral on the subject," Clara noted. "What do you really think of the Harringtons?"

Fisher sighed. "They're not friendly people. Stuck up, disdainful of everyone else. Didn't surprise me when most of them left. This isn't much of a kingdom to be proud of anymore. Honestly, if Liam would just follow suit the town would be a much better place."

"Why doesn't he, then? Can't imagine it's very comfortable for him living here."

"Pride. Stubbornness. Who knows? Probably has visions of grandeur, restoring the family to past glories."

They lapsed into silence again; the only conversation left to the metronome of rain and the churn of tires on wet asphalt. Clara watched the trees flick past, blurred to the point of abstraction, and pondered how anyone could navigate a place this dark without getting lost.

The station came into view, its sign backlit and flickering, the parking lot an island of yellow light in a sea of black. Fisher coasted to a stop, engine idling, wipers finally allowed a moment's rest.

For a moment, neither moved. The car's interior felt suspended in time, as if the weather and the memories might never let them out.

Fisher cleared his throat. "Tomorrow's another day," he said, but the words ring as hollow as the car's battered interior.

Clara tipped back the last of the cold coffee, savoring the bitterness, and nods. She watched the water bead and race down the side window, each droplet carving its own doomed path.

She gathered herself, then opens the door to the world's chill and the ever-present sound of rain, leaving behind the warm fug of pine and disappointment for the brighter, if only marginally more hopeful, light of the sheriff's station.

Chapter 7

The pub felt small, like the town. Cramped with the worn wood of its tables, the dim lights and damp air, the knowing eyes of its patrons. It smelled of beer and the desperate expectation of a community determined to break apart.

Emma sat with an enthusiasm that spilt over, excitement bouncing in the curl of her words. Clara sipped and scanned, knowing the questions will come. Knowing she won't answer. She will hold her secrets but pry the town's loose.

Emma beamed across the table, and the pub's dim light caught the excitement in her eyes. "It's so good to be out like this, just like old times. I've missed you, Clara."

Clara watched the conversations around them. Too many were glancing in their direction. Her own voice felt cautious, thin. "Yeah. We should do this more often."

"You're really back at it, then? With the case?" Emma leaned forward, her curiosity quick and warm.

"Sort of." Clara let the words hang.

"Probably not what you expected, huh?" Emma was relentless in her gentle way. "Jumping right back in like this?"

"That's for sure," Clara said. The tension wound around her like a second skin. "How's Russ feel about me dragging you out on a Friday?"

"He's fine," Emma waved it away. "He's still at the logging site anyway. Probably drinking with the boys." Her voice lowered, a friendly nudge in its tone. "So? How many killers have you caught anyway?"

Clara deflected with a sip of beer. "I don't work murder cases all that often. The job is nothing like on TV."

Clara's maneuver didn't slow Emma down. "Compared to a small town bookkeeper like me your life seems positively thrilling. You must work kidnappings—"

"Tell me about Robert Kane," Clara cuts in.

Emma looked momentarily lost, Clara's shift threw her off balance. But her smile didn't fade. "Robert Kane?"

"What's his deal?" Clara asked, redirecting again, keeping the conversation off herself.

Emma settled back in her seat. "I guess you don't know his story," she said, leaning in with the promise of a good yarn.

Clara watched the room, listened to Emma's voice over the clatter and hum of the crowd.

"Kane's a local boy. Did you know that? He grew up dirt poor on the edge of town," Emma explained. "Took over a tiny construction business. It was almost dead when he got his hands on it, but look at him now." She gestured vaguely, as if all of Cedar Hollow is the proof. "One of the most successful men in the county."

Clara thought back to Kane's show at the town hall. How he had the town eating out of his hand.

"He built all those houses on the west side, all the new buildings," Emma continued. "He practically owns the town. Well, except for the Harringtons, and maybe not for long."

"His announcement caused quite the stir," Clara observed, her voice neutral.

"Of course it did," Emma said. "Did you see him? He's made for that. Always at the center of things."

Clara nodded. "I take it he has political ambitions?"

"He was president of the Rotary Club, then pushed them to open a new branch and take on younger members," Emma said. "He's on the church board, the planning commission. Mayor is probably the next step. They say he has his eyes on the state senate too. He might just do it. I've never seen anyone as determined."

"He's really that involved in everything?" Clara asked, considering what she's heard so far.

Emma laughed. "You'd think it'd be impossible to manage all that, but somehow he makes it work."

Clara thought back to how easily Kane manipulated the town's suspicions at his press conference, the subtle challenge he threw directly at the police.

"He knows how to run a campaign," she said, more to herself than to Emma.

"He should," Emma replied. "He's been working on his image since the day he made his first dollar."

Clara sipped her drink. The eyes of the pub feel heavy on her, as if the murkiness outside has crept in and thickened.

The sensation started as a tingling at the nape of her neck—Clara knew exactly what it means to be the subject of slow, deliberate observation. In the pub, the feeling grew sharper, refined by the close geography of regulars who have nothing better to do than pick apart the stories and gestures of others. Every time she glanced up, she found a pair of eyes darting away, pretending to be invested in old sports highlights on the mounted television or in the foam patterns of their pint glasses. But the moment she focused elsewhere, the gaze returned, probing and prodding, looking for something beneath her casual posture and forced neutrality.

She tried to anchor herself to the table, to Emma's stream of commentary, but her attention kept fragmenting, split by the subtle choreography of suspicion that ripples out in concentric circles from their booth. She saw the couple at the bar, mid-sixties, who have probably watched three generations of Cedar Hollow grow up and out and sometimes disappear. Saw the laborers with dirt still fresh under their nails, who'd earlier nodded at Kane's name with a mix of envy and something darker. Saw the bartender, who wiped the same glass for a full five minutes, eyes never leaving the side of Clara's face.

Clara catalogued the faces, her instincts reflexively sorting them into the categories she used back at the precinct: the outright hostile, the skeptical but fair-minded, the ones who would fold under direct questioning. But tonight, there was no questioning to be done; she's the object, not the subject.

Emma noticed none of this. Or if she did, she's elected to ignore it, keeping the conversation on Kane's rise and the oddities of small-town social climbing. But Clara's drink was already warm in her hand, and her skin prickled with the effort to not react. She felt the stories being built around her, brick by brick, by every glance and every shared nod. In the city, you could disappear into the background; here, the background itself seemed alive, sentient, and deeply invested in your every move.

She pushed her glass away, untouched for the last several minutes, and leaned in closer to Emma, lowering her voice even though she knows it won't really change anything.

"People are watching us," Clara said.

"Don't let it bother you," Emma said. "They're just not used to strangers."

Clara knew it was more than that. She remembered how the crowd at the town hall took notice when Kane caught her eye. It was almost too quick to catch, but not for Clara. Now the same thing was happening here. It made her skin crawl.

Emma seemed not to notice, absorbed in their conversation.

The noise in the pub ebbed, only to rise again like the gloom outside. She saw the tension in the room play out, felt herself at its center. Emma continued her description, more certain of her footing, now that the talk had drifted away from Clara and her time at the Bureau.

"Kane's not easy to pin down," Emma said. "All that work, you'd think people would know him better."

Clara tried to picture Kane's next move, how he'll play his cards. He'd already managed to direct the town's suspicions against the Harringtons.

Emma saw Clara's focus drifting. "What?" she asks, worried she's said too much or too little.

Clara didn't answer right away. Her attention turned to the shifting dynamics in the room, to the weight of every curious glance.

"Never mind," she said. "It's nothing."

Clara continued watching the bar and letting Emma fill the space between them with the ease of her words. "What about the Harringtons?" Clara asked, breaking her own quiet. She saw how quickly Emma folded into the familiar. The subtle way her shoulders relax when Clara pulled the topic away from herself.

"The Harringtons are always a hot topic," Emma said, her inflection flickering between excitement and wariness. The name alone has a sound in Cedar Hollow—like a match struck or a bone snapped. Clara felt the room sharpen in its attention, the air around them quickening with a static charge that wasn't there a moment before. If Kane was the logical center of town, the Harringtons were the emotional weather system, brewing a thousand small storms in every house.

Emma sipped at her cider, trying to keep her tone casual with the practiced ease of a local, but Clara could hear the old stories packed into every phrase. "Every family has either worked for them in some capacity or knows someone who has. If you want to succeed in this town you need to be on their good side. It's almost like everyone here can chart their own rise or fall based on a Harrington whim.

"At least Russ says that's the way it was before Kane," Emma goes on. "You know people call it the 'quiet war'? Kane's always pushing for new developments, and Harrington is always leveraging historical ordinances to block him. It's all very polite, very Cedar Hollow. But people want to see Kane win out in the end, even those working for Harrington."

"They think they'll have it better when Kane takes over," Clara mused, not looking up from the slow rotation of her glass.

Emma grinned. "Exactly. You're getting it. People act like Liam is some sort of ghost, but that's just because no one wants to admit how much he still runs the place. Still, he's the only one left, and if he goes too then the Harrington influence will be finally gone for good."

As Emma kept talking, more heads turned, and the pauses in the background conversation got longer and more pointed. The Harrington name did this to people, it opened old wounds that are never quite scabbed over.

Emma's voice softened. "I'm glad you're here, though. We need someone from the outside to look at things. People talk, but they don't see their own patterns anymore. They just… repeat."

"How did it get down to just Liam?" Clara asked, pressing gently past the boundaries of Emma's comfort. "There were brothers. Cousins."

"Well, you know how it is in old families," Emma said, but she's already off balance. The words come out slower, as if the conversation has moved into a stretch of road she's not sure is safe. "There's always… something. Something that makes people just fall away, I guess. Russ' grandmother used to be the housekeeper for the Harringtons, back when there were more. Three brothers, two sisters. Big Thanksgivings. Big fights."

"Why did they stop?" Clara watched Emma struggle with the question, like she was digging up a root she half expected to break off in her hands.

"She said it was the oldest brother, William. Liam's uncle. He was the crown prince, always dressed up, never a hair out of place. He was supposed to take over the whole thing. But then there was the murder. The girl." Emma glanced furtively to the side.

95

Clara nodded, thinking about the rhythm of the town, how every story pointed back to a handful of names and faces, how trauma calcified into myth until no one knew what really happened.

"What about the rest of them?" Clara pressed, knowing how far Emma will go with the right push.

"You know, rumor has it Liam won some kind of power struggle." Emma scanned the room as she said it, aware of the impact the Harrington name has in Cedar Hollow. "With the rest of the family. Years ago."

Clara tracked the subtle shift in the room, how it tightened when the talk turns to the Harringtons.

"No one knows exactly what happened," Emma said. Her voice drops to a near whisper. She traced the condensation on her glass, leaving vague and temporary shapes. "But people think it has something to do with his refusal now to marry. Anyway, the others packed up one by one to someplace in Europe. The ancestral home, supposedly."

Clara noticed several patrons staring now, the noise in the pub thinning to an expectant hush. It wraps around them like a damp cloak. The specifics of anything that happens in this town seem to elude people, she thought to herself.

"I can see you're hooked," Emma said, ignoring the sudden quiet, the way it made Clara shift in her seat.

"I can see you love this stuff," Clara replied. She tried to keep her discomfort hidden, but Emma knew her too well.

"The days get monotonous after a while," Emma mused. "We need something to occupy our thoughts.

Clara focused on the way the room turned in her direction, the feeling that every word made its way through the town in hushed ripples. The other patrons seemed closer now, almost like they were sitting at the same table, leaning in to catch each line of conversation. Each reference to the Harringtons, to Clara's involvement, to Cedar Hollow's history brought their attention sharper into focus.

"How are your folks doing these days?" Emma asked suddenly.

Clara deflected with a practiced ease. "Same as always."

"Isn't it weird that I never think much about childhood?" Emma said. "Sometimes it's like I forget it even happened. And I didn't have it nearly as rough as you did growing up. Still, you must visit from time to time to check up on them."

Clara knew where this was leading, but then Emma surprised her, returning to the gossip she lived and breathed.

"I've heard some people say that Kane isn't as squeaky clean as he pretends to be."

"Huh," Clara said, playing off the confirmation of a hunch that she'd been angling for all night.

"As long as the Harrington family is here Kane will never really be 'the guy' here, you know? Even with just Liam left he can't exactly wait it out. He's bound to start playing dirty."

Like setting Harrington up for murder? Clara wondered. It seemed like a long shot, but she intuitively felt it was important that John Mills worked for Kane. Or maybe she was just trying to will some elaborate plan into existence, to justify her continued work on the case.

The weight of the room pressed on her with an insistence that threatens to break her concentration, her composure. Each look her way intensified the feeling that her every move will feed the town's insatiable gossip mill.

The pressure was too much. It was supposed to be an escape, this time in Cedar Hollow. Now it felt just the same as everything she had run from. Like all the stares and the questions and the uncertainty that had caused her to flee here in the first place. She wasn't ready for how deep it pulled her, how quickly it spun out of her control.

A chair scraped, jarring Clara into action.

"We should go," she said abruptly, standing and reaching for her coat.

Emma looked up, surprised by the suddenness of Clara's decision but not by the decision itself.

"We've only had one round," Emma protested to get Clara to reconsider. Clara didn't. She hears the note of frustration in Emma's voice, the concern that blended with it when she brought up Alex at the house. Clara tried not to flinch at the thought.

They left. The cold air of the evening was a slap in the face after the cloying atmosphere inside. Clara felt the shroud surrounding her, every bit as heavy as the questions.

Emma's steps slowed to match Clara's. The disappointment still showed, but so does her knowing smile.

"So, you're staying until you catch the guy?" Emma's voice lifted with hope.

"At least until I know more," Clara replied.

Emma nodded. "Maybe it's better than just running." She let the words land gently, carefully, in the damp air.

"Maybe," Clara said. She doesn't know if it's true, but she wanted it to be, wanted an unexpected success to erase all the previous failure. She took a long breath, pulls the thick air deep into her lungs. Her words were a thin wisp. "Maybe it is."

She knew she was tangled up in the town's stories, in the rumors she'd heard and those she hadn't. Emma walked by her side, still saying something about the night's plans, about how Russ would be glad she didn't keep Clara too long. Clara heard the conversation in pieces, fragments that float between the other fragments she's sorting out in her mind.

She couldn't stop thinking about the connections Emma mentioned, the links between past and present. The speculation about the fall of the Harringtons and the rise of Robert Kane. Strange symbols nobody knew anything about, again tied to murder. It all felt too deliberate to ignore, like the echoes of history are more than echoes. Like they're something she could solve.

The windows of the pub blurred with condensation as they passed, a ghostly glow marking their retreat. Clara imagined the eyes behind them, watching as she made her way into the night. Her thoughts were already on the next step, the next move. Emma's chatter faded, drowned out by the thrum of her own need to prove herself again.

It was more than just the case. It was more than she was ready to admit.

The choking vapor folded them in, silent and consuming, each tendril wrapping tight around the story she left behind.

Chapter 8

Clara felt every moment extend into the next as she approached the Harrington estate for the second time. Each step seemed to slow her more, dragging her deeper into uncertainty. Sheriff Fisher was a steady presence by her side this time, patient and silent. They were met by a housekeeper whose silence spoke volumes, echoing through the cavernous mansion and magnifying Clara's sense of not belonging. The vast halls closed in on her, a maze of power and history. A reminder of how easily she could lose her way. Of how much she had at stake.

The same large room, the same rigid posture from Liam. Seated, commanding, watching her with a mix of contempt and curiosity. His eyes flicked to Fisher with recognition, as if noting the sheriff's presence and recalibrating his strategy. Clara braced for dismissal.

"Miss Reynolds," Liam began, skipping any pretense of politeness. "And the sheriff. To what do I owe the pleasure?" His voice dripped with irony.

"Thanks for seeing us," Fisher said. His tone was calm, belying Clara's tension. "We need a bit more of your time."

"Must we go through this charade again?" Liam's irritation was immediate. "Unless you've found something?"

"We're looking at all possibilities." Clara took the opening, unsure of where it would lead. "Including rumors of an affair."

Liam's eyes narrowed. "Rumors," he said, incredulous. "Why am I not surprised?"

"That's why we're here," Clara said, trying to match Fisher's calm. "To get the truth."

"You accuse me of an affair with a dead teenage girl," Liam snapped. "And call that getting the truth?"

"Just tell us," Clara pressed. "Were you involved with her?"

"No." The word was a knife. Sharp and final. "I was not."

Clara saw the anger simmer beneath his composed exterior. It was more than she expected, and it pushed her forward.

"Then why the reaction?" Clara asked, pushing him closer to the edge.

"Because I can see you're as desperate as everyone else," Liam replied. "Wasting my time with stories."

He stood, the move sudden and dismissive. But Clara noticed the crack in his composure, the way he fought to maintain control.

"Let's try another story," Clara said. "Kane has been trying to buy out your land for years, hasn't he?"

Liam hesitated, then a wry smile crept across his face. "Ah," he said. "And now the game reveals itself."

Clara was silent.

"Miss Reynolds," Liam continued, "you are a pawn."

"That's not what this is," Fisher butted in. His words were strong, but Clara doubted them even as he spoke.

"You're the outsider," Liam said to Clara, ignoring Fisher. "You have no idea how this town works." His voice held a mix of pity and arrogance.

"I know how these things work," Clara replied, steadying herself. "Business rivals, each casting aspersions on the other. There's a lot of money on the line, isn't there?"

"Yes," Liam agreed. "Kane's been trying to buy up our land for years. He's got several development deals waiting for the green light. Trying to turn this town into something it's not. And you're doing his bidding chasing around after this nonsense."

"I'm after the truth," Clara said, her voice a measure more certain than before.

"Then find it and stop wasting my time," Liam shot back.

Clara felt the tide turning. "I think we're getting somewhere," she said, almost to herself.

Liam's jaw tightened. "Not with me," he retorted.

"You don't care who killed her?" Fisher asked, finally interjecting again. "Or what happens next?"

Liam met the sheriff's gaze, then Clara's. "I don't particularly care who killed her, no. As to the rest of it, Kane wants me out of Cedar Hollow," he said. "He doesn't care how."

"Maybe you should care," Clara replied. "Unless you're hiding something."

The words hung in the air, a challenge and a truth. Liam's expression was stone, but Clara saw it waver, if only for a moment. He didn't have the upper hand. She almost felt bad for him. Almost.

"Kane is the one hiding something," Liam insisted, a final push to turn the suspicion away from himself. "How do you know he isn't lying about the boy's alibi?

"That's something we're checking," Clara said.

"See that you do," Liam replied. He motioned to the door, signaling the end of their visit.

Clara and Fisher exchanged glances. They knew better than to press further, at least for now. As they left the estate, Clara felt the cold air wrap around her like the questions she couldn't yet answer.

"That went well," Fisher said, his voice tinged with humor.

Clara shook her head. "I don't know," she replied. "I believe him about the affair with Lila. Still, I think he's rattled somehow."

"You got to him," Fisher said.

"I got something," Clara agreed. But she didn't know what it was yet.

She knew only that Liam's insistence carried the weight of truth and deception in equal measure. She couldn't decide which, and it gnawed at her as they left the Harrington property. Each step back to the car left her with more questions than answers. But it was a start. Maybe even a break.

———

Clara arrived at the construction site at dawn. The skeleton of the new church loomed through the morning haze like a rumor, its half-built beams the bones of another dead end. She ducked into the foreman's trailer. It smelled of burnt coffee and cold ambition.

"Clara Reynolds, here on behalf of Sheriff Fisher," she announced. The man looked up, eyes as bloodshot as the sky. Clara asked for the shift logs. She read aloud: Four to eleven. Exactly what she feared. Clara moved outside to question the workers.

Clara approached Maria Diaz, her boots crunching over gravel. The site felt mostly deserted, only the looming crane and a scattering of people bearing witness to her investigation. "Maria, is it?" Clara asked, her voice piercing the morning hush. Maria's face was tired but not unkind. She gave a nod, resigned.

Clara went straight for it. "What do you remember about John Mills on the night of Lila Hays' murder? Anything unusual?"

Maria rubbed her arms against the chill. "I told the police everything already." Her words were clipped, practiced.

"Tell me," Clara pressed. "Did he leave the site? Was he distracted? Any phone calls? Anything you didn't remember at first?"

"Nothing like that," Maria replied, her eyes avoiding Clara's. "He was working is all."

"Working," Clara echoed. She knew this part. She wanted more. "Walk me through it," she said. "What exactly did John do? Hour by hour."

Maria hesitated, then sighed. "Measuring studs," she began. "Handing off plywood. Took one break, maybe fifteen minutes, then back to it." She met Clara's gaze finally, her expression resigned. "Til the end of shift."

"Break was when?" Clara asked, sharpening the questions.

"Around eight. Maybe a little after." Maria looked off, her stance guarded. Clara saw it for what it was. A small rebellion against her need for certainty.

"What about after?" Clara pushed. "Are you sure he didn't slip away?"

"He stayed," Maria insisted. "Whole time. You can check the logs."

"I am," Clara replied, "But it's more useful to hear it from you. Are you covering for him?"

Maria flinched at the accusation. "No."

Clara stayed silent, watching Maria shift from one foot to the other. The pressure was deliberate, a tool she'd used often before, though never with certainty. It paid off.

"Look," Maria said, her voice flat with reluctance. "He was here, okay? Why else would we say it?"

Clara's gaze lingered a moment longer, then she left Maria with her defenses up and moved toward Tony Fletcher. His back was to her, head down in concentration. He sorted rebar with a steady rhythm, unaware of her approach until she cleared her throat. He turned, a young man's face with old wariness etched into it.

"Clara Reynolds," Clara said by way of introduction. "I've got some questions."

"Figures," Tony replied. He dropped the rebar, his reluctance audible in the clatter of metal against the ground.

"I need to know John Mills' whereabouts on the night of the murder," Clara began.

Tony crossed his arms, holding his silence as long as he dared. "I told the deputy," he finally said.

"Tell me," Clara insisted, her voice sharp enough to puncture his hesitation. "Start at the beginning. What did you see?"

"Nothing special," Tony said, his tone flat. "He was just there. Working like the rest of us."

"The whole time?" Clara asked. "Nothing unusual?"

"Yeah. Working," Tony repeated, sounding bored with the question and his own answer.

"Breaks? Phone calls?" Clara pushed, changing her angle.

Tony scratched the back of his neck, thinking. "Just one break. Don't know about calls."

"Walk me through it," Clara said, her patience thin. "Where was he? When?"

Tony eyed her, unsure if his answer was the right one. "By the frames, measuring and stuff. Then handing plywood to Joe. Just a normal shift."

"Maria said the same thing," Clara informed him, watching for cracks in his composure.

He shrugged. "Well, it's true."

"When was the break?" Clara asked.

"Right after eight," Tony replied. "A piss and a quick bite, not much more than that." He met her gaze now, defiant. "That what you need to know?"

"I need to know if he left the site," Clara said, staring him down.

Tony hesitated, then shook his head. "He didn't."

Clara took a step closer. "Why do you remember so well?"

"It's just what happened," Tony shrugged, shifting his weight.

Clara saw the possibility of a lie in the same precision that riddled Maria's statements. But she had no proof, nothing more than a gut feeling that was as worn as her resolve. She exhaled sharply and moved toward the trailer again.

————

Clara found Greg Jacobs at his desk, pouring over a stack of blueprints. "I need security footage," Clara said without preamble. She wasn't in the mood for more dead ends.

Greg leaned back, his chair creaking with fatigue. "I explained already," he said, as if every word were an effort. "We don't have cameras at this site. Blame the old priest, I don't like it either."

"Of course not," Clara muttered. "So, I've got nothing to work with but your logs."

"And the crew," Greg added, sounding annoyed at her persistence. "Joe, Maria, Tony, Al, Ricky, Mark and Zeke all on that second shift with John. They got no reason to lie."

"That so?" Clara asked. "Same story from all of them. Down to the minute."

"Then maybe you've got your answer," Greg said, shrugging.

Clara didn't reply, didn't want to give him the satisfaction. She left the trailer, the morning haze seeping into her clothes and her mood.

She needed a hole in their alibi, but each attempt only closed the net tighter around John's innocence. She turned, her disappointment trailing her like the drifting fog. She made her way to the car, boots dragging through the morning damp. The crane cast its shadow over the site, a silent judge of her failure to crack the alibi. She hesitated by her car, looking back at the workers. They pretended not to watch, but she knew better.

———

The smell of money and self-importance filled the air, crowded and clinical like Kane's brand-new office. Clara waited, knowing the businessman would orchestrate a grand entrance, just as he'd orchestrated the press. The whole town.

He appeared, larger than life, his handshake firm and insincere. "What can I do for the FBI?" he asked, words coated with concern. Clara caught the glint of calculation behind his eyes.

"Tell me why you're offering such a large reward," she said. "Not getting enough press?"

Kane's smile grew. "I have the resources," he replied. "It's the least I could do."

Clara watched Kane as he settled into his role, as comfortable behind his desk as on stage at the town hall. She tried to pin him down, to decipher his motives, but he was a moving target. His smile was steady and infuriatingly confident.

"You subtly implicated the Harringtons. Only in this town it's not so subtle, is it? You had to know the chaos you would cause."

"Someone knows the truth," Kane continued, leaning forward, his hands clasped with rehearsed urgency. "Maybe they feel afraid, need an extra incentive to come out with it. We've lived under the Harrington shadow long enough to fear it."

"And you're the one to change that?" Clara asked, challenging his savior complex. She measured his response with every sense, alert to the hidden message beneath his practiced words.

"I'm the one with the courage to speak up," Kane replied, ignoring the hint. "This is bigger than you realize, Miss Reynolds." His tone was rich with implied knowledge, with a history Clara was only beginning to unravel.

She cut to the heart of it. "This is about Lila Hays," she said, pushing back against the weight of his certainty. "But you made it about the Harringtons."

"They're not separate issues," Kane insisted. His voice rose with dramatic fervor, a calculated conviction that mirrored the man. "You're not from here. You don't know the damage that family's done."

Clara's skepticism showed in the lift of her eyebrow. "But you do."

"I've lived it," Kane declared, passion seeping into his voice, as if he were testifying to a great injustice. "And I'll make sure we don't suffer another tragedy at their hands." He studied her, gauging her reaction, confident that he was pulling her into his narrative.

"Maybe it's personal," Clara suggested. "Like your ongoing business conflicts with them."

"Of course it's personal," Kane shot back, seizing the opening. "It's personal to everyone in Cedar Hollow." He watched her closely, as if daring her to contradict him.

"It sounds like more than just concern," Clara observed. "You've been trying to get rid of them for years."

Kane didn't flinch. "We've all been trying," he said, his voice a conspiratorial whisper. "But this time, with what's happening..." His eyes flashed with zeal. "It's our best chance yet."

Clara weighed his intensity, unsure if it was real or another act. Another way to manipulate the town. "And what is happening?" she asked, playing into his sense of drama.

Kane's expression turned grave, a well-played mask of seriousness. "History," he said, "is repeating itself." The words hung between them, thick with implication.

"Another murder?" Clara pressed. She held his gaze, refusing to be swept away by his theatrics.

"Another Harrington cover-up," Kane replied, leaning back in his chair. His confidence filled the room, suffocating and absolute.

Clara leaned in, narrowing the gap between his words and her doubt. "You don't believe John Mills might have done it?" she asked, knowing he'd have an answer ready.

"Not for a second," Kane said. His voice was smooth, almost too smooth. "The boy and his father work for me. If they're lying, I would know."

"You think Liam is guilty," she said. She didn't ask. She knew his answer already.

"I know he is," Kane replied, the edge in his voice a weapon he wielded with precision. "He's hiding more than you can imagine." He stood and moved to the window, gesturing to the construction site a few blocks down. The skeleton of the new church stood against the gray sky, a monument to Kane's ambitions.

Clara followed his gaze, saw the physical manifestation of his drive. "So, you take it upon yourself to fix it," she said, sensing the depth of his conviction, if not the sincerity.

"Yes," Kane said simply. He turned back to her, his expression one of unwavering resolve. "Because I'm the only one who can."

"You're really that sure of yourself," Clara observed, her tone incredulous, skeptical. "Or are you just using this for leverage?"

Kane returned to his desk, a flash of triumph in his eyes. "The community needs protection," he said. "And no one else has the courage to challenge them. Especially not the police."

"The police have the will to do their job," Clara replied. "I can promise you that."

Kane seemed amused, as if her insistence proved his point. "The reward will help bring out what's hiding in plain sight," he said, his confidence infecting every corner of the office. "And that's exactly what I want."

Clara watched him carefully, trying to catch the slip that would tell her more than Kane intended. But the man was as practiced as his words, every movement deliberate, every sentence placed with surgical precision. "What is it you're hoping to find?" Clara asked, letting her question hang.

"What the town's been ignoring," Kane said, his voice dropping to a confidential tone. He saw the doubt in her expression but pressed on. "And it's more than just the murder of Lila Hays."

"You sound like you know a lot," Clara said. Her eyes narrowed with suspicion. "But it also sounds like a lot of vague accusations."

"They're not accusations if they're true," Kane replied, his intensity growing. "I know it's hard for you to understand, but the Harrington influence is real. It's poisoned this community for generations." His passion bordered on the fanatic. Clara wondered how deep it went.

"You really think it's all their fault," Clara said, still measuring every word, every shift in his demeanor.

"They believe they're untouchable," Kane answered, leaning forward, his voice charged with energy. "But this time we'll prove they're not."

Clara was torn between disbelief and reluctant curiosity. Kane's insistence was infectious, but his sanctimoniousness was hollow, devoid of the facts needed to substantiate it. She studied him, the way he projected certainty, the way he crafted his words to sound inevitable.

"And you think the symbols on the tree tie back to them?" she said, less a question than an invitation for him to reveal more.

"I know they do," Kane stated, his expression one of near-religious fervor. "We all know it. This is a fight against the darkness they brought into our town."

Clara heard the echoes of Father Callahan's warnings, the whisper of a cult that Kane seemed more than willing to believe. "You're referring to the cult I've heard rumors of?" she asked.

"It's more than rumors," Kane said. His voice dropped again, filled with gravity. "It's evil."

Clara took a long pause, letting his words sink in, unsure if he was driven by faith or strategy. Either way, she didn't find him trustworthy. "And you're the only one who can fix it," she said, repeating his earlier claim, letting him decide how she meant it.

"Yes," Kane said, without hesitation. "Because I'm the only one who dares."

Clara felt the air thicken with his conviction. It was more than she'd anticipated, more than a businessman's careful game. "This means a lot to you," she said, unsure whether to trust his zeal or dismiss it, repeating platitudes back at him until she could figure it out.

"It means everything," Kane replied, standing once more, this time to signal the end of their conversation. "I won't let the Harringtons ruin us again." His certainty was chilling.

"You sound awfully sure of yourself," Clara said, repeating the challenge.

"I have to be," Kane answered. "For all of us."

Clara left the office, her mind a knot of suspicion and intrigue. Kane had given her much to consider but not enough to believe him. Not yet. In person he does have a command, an ability to make you see substance in his words that aren't there. Almost.

Clara paused by her car, breathing the cold morning air, the residue of her conversation with Kane clinging like mist. It was too convenient, too calculated. But she couldn't dismiss the core of his claims, as wrapped in doubt as they were. Not when there were no other leads.

———

The permeating gloom was thick as she returned to Emma's, as heavy and lingering as her unanswered questions. Clara thought back on Kane's words. That history was repeating itself. She wondered how deep his belief went, and how far he'd take his claims.

The house was still, shadows lengthening in the growing darkness. Clara entered quietly, unsure if she wanted solitude or if it scared her. She'd come here to escape. Now she didn't know if she ever would. Her own past wrapped around her, the uncertainty of the future just as heavy. Clara felt the specter of old failures pressing in, as solid as any alibi.

A light switched on in the hall, and Emma's voice called out, tentative and warm. Clara let herself be drawn in, drawn away from the spiral of her thoughts. She took a breath, letting Emma's concern fill the spaces left by Kane's manipulation. By the questions she couldn't answer. By the stories that lingered, unburied and haunting.

"We're getting ready for dinner," Emma said, meeting Clara's eyes with concern. "You joining us?"

"Yeah," Clara replied, feeling the complexity of the word as it left her mouth.

She knew she was as trapped as she was welcome, and she didn't know how to leave without doing any more damage. She followed Emma into the light, leaving the darkness behind. But it was still there, as heavy and inescapable as everything she'd tried to forget.

Chapter 9

Clara slipped out before breakfast, the thick air seemed to choke her as she walked. At the police station the deputies were tangled in phones, files, and frustrated exclamations. Fisher hunched over his desk, shuffling paper with a steady intensity.

"You get anything out of Kane?" He was weary but curious, a note of challenge behind his even tone.

Clara dropped into a chair, ready for the next round. "More words than evidence. He acts like a messiah." She shook her head, half-amused, half-wary. "Seen anything to back his crusade? Any evidence of this cult or whatever it is that the Harringtons supposedly control?" Her question twisted through the air between them.

"We've seen no evidence of that so far. Not sure where it came from."

"When did those specific rumors start up?"

"People whisper about the Harringtons every day, but the cult thing is more recent. Last couple of months at most."

"There must have been a reason," Clara thought out loud.

Fisher shrugged. "All these rumors have to twist and morph every so often to stay alive."

"Convenient, in a way," Clara continued to muse. "Almost like they were put out there on purpose, to act as a setup for the murder."

She registered Fisher's skepticism and didn't give him time to voice it.

"But that would mean the whole thing was planned far in advance. That's a reach I know. These kinds of murders are almost always crimes of passion. Still, those symbols suggest some kind of intent. Let's say it's one of two things—a cult leaving its signature, or someone trying to make it seem that way."

Fisher sat back, a pause settling as he organized his thoughts. "Forty years apart is not a signature. Even if the cult rumors are true, I don't see Liam drawing the parallel to the older murder. If he was guilty in any way, he'd want the opposite. Why risk making it look like the same thing again?" His expression challenged her to accept his reasoning.

"You really think he'd care?" Clara knew how easily men like Liam dismiss what they can't control. "Despite his shows of frustration, he must revel in the attention. Otherwise, he'd make more of an effort to change people's perceptions of him."

He looked up, his gaze steady. "We don't have a motive right now, just speculation upon speculation."

"Kane, then," Clara pivoted. "He's got clear motive against Harrington, could have set the whole thing up to bring him down."

"His righteousness is real," Fisher said, contradicting Clara's thought. "At least he believes it. No way he'd go that far, not just to pin something on Liam."

He met her gaze, waiting for a response. Clara chewed on the idea. She knew Fisher trusted his judgment of people but thought he didn't realize the limiting effect that could have. "History is full of righteous men doing unrighteous things in the name of their righteousness," she said.

"It's a distraction," Fisher insisted. "If we focus only on their feud, we'll miss the real angle."

Clara wanted to push back, but she sensed the firmness of his belief. "What other angle do we have?" she asked, wary but willing to hear it out.

He leaned in, the movement decisive. "My take is that Lila was having an affair. Just not with Harrington." Clara listened, waiting for him to fill in the blank. "My bet is on the man in the old pickup truck.

"You think this man killed her?" Clara tried the idea on, measured how it fit against what they knew.

"It makes more sense than Kane or Harrington," Fisher replied. He talked it through as he would any theory, with methodical conviction. "Someone older, married. Maybe she threatened him, maybe he got scared."

Clara watched him, sees the theory take shape in the air between them.

"And he carved the symbols because he knew that we—hell, the whole town—wouldn't be able to resist the implications," she added, hearing how plausible it sounds when she says it aloud. She let it sit with them, a possibility more than an answer.

"Exactly." Fisher's agreement carried a note of confidence. Clara weighs it, feels herself tilt towards believing, then catches the pull of uncertainty and stops it.

"Problem is we have no proof of another lover." Clara's voice landed heavy, the burden of every unproven case she's ever touched. "It's all speculation. That magic word again. Here we are a week into the investigation and everything is still speculation."

Fisher looked intent, unwilling to give up what he saw as the most promising lead. "Maybe, but it's the simplest explanation."

"Maybe." Clara echoed his words, softer, uncommitted. She knew better than to rely on maybes, even when they were all they have.

"But we've got no clue who this jealous lover could be. Until we know more," she said, circling back to where they started, "the cult angle is the only actual lead. Tenuous though it is." She wanted to keep all possibilities open, afraid of closing off the wrong one.

"I still think it's a setup," Fisher said. He was less certain now, Clara's influence tugged at his certainty. "Lila threatened this guy somehow, and he panicked. The symbols are nothing but a smokescreen. Any local with a brain could have thought to do that."

Clara stood, ready to let him follow his path even as she's unsure of hers. "You could be right," she said. Her tone is tight with the weight of doubt.

"Let's go talk to Mr. Tasker at the diner tomorrow," Fisher replies, confidence creeping back into his voice. "He drives a sedan. Can't see him up to that kind of thing anyway, but he might have seen who picked her up."

Clara nodded, more to keep things moving than to agree.

———

Clara pushed the station door open with her shoulder and emerged into a dense curtain of sightless air, the kind that felt less like weather than a living presence. The air had thickened since dawn, softening the world to a series of vague silhouettes and muffled sounds. She drew in a lungful of sharp, mineral-scented air, the taste of damp concrete and decaying leaves as familiar to her as her own breath. It was a cold she felt in her gums and her bones, a cold that didn't care how many layers she wore. She let the door clatter shut behind her and paused on the steps, uncertain where to go next.

She started walking, boots clicking on the wet sidewalk, the town flickering in and out of existence as the pall closed in and then eased, each breath of wind rearranging her world. She recognized the hollow tap of a crosswalk signal up ahead, but the street itself was invisible. The air absorbed sound and light. The feeling was one of exile: a city shrunk to the size of a memory, emptied of witnesses.

Clara didn't have a destination in mind, not really. She paced in circles, replaying the conversation with Fisher in her head, hunting for flaws or tells or anything that would give her a reason to believe—or to stop doubting. She could still see his face, the calm certainty of his statements, as if the rightness of his theory made it true. But Clara had lived through too many "obvious" cases that turned out to be smoke and mirrors. She had followed too many bad instincts, trusted too many facts that dissolved under the light. Over time, she'd learned that the simplest explanation was almost never simple, and rarely an explanation.

Her mind snagged on Kane's name, then on Harrington's. She pictured Robert Kane as he'd looked at his desk: ramrod posture, voice measured but never raised, eyes constantly scanning, hungry for leverage. The man was a machine for building and breaking deals; he didn't operate on impulse. Then she replayed Liam's interview, every gesture analyzed and catalogued. He hadn't seemed especially rattled, but Clara knew how easily a man like Harrington could mask emotion, how many years he'd spent learning to project confidence and mask desperation. Even so, the idea of him orchestrating a murder to echo the old one—which implicated his own family—felt off.

Voices materialized behind her, two teens laughing, their shapes indistinct until she saw the flash of a phone screen. They veered away, shaking off her presence as if she were part of the landscape. Clara heard her own name whispered in their wake; she pretended not to notice. The town had its eyes on her, even if no one would admit it.

She detoured down an alley beside the old bakery. The alley was narrow enough that the murk pooled thigh-high, and the walls sweated from constant condensation. She pressed her back against the brick, closed her eyes, and tried to reconstruct the crime scene: Lila on the ground, the absence of struggle, the freshly carved symbols. Someone had either earned her trust or moved so quietly she never saw them coming.

She thought of the phone in her pocket, the endless list of unanswered emails and messages. The bureau's official silence was louder than any reprimand, and it stung more than she wanted to admit. Clara wondered how long it would take before she was back in Omaha, whether she ever would be. Either way, right now she was alone in the haze, chasing a story that refused to resolve.

She needed to do something, anything. If she kept walking, she might never stop. Clara pulled out her phone and scrolled to her saved files, flicked through the photos from the night of the murder. She zoomed in on the symbols, on the lines so sharp and deliberate they seemed to glow against the bark. Someone wanted them to be seen. Someone wanted to start a new rumor or keep an old one alive. Clara stared until the shapes lost meaning and became only pattern and threat.

A voice startled her; she snapped the phone shut and stepped out of the alley. She'd circled back to Main Street without even aiming for it. The world had a way of pulling her toward the center of things, toward the place where old stories got recycled and new ones began. The hardware store was open early, lights blazing in defiance of the season. Across the street, the old church looked like a ship drifting through a white sea, its steeple the only thing rising above the fog.

Clara kept moving, her steps methodical. She saw herself as a dot on a blueprint, a variable in the story she was trying to diagram. The more she tried to impose order, the more the facts repelled her. She didn't know who to trust—not Harrington, not Kane, maybe not even Fisher—and she didn't know if that was a flaw or a survival instinct. Maybe both.

She paused at a crosswalk, waiting for a delivery truck to materialize out of the void and lumber past. Its exhaust added another layer of haze, and for a moment, she welcomed the obscurity. The world was easier to manage when you didn't have to see everything so clearly. She crossed, hands jammed deeper into her pockets, and let the restless energy carry her.

Up ahead, the coffee shop was open, a beacon through the gloom. She could sit, pretend to work, watch the town filter in and out of sight from behind a plate glass window. She could build a new theory, or at least a new defense. But the idea didn't appeal to her, not yet. She needed to be in motion, to keep her thoughts from congealing into fear or certainty. Clara passed the shop, sidestepped a young mother wrangling a stroller, and drifted toward the park at the edge of downtown.

She was nearly back to the central cross-street when she noticed a shape detaching itself from a fence post and drifting into her path. Old, small, bundled in a purple coat with fur that's been chewed bald by time and moths. The woman's hair was a haze of white, her eyes bright and wet, sharp with the kind of awareness that survived only in the town's oldest inhabitants.

"You the detective?" the woman asked, voice brittle but sharp enough to cut through the enveloping thick. No greeting, just accusation, and Clara instantly recognized the chemistry of across-the-street scrutiny, the veteran busybody with the town's inventory of pain neatly cross-referenced in her skull.

Clara gave her a slow once-over, cataloguing the purple coat, the battered clogs, the rheumy yet laser-honed glare. "Agent. I'm assisting with the investigation," she said, calibrating her tone to neutral. "Is there something I can do for you?"

The woman shook her head, but with a stutter, like her neck is refusing to let go of what's inside. "Not here," she hissed, glancing up and down the washed-out corridor of the street. "These houses have ears. Walk with me."

Clara hesitated, but only for the optics; she has been on enough small-town streets at 2 a.m. to know danger when she saw it, and this was not that. She fell in, keeping a respectful interval, and matched the woman's pace as they moved deeper into the neighborhood—past the same sunken porches and lichen-stained lawn ornaments she'd ignored on her walk up. In the murk, even the familiar is uncanny; every porch light buzzes like a threat, every shadow seems to lean in to listen.

"My name's Mrs. Gunther," the old woman said after a while. "I know things about the murder. But I don't want your reward."

"I appreciate that," Clara said. "What do you want?"

The old woman hunched in on herself, as if there was a kernel of warmth she wanted to shield from the night. "I want the truth. I want it in the paper, in the record. I want people to know what's been happening here all these years. My grandkids live two blocks from here. They deserve more than this." Her hand gestured vaguely, as if she could dismiss the whole town with a flick.

Clara nodded, though she's already bracing for the swivel into conspiracy. "What is the truth, Mrs. Gunther?"

"It was the cult. The same as always." Her use of 'cult' wasn't casual; she meant it in the old sense, with robes and oaths and the promise of consequences.

"I've heard about the rumors," Clara said, her own voice steady, "but so far that's all I've seen. Rumors."

Mrs. Gunther gave a small shake of the head, as if the answer was an insult to local history. "They pick a night when the moon is dead. They go out to the ruins, the ones by the mill. You know the place?"

The details of the case crackled through Clara's memory: symbols carved into old trees, the spiral of salt in the damp soil, an echo of a story she didn't quite believe. She could vividly picture the place in her mind, with its crumbling altar and moss-covered stones. "I know it."

"Then you know what they do there. You know what they want." Mrs. Gunther's words have picked up a rhythm, a cadence of recitation. "They come back every so often, whenever they want something. Blood, that's what they use. Blood to keep the devil at bay."

She's recited these lines before, probably to anyone who would pause long enough to let them land.

Clara watched her carefully, parsing the line between folklore and evidence. "You ever seen them?"

Mrs. Gunther shook her head, her expression twisting. "No, no one sees them and lives, not for long. But I know. The priest, Father Callahan, told me weeks ago that they were back." Her voice wavered on "priest," as if the word itself might summon something from the air.

Clara filed this away, unsure of its worth. "What did he say, exactly?"

"Said we needed to watch ourselves. Said to keep our pets inside, not to go out after dark." Mrs. Gunther shivered, and it was impossible to tell if she was cold or frightened or just vibrating with her own nerves. "He's a holy man. He'd know."

"Did he say who was involved?"

The woman's laugh was sudden and sharp, a little too loud for the atmosphere. "Do you think a priest would name names? You're not from here. You don't know how it works.

"My mother used to warn me, every time there was a full moon. She'd say, 'Don't go into the woods, don't look at the stones, don't answer if you hear someone call your name at night.'" She closed her eyes, lost in some memory that Clara knew she'd never access. "But they're not just in the woods anymore. They're everywhere."

"You remember when Margaret Dooley was killed?" Clara asked.

The old woman's eyes opened wide, the whites were webbed with red. "Of course I do. My mother made us pray every night until the snow melted. She said the cult had gotten greedy, that they'd let something loose." She lowered her voice to a whisper. "It was the same then as it is now. A girl,

133

pretty, too curious for her own good. Her blood was the key, they said. That's why they chose her."

"Who chose her?" Clara asked, but Mrs. Gunther was already onto her next thought.

"All the girls wanted to be Margaret. She had that hair, that smile. And William was the prince of the town." The woman's mouth twisted, half-admiring, half-envious. "Everyone thought he'd marry someone from the city, but he picked her. And then she died."

"You think he was involved?"

Mrs. Gunther's face screwed up in revulsion. "No, no, not him. He was too soft. His father, though..." She let the thought trail. "Old Mr. Harrington was the real monster. He had the eyes of a wolf, they used to say. I saw him once, in the woods. He was marking the trees. With what, I don't know, but it smelled awful. Like rotten eggs and iron."

Clara's brain sifted through the layers of accusation, myth, and malice. "You think William left because of what his father did?"

The woman's mouth set in a hard line. "You'd have to, wouldn't you? If you found out your own father was... one of them." She exhaled a wet, reedy breath. "He ran as far as he could. Some say he never stopped running."

The conversation was surreal, a relay race between facts and delusion, but Clara held on, picking out the parts that might fit together. "If it's the same cult, do you know why they'd start up again now?"

Mrs. Gunther laughed again, softer this time. "This town is sick. Always has been. You can bury the symptoms, but the disease will surface eventually." She leans back, squinting at Clara. "That's why you're here, right? You don't want to leave until you've seen it for yourself."

Clara felt the bite of truth in that, and the absurdity, too. "I just want to solve the murder."

"You can't," the old woman said, simple as that. "Not unless you're willing to see what's really behind all this. Not unless you're willing to see them."

"Who's 'them'?" Clara asked, voice pitched for patience.

Mrs. Gunther lifted a trembling hand and waves it, taking in the houses and the hedges and the horizonless miasma. "All of them. The men who run things, the ones who built this place. They let the rot in so long ago, they can't even tell where it ends and where they begin. That's why the symbols are back. It's like a warning, or a promise."

Clara watched her, fought the urge to dismiss every word. "Why are you telling me this, Mrs. Gunther?"

The old woman's face creased, and for a moment there was something vulnerable there. "Because no one else would believe me. My daughter thinks I'm losing it. But I know what's real, and what's just pretend. I want you to catch them before it happens again."

Clara weighed her options. She could push for specifics, dates, names, but it was clear this woman was more attuned to the logic of superstition than the hard structure of evidence. "Thank you for telling me," she says, honest enough.

Mrs. Gunther stepped out of the alcove, back onto the street, looking both ways before she added, "If you need me, I live just behind the post office. The blue house. Don't come at night." She said it with a finality that closes the topic.

Clara watched her disappear, swallowed by the same suffocating air that conceals everything in this town. For a moment, she wondered if the woman was even real, or just a hallucination conjured by the endless, repetitive whisper of Cedar Hollow.

When she finally turned back for her borrowed car, she felt a pinch of paranoia: the sense that the town was not only watching her, but weighing her, measuring whether she belonged to the rats or the birds. Maybe both.

She was halfway down the block when a second figure emerged, this one taller, broader, younger. She braced, but it's only a man walking his dog, the leash a thin thread of normalcy in the damp. They exchanged nods, nothing more, and Clara quickened her pace until the cross-streets were behind her.

She let herself into the rental, closed the door, and took inventory of her new information. She was exhausted, but adrenaline hissed in her blood, not letting go of the old woman's warnings, the ancient names, the implication of a legacy that refuses to die.

Cedar Hollow was a town built on secrets, and tonight it felt as if the surface tension was about to break. She wondered how many Mrs. Gunthers were out there, waiting for someone to take their story seriously.

She thought through the layers of the story. It was the cult, it was William's father, it was the town itself. The town is the rot, the town needs sacrifice. None of it fit Lila's murder, but parts of it might point somewhere near the truth.

Chapter 10

The diner leaked fluorescence into the veil of white, one of the only places in Cedar Hollow with hours as long as its memory. Clara and Fisher entered through a veil of mist that hung just below the peeling awning, the wet cold pooling around their ankles as they stepped inside. The door's bell, newly shrill, announced them to the scattered clientele, made up of a handful of graveyard-shift loggers and a couple retirees who looked like they'd been sitting since the place opened in '72.

Clara scanned the space automatically. Booths that haven't been bussed; a counter lined with silent men, hunched over chipped mugs. The air was thick with bacon grease, burnt coffee, and the low murmur of talk radio filtering through an ancient speaker. It all felt like a scene waiting for the punchline, one she was now forced to deliver.

The man behind the register, Joseph Tasker, fit the diner so well it was hard to imagine him elsewhere. His arms were thick with sagging muscle, his hair a wire brush graying at the temples. Tasker wore a short-sleeve work shirt open at the throat, revealing a splotched tattoo that Clara guessed predated even his wife. He saw Fisher first, gave a nod of the chin, then let his eyes glide right past Clara. She felt the intention of the dismissal.

"Sheriff," Tasker called, voice gruff but not unfriendly. "Everything alright?"

Fisher nodded, then gestured Clara forward. "This is Agent Reynolds. We have a couple questions about Lila Hays."

Tasker's attention returned to the register, hands busy counting and recounting bills. "Already told the deputy what I know," he said. "Unless Lila's ghost has been clocking in after hours, there's nothing to add."

Clara kept her expression flat. "We appreciate your time," she said, as neutrally as possible. "Can we sit?"

Tasker waved at a corner booth, the one with the duct tape patching a split in the vinyl. "Suit yourselves. Coffee?"

Clara declined. Fisher didn't.

Tasker poured two mugs anyway, carrying them over with a resigned shuffle. He set them on the table with enough force to suggest impatience, then leaned back, arms crossed over his chest.

"So?" he said, eyes pinning Fisher.

Clara let the silence stretch, waiting for Tasker to acknowledge her. He didn't.

She pressed on. "Lila worked closing shift the night she died?"

"That's right."

"Was there anything unusual about her behavior that day? Anything she said or did?"

Tasker shrugged. "She was quiet. But she was always quiet, at least with me. Did her work, smiled at the customers. What do you want me to say?"

Clara kept her pen poised. "We're interested in anything that stands out. Even small things."

Tasker's jaw clenched. "Small things," he echoed, as if the phrase tasted bad. "Alright. She made a couple extra pots of coffee for the regulars. She stayed after to help bus tables, even though it was the busboy's job." He paused, eyes flickering with something like regret. "She left her apron in the back. That ever come up?"

Fisher glanced at Clara, but she just wrote it down. "Not until now," Clara said.

"Was she upset?" Fisher asked. "Seem nervous, distracted?"

Tasker took his time answering. "If you're asking if she was scared, I don't think so. But I'm not a mind reader. She said bye and went out through the kitchen. That's it."

Clara tried a different tack. "We heard she sometimes got rides home when it was late. Did you notice who picked her up?"

Tasker's eyes sharpened, and now he looked directly at her. "She usually biked," he said. "Sometimes she'd get a ride from one of her friends."

"What about in the weeks before the murder? Anyone stand out?" Fisher again, giving her a break.

Tasker didn't even look her way this time. "She was friends with a couple girls from school, but I don't really know their names. Sometimes the Mills boy picked her up. Nobody else I can recall."

Clara tried not to show her frustration. "What about an old pickup? Dark color, maybe black or silver. Anyone like that come through?"

Tasker seemed to think about it seriously for the first time. "There was a night—maybe two, three weeks ago before it happened—when I think Hoffman drove her home."

"You mean James Hoffman, the math teacher at the high school?" Fisher asked.

"Yup, same one," replied Tasker.

Fisher's face betrayed nothing, but Clara sensed the hint of surprise.

Tasker leaned in, forearms pressing the tabletop. "They were very chit chat every time she went to his table. Probably in his class, I'd wager."

Fisher nodded a confirmation to Clara. The conversation lapsed into a silence broken only by the clack of ceramic against Formica as Tasker cleared away the mugs.

"I've got a business to run," he said, standing up.

"We appreciate it," Fisher said, rising with him.

Clara remained seated, gathering her notes. Tasker's shadow loomed, then receded as he moved behind the register, already erasing them from his world. She watched him go, caught the flicker of his gaze as he looked past her for the last time.

Outside, the murk had thickened. The world beyond the diner was a soft, gray smudge. Clara walked beside Fisher to the cruiser, their footsteps muffled by wet gravel.

"He likes you," Clara said, voice deadpan.

Fisher gave a noncommittal grunt. "He likes the badge."

"He didn't like me," she added.

Fisher looked at her, the first genuine eye contact since they entered the diner. "This town doesn't like anyone new. Especially anyone who asks too many questions. Let's head over to Hoffman's place."

Clara let the comment hang, then slid into the passenger seat. She felt the night press close again, the diner's warmth already a memory. As Fisher turned the key and the cruiser growled to life, Clara thought about the way Tasker had dismissed her, the way everyone here expected her to fade quietly into the fog. If it hadn't been for this case she very well may have disappeared into it entirely.

Mr. Hoffman's house stood at the terminus of a dead-end street lined with identical ramblers, each with a yard the color of a chewed pencil. The place looked like it had been inherited from a relative no one liked, the paint halfway between green and gray, the roof threatening to shed shingles at the next strong wind. A porch light flickered at odd intervals, as unreliable as a witness in this case.

Clara and Fisher parked in front of the house, windshield wipers brushing away a fine spray of drizzle. The walk up to the door squelched underfoot, the lawn saturated and unkempt. A cheap brass nameplate beside the doorbell read "J. Hoffman," the adhesive curling at the corners.

Clara glanced at Fisher. "Ready?"

He nodded, already bracing for the odd defensiveness of an academic with something to prove.

She rang the bell. After a pause, footsteps approached. The door opened to a blast of over-warm air and the smell of black coffee. Hoffman himself was a slim man, his face pale and almost sharp, with the vestigial beard of a week's distraction.

He opened the door no wider than necessary. "Yes?"

Clara introduced herself. "We'd like to talk about Lila Hays."

Hoffman blinked. The lines at the corners of his eyes deepened, as if he'd practiced being skeptical in a mirror. "Of course. Please, come in." He stepped aside, holding the door but never turning his back.

The living room was a textbook case of organized neglect—books stacked in neat columns, papers fanned out across every horizontal surface, but the floor was vacuumed, and the furniture appeared to have been chosen for its resistance to stains. There was no television, only a battered upright piano and a small army of houseplants, most of which looked thirsty.

Hoffman motioned to the couch, then perched on the edge of an armchair across from them. "I already spoke to a deputy last week," he said, folding his hands in his lap. "But I'm happy to clarify anything."

Fisher led. "We're following up on your relationship to Lila Hays. You were her math teacher?"

Hoffman nodded. "AP Calculus. She was gifted. Best student in the class, maybe the best I've had in years." He sounded proud, but there was an undertone of something else. Regret, maybe, or disappointment in the universe for letting such a promising variable fall out of the equation.

Clara took a notebook from her pocket. "We heard from her employer at the diner that you gave her a ride home a few weeks ago."

Hoffman seemed unsurprised. "Yes. Her bike was flat. She didn't ask for help, but I offered." He said it as if that was supposed to explain everything.

"Where did you drop her?" Clara asked.

"Her house." He recited the address from memory. "It was less than ten minutes from the diner. I didn't think it was relevant to the case, or I would've mentioned it. I'm not hiding anything."

Clara noted the defensive edge. The emphasis was subtle, but it told Clara everything about where he expected the conversation to go. "Can you walk us through that evening?"

He shrugged. "I went to the diner after class to grade and have some coffee. She was on shift, we said hello, talked a little about college applications. She mentioned her parents weren't supportive of her leaving town, particularly her mother. I saw her struggling with the bike as I was leaving. She looked

145

embarrassed, honestly, but I insisted. It seemed silly to let her walk home alone."

Fisher's tone was neutral. "Did you stop anywhere along the way?"

"No." Hoffman smiled, but it was thin, more like a facial tic than an expression of pleasure. "There isn't anywhere to stop between the diner and her house, unless you count the gas station."

Clara wrote this down, not because it was useful, but because it gave her time to gauge the man. "What did you two talk about on the drive?"

For the first time, Hoffman hesitated. "She asked about college and what it was really like to leave home. She was nervous. Excited, but scared." He rubbed his palms together, as if he were cold. "She talked about wanting to escape. Not just Cedar Hollow, but her family. She said her father didn't care and her mother was… intense."

"Did she mention any problems at school? Or with friends?" Fisher asked.

Hoffman gave a little half-shrug that was almost apologetic. "She didn't have problems, not academically. She was at the top of every class. If there were social issues, I never heard about them. Frankly, she seemed bored by most people her age." He looked at Fisher, then at Clara, measuring how much empathy would be too much.

Clara tapped her pen. "What about John Mills? They were dating, according to most people we've talked to."

A shadow crossed Hoffman's face. "She mentioned him. Said he was kind of boring but it was something to do. I got the feeling she didn't particularly care for him." He offered a small, bleak smile. "Teenagers date for reasons that don't always make sense to adults."

Clara caught the glance he threw at Fisher, as if fishing for agreement. Instead, Fisher just waited, letting silence colonize the space.

The clock on the wall gave a single, abrupt click, and all three of them registered the seconds bleeding away. Clara could hear the pulse of rain at the window, the shroud outside thickening more and more. She pictured Lila in those last months—half in, half out, dreaming of escape but afraid of the unknown.

She leaned in. "Did you ever see her with anyone else? Or did she mention anyone?"

"I never had the sense she had a large group of friends." Hoffman offered a smile now, less forced. "I know it sounds cliché, but she was genuinely focused on getting out. Cedar Hollow wasn't built for people like her."

Fisher switched topics. "You said earlier you didn't think your ride with Lila was relevant. Why is that?"

Hoffman's eyebrows rose. "Because it was a few weeks before the…you know."

Clara studied him. She believed him, mostly, but she knew too well how people hid their guilt in the folds of technicality and semantic games.

"Were you aware of the rumors about Lila and Liam Harrington?" she asked.

Hoffman scoffed lightly. "I heard something about that the other day. I wouldn't take that nonsense seriously."

Fisher closed the notebook. "Thank you, Mr. Hoffman. We may have more questions later."

Hoffman nodded, already standing to show them out. As they crossed the threshold, he paused.

"She was a good kid," he said. The words were soft, almost inaudible over the drumming rain. "I wish I could have done more."

They walked to the car in silence. The street was darker now, the creeping fog swallowing the houses and the weak glow of porch lights. Clara slid into the passenger seat, shut the door, and let the hush of the interior calm her.

As Fisher started the car, Clara found herself thinking less about the case, and more about the way every answer only added to the confusion. In Cedar Hollow, you never really got clarity. Only the promise of it, always just out of reach.

———

The drive back to the station was a slow churn, the headlights flattening every shape into a ghost of itself. Cedar Hollow seemed to have gone completely still. There were no kids on bikes, no one out walking, even the ever-present dog-walkers absent from the sidewalks. The case seemed to have spooked the town, as if every resident was hiding away, waiting for the next rumor to decide their fate.

Fisher drove one-handed, elbow braced on the door, thumb drumming the wheel in time with the wipers. For a while neither of them spoke. It was a familiar silence, the aftermath of a dry interview, the kind that left more questions than answers.

Eventually, Fisher broke it. "You believe him?"

Clara angled her face to the glass, watching the way the world blurred by. "Maybe."

"He was a little too prepared for every question," Fisher said. "I know the type. Had his lines rehearsed."

"You think the two of them?"

"No," Fisher grunted. "There's never been talk of him having romantic entanglements with women, if you know what I mean."

"Regardless, I don't buy the idea that she was seeing anyone else. She doesn't seem the type," Clara said.

Fisher grunted again, this time with a little more conviction. "Still. Maybe it's got nothing to do with that. Maybe he resented her. Maybe she reminded him of himself, what he could've been." He gestured vaguely with his free hand, as if brushing off the thought, but Clara could tell he'd been stewing on it for a while. "Suppose you're a guy in a dead-end town, watching someone you admire get ready to leave. You drive her home, you get to talking, and you realize you'll never have her hope. Maybe it pisses you off."

Clara chewed on that. "A projection thing," she said. "He can't let her leave town because he couldn't himself."

It sounded plausible enough, but she didn't entirely buy it. There was something about the way Hoffman had looked at her—measured, cautious, a little sad—that didn't read as predatory, or even desperate. Just tired. But she let Fisher's theory settle between them, a working hypothesis.

They hit a stretch of road where the trees pressed in close, branches making a cage of gray air.

150

Clara closed her eyes, replayed the interview in her mind, looking for gaps. "You really think he's our guy?"

Fisher didn't answer immediately. "No. But if it was an older man, someone she trusted…" He trailed off, letting the list finish itself.

Clara watched his profile in the dimness. She wanted to agree with him, wanted there to be a simple answer, a single villain to hang everything on. But she knew the facts never lined up so clean.

Fisher's voice cut in again, softer. "There's something we're missing, you know."

"There always is." Clara's mouth curled at the corner.

They lapsed into silence again, the only sound the hum of the tires and the faint click of Fisher's tongue when he was deep in thought. Clara leaned back and let herself drift, mind picking at the edges of the puzzle.

Fisher pulled into the station lot, the building's low yellow glow seeping through the haze. He killed the engine and stared through the windshield, eyes narrowed.

They sat a while longer, the engine ticking as it cooled, neither one ready to go inside and face the war of paperwork and rumor waiting for them. Clara felt the exhaustion in her bones, the familiar ache of another day spent chasing ghosts through a dampening gloom that would never clear.

"What next?" Fisher asked.

She looked at him, saw the way the years had etched patience into every line of his face, and she envied it.

"We keep talking," Clara said. "Someone out there knows. They always do."

Fisher nodded, put a hand to the door, then paused.

"Good work today," he said, not quite meeting her eyes.

"Thanks," Clara said, meaning it.

They stepped into the chill together, the shroud closing in behind them.

Chapter 11

Clara's heart spiked as she turns off the road and up toward the Harrington estate. The climb feels steeper than before, as if the earth itself is bracing against her. By the time the estate emerged, the old iron gates hung askew, one bent as if by violence, and the stone pillars looked daubed in clownish red paint—except it wasn't just paint, not at this saturation, not at this ferocity. The car rolled to a halt under the icy gaze of a marble nymph whose bare torso was now adorned with the word "Pervert" in hurried, blocky strokes.

Clara stepped into the driveway. Her shoes crunched on a mosaic of shattered glass, and the air shivered with the ozone tang of vandalism still fresh. The mansion, once a study in restraint, was besieged. Spray-painted slurs ("Coward," "Freakshow," "Murderer") ran in arterial streaks up the colonnades, across the garage, even onto the tail end of an oxidized bronze deer. Entire phrases snaked along the porch rail: "WE KNOW," "LIAM KILLS," "NO MORE HARRINGTON LIES."

She paused, inventorying the carnage, the way someone might slow to consider a multi-car pileup. The phrase "Arbiter of Decay" glistened on the front door. Someone had thrown eggs too, and the yolks congealed in yellow gobs that smell faintly of sulfur and rot.

Down the hill, through the trees, she spotted two or three cars idling, headlights dimmed, occupants barely visible behind fogged windshields. Word had gotten out. Cedar Hollow's appetite for spectacle was insatiable, and now the Harrington family house was its main event. Clara studied the rhythm of the damage, the symmetry of attack. This wasn't a random outburst. It was targeted and strategic, executed by people who knew exactly what message they intended to send.

She took a breath, exhaling vapor. With every step up the porch, she felt as if she was trespassing on holy ground, or a crime scene. Maybe both.

The porch itself was a battlefield. Fragments of a decorative wreath littered the welcome mat. The doorbell was unplugged, wires yanked, and a dead bird lied flattened in the corner, wings splayed, breast still damp and sticky from a thrown tomato. Clara tucked her hands into her pockets, unwilling to smear herself with the residue of the town's loathing.

She stood before the front door, steadying herself. Fisher told her to check it out and report on the situation, but she's not sure if she's here to mediate or witness, to confront Liam or to protect him. Her own motives feel as fractured as the glass beneath her boots. It occurred to her that the FBI never taught her about small-town sieges, about the physics of rumor or the chemistry of hatred. The curriculum skipped the days when a town turned on itself, and all the old rules go primal.

Clara raised her fist to knock, and for a suspended instant her reflection blurred in the high-gloss black of the door, the spray paint refracting her features into something monstrous. Before she made contact, the knob turned, and the door glided inward with the smoothness of ritual.

Liam Harrington stood in the foyer, backlit by the cool, controlled glow of a chandelier. He was in a tailored navy shirt, sleeves rolled just so. His face was careful, as if meticulously arranged for her. He glanced down at her shoes, at the muck on them, and then back up, meeting her eyes with the steadiness of a practiced host.

"Miss Reynolds," he said, as if she were merely stopping by for tea. His composure contrasted with the wreckage outside. "I wasn't expecting you this morning. I suppose you've seen the latest."

Clara matched his calm, masking her own uncertainty. "Vandals?"

"Or," he replied, "just the effects of a rumor that's ripened a bit too well."

The sudden hush as the door swung closed behind her was so seismic that Clara momentarily wondered if Harrington manor had been designed expressly to smother voices. The threshold became a dam—everything outside shrieking with agitation, while within, every surface gleamed, every stair runner and polished floorboard radiated silent rectitude. It was the kind of place where nothing out of order ever lasted long; even now, the only sign of the chaos was a faint chemical tang of cleaning solvent, as if the staff had anticipated the need for containment.

The hush pressed in, heightening the click of her shoes on marble, the clang of distant central heating, the way Liam's measured breathing filled the foyer as he regarded her. He closed the door gently, one palm splayed against the lacquered wood for a heartbeat longer than necessary, as if communing with the old house, promising it that order would prevail.

Liam's calm in the face of siege felt like a performance, but Clara didn't think it was meant for her. He wasn't posturing for her benefit, not entirely. The set of his mouth, the precision of his composure, suggested a man so acclimated to scrutiny that even at his most exposed, the act was indistinguishable from the person. She wondered if he knew the difference anymore.

There would be rumors that Harrington staged the whole thing, or else was hiding bodies in the wainscot. Both stories would circulate. Both would serve their purposes.

He ushered her into the library, and the door thudded softly shut behind them, decanting warmth and old paper into the air. Liam gestured to a deep armchair beside the fireplace and positioned himself in the opposite seat, crossing one long leg over the other and folding his hands in his lap with practiced serenity.

For a moment, neither spoke. The mantel clock ticked in the silence, its metronome pulse aligning with the seconds Clara spent rehearsing her opening question. But Liam beat her to it.

"What do you think they're hoping for?" he asked, voice so low it harmonized with the clock.

She blinked at the shift in protocol. "Who?"

"The town." He nodded toward the window, where the warped reflection of torchlights leaked in through a slit in the drapes. "The ones painting the gates. The ones who called the press, or left bird corpses at my doorstep. Surely you don't think this is about simple property damage."

Clara hesitated, then leaned into her chair, adopting the posture of the interrogator. "People want a villain. They want a story that makes sense of things they can't control."

Liam's lips twitched. "Ah. So, they make one up, if none are available?"

She shrugged. "Or they pick the oldest one on the shelf and dust it off."

A moment stretched, punctured only by the pop of a log in the fireplace. Liam watched the flames, the light carving the hollows at his cheeks into something foxlike. "It's almost flattering, the persistence," he said at last. "We tried so hard to move past all this, Clara. As children. As adults. Cedar Hollow wouldn't let us." He swiveled back to her, eyes bright. "You came to see if I'm dangerous."

It was not a question, so she didn't answer. Instead, she shifted to the matter at hand. "What are you going to do about it?"

Liam drew a slow breath, as if parsing a more complicated answer than what he wished to give. "What I've always done, I suppose. Endure." He said it lightly, but Clara heard the fatigue beneath. "Let them exhaust themselves. Wait for the next spectacle to divert them." He smiled, but it was the smile of a man who'd practiced being gracious while cornered since childhood.

She watched him, measuring the way he seemed both vulnerable and unbreakable. The juxtaposition made her uneasy and invited her to drop her guard, even as every instinct screamed not to. There was heaviness in his gaze, a readiness, as if he'd rehearsed every possible outcome of this meeting and was prepared to shed one mask for another, depending on what she said next.

"You knew it would come to this," Clara pressed, not out of suspicion but because she sensed he'd already mapped the entire shape of this conflict.

"Yes," he admitted. "Though I hoped otherwise. People can disappoint you in both directions, I've found." He uncrossed his legs, leaning forward, elbows on knees. "Would you join me for dinner tonight?"

She blinked, caught off guard. "Dinner?"

"Your investigation. I believe I can help." He flashed another smile, more genuine this time.

She was suspicious of his certainty, and of what this offer meant. She remembered Fisher's words, Kane's theatrical humility, the way everyone in Cedar Hollow seemed to circle each other in orbit. She thought about the vandalism, about the crime scene, about how none of it fit together cleanly. If Liam had information, was it truth or misdirection? Was she being recruited, subtly, into the Harrington cause?

"I'm not sure I should—" she began, but Liam raised a palm, forestalling her with polite insistence.

"I have information," he said, voice tightrope steady. "You can decide how to use it. But if you want to understand what's really going on in Cedar Hollow, you should hear it from me first." His eyes held hers, the challenge and the bargain both plainly visible.

Clara felt herself bending toward the center of the storm, toward the place she'd told herself she wouldn't go. She let his words circle her like a noose, then exhaled. "It might save you some time," Liam added, softly.

She waited a beat, then nodded. "Okay. I'll be back this evening."

"Very well," Liam said, standing. His face shifted, a flicker of gratitude and something else. Indecision perhaps, or relief. Clara watched him, trying again to read the man behind the performance. "You may be surprised," he added, almost as an afterthought.

He nudged the library door for her, and Clara retraced her steps through the echoing house, each room a vault of quiet. At the threshold, she paused, looking back into the curated gloom. Liam lingered in the entry, hands clasped behind his back, head inclined in what might have been deference or dismissal.

Outside, the world was raw and unfiltered. Clara pulled the door shut, sealing his promise in the heavy air. She lingered a moment on the porch, letting the derision and the anger in the vandalism settle over her like a dusting of radioactive ash. She could still feel the pressure of Liam's gaze, twin points of heat boring through the safety glass.

She walked back down the ruined steps, the glass crunching underfoot with every stride. At the driveway's bottom, she paused. The onlookers' cars were still there, their occupants emboldened by the spectacle. Someone filmed her with a phone, the blue glare reflecting off the windshield. Clara stared at the lens until the watching face, startled, snapped the device down. The engine revved, but the car didn't leave.

She made a show of checking her watch, then turned her back on the crowd. There was nothing new to glean from surveillance, not until she'd heard what Liam had to say. Still, Clara scanned the tree line, the outlying hedges, alert for movement. Rumor and violence always traveled in packs.

The wind off the valley hit her, sharp and invigorating. She inhaled, tasting woodsmoke and the metallic tang of fear in the air. She hated that her pulse stuttered at the hint of being watched, but she didn't break stride as she reached her car. She got inside, locked the doors, and breathed in the cold, sterile silence. Only then did she allow the adrenaline to subside, the afterimage of Liam's offer playing back in her mind.

She sat for a minute, knuckles whitening around the steering wheel, as she tried to transpose her own motives onto the evening. Was she really doing this to solve a murder, or to satisfy the gnawing curiosity that had taken root since Lila's death? Was she an agent of justice, or just another voyeur in a town built on secrets?

———

Clara returned to the estate just as the last of the twilight fractured into dusk, exposing the full raw wound of the day's vandalism.

The dining room was immense. Twelve-foot ceilings, flocked wallpaper the color of dried blood, a table so long she could imagine wars waged over its center. The only participants tonight were Clara and Liam, and the expanse of dark wood between them was less a buffer than a challenge.

He stood as she entered, imposing and flawless in a dark suit, his posture unstudied but somehow classical. He looked tired, the sharpness in his jaw overtaking any hint of softness, yet his eyes remained a clear, deeply blue, and fixed on her with an intensity that suggested the meal was happening entirely for her benefit.

"Clara," he said, dropping the formal address as if to signal a ceasefire. "I appreciate your willingness to return, in spite of…" He gestured vaguely at the windows, at the simmering threat outside, then let the hand drop.

She took her seat. He'd placed two chairs together, close enough to conspire, not so close as to implicate. The table was already set: mismatched candles burning low, long-stemmed crystal catching the light in shivers, the service old enough to carry the ghosts of a hundred brutal gatherings. Clara noted the presence of a single decanter, a bottle of Bordeaux already breathing, and the way the lacquered wood surface had been buffed to an obsidian shine.

They exchanged no small talk; there was nothing trivial left to say. Instead, Liam poured the wine with a steadiness that bordered on ceremonial. He filled her glass first, then his own, then raised his in salute. The motion was fluid but careful, like someone who had practiced this gesture many times in front of a mirror.

"To the truth," he offered, voice smooth as the wine. "And to not running from it."

Clara hesitated. She regarded the glass, the garnet swirl of its contents, and wondered whether the toast was an invitation or a warning. "Cheers," she replied, the word dry in her throat.

They drank. The wine was excellent, smoky and layered, the sort of thing meant to mark a turning point.

He watched her, gauging the effect of his words. "Do you know what it's like," he began, "to be accused of something you didn't do?"

She met his gaze, saw the vulnerability peeking through the cracks in his confidence. "Sometimes," she answered, guarded.

"The stories they tell about us," Liam continued, "they've shaped this family more than you know." His voice held a mix of defiance and regret.

Clara waited for more, though he seemed momentarily lost in thought.

A first course arrived, silent as a shadow. Delicate slices of venison, garnished with wild mushrooms and something fernlike. The servers did not speak or make eye contact with Clara, as if she were another artifact, as if they had long since learned to avoid becoming part of the story.

Clara cut into the meat, the blade meeting only the mildest resistance, and waited for the next move. She had learned to let suspects fill their own silences.

"Ah, yes, I have a proposal for you," Liam said as he snaps out of it. "I will reveal a family secret, but first you must reveal one of your own. Specifically, what drove you to this little town to begin with."

"I'm not here to play games with you," Clara said, seething outwardly. "You told me you had information, now you tell me or I leave."

"Worth a shot." He breathed out slowly, the exhale a release. "Margaret was killed by my uncle William. The truth everyone assumed, but we denied." The admission hung in the air, heavy and raw.

"And blamed this cult?" Clara pushed, her interest sharp.

Liam nodded, the movement filled with shame. "A group of amateur historians, really. A ridiculous theory but my grandfather needed a story that was plausible enough to distract, yet fantastic enough to burn through the rumor mill before it got too close to home. All the while, the real secrets were more pedestrian and much less interesting."

"Seems like it didn't work out that way. Rather than burning out, it led to four decades of suspicion."

"Yes," Liam admitted. "It took on a life of its own my grandfather didn't expect. All the sudden we were the ringleaders of this made-up group. Poetic justice, perhaps."

The second course arrived. More wine was poured. By the time the plates were cleared, Clara found herself not feeling lulled, exactly, but changed. The hostility she brought to the table had mutated into a reluctant curiosity. Liam was performing, yes, but so was she. In Cedar Hollow, no one survived by staying transparent.

"Why tell me?" she asked.

Liam's eyes met hers, clear and unflinching. "Because I'm tired of it. I was very young at the time and didn't really understand what was happening.

When I finally realized the full weight of it all I saw how trapped I was."

"Trapped, how?" Clara asked.

"There are certain expectations of behavior that come with being part of this family." His eyes were no longer meeting hers. "I thought perhaps that I could change that, but when I finally had the chance, I found that I couldn't after all. I'd be happy for the truth to come out but, to my shame, I couldn't bring myself to share it."

"Until now."

"I thought you might understand. You're not one of them, don't have the weight of years of bias and hatred. I thought I sensed something in you that I recognized, the deep sadness that comes from not having control over your fate. Maybe I'm wrong, but there's something there—I see it in your face—and that's why I'm curious about you."

Clara's fingers traced the ridges of the wine glass without lifting it, circling repeatedly as if she could grind the memory of Liam's words into the crystal. She felt the surge of empathy in her chest, but she fought to contain it, to limit its spread.

"You want my story?" she asked, trying to summon the clinical tone that had gotten her through hundreds of interviews, dozens of cross-table confessions. The trick was to keep the information flowing in one direction, never backwards, never into herself.

But this wasn't an interrogation. His gaze unsettled her, not because it was predatory, but because it was too open. It reminded her of those rare moments at Quantico when a classmate would admit, in the quiet between drills, that they were a little bit afraid of becoming an agent, of whether they could handle it emotionally. The raw voltage of that fragility haunted her even now.

"I want you to stay," Liam said softly, not breaking the stare. It was a statement with no strategic edge, no expectation. The directness of it caught her off-guard.

Clara's pulse hammered through her wrists, the sensation so strong she half expected the fork on the table to tremble. She felt the old urge to run, to vanish into the night and leave this place and its decaying grandeur and its impossible inhabitants behind. But she stayed, because she needed the answer to the question even more than he did.

Instead of speaking, she drank. The wine was heavier now, the taste of oak barriques intermingling with some volatile note she couldn't identify. Maybe the bottle had soured, or maybe she was tasting her own anxiety.

She watched the candle stub flicker at the far end of the table, the way the melting wax pooled then overflowed onto the antique runner in a slow, viscous disaster. She wondered how long before it burned through. Everything in Cedar Hollow felt like it was measured in time-to-rupture.

"You're wrong," Clara said finally, voice trembling despite her effort to keep it steady. "I don't know what it's like to be accused of something." She let the edges of the admission harden as she continued, "But I know what it's like to be a victim. To lose someone. To blame myself for not being there."

Liam flinched. Nothing more than a twitch of jaw and eyelid, but the reaction was real. Clara felt it hit the center of the table, spiraling out from the spot where neither of them had set down their forks.

"My brother Alex," she said. The words tumbled out before she knew to reel them back. "He was abducted. On his way home from a friend's house, three blocks from our street."

She saw the memory in full color. Alex's face, open and mischievous, the mop of hair perpetually falling into his eyes, the way he'd dart down the warped sidewalk with a plastic bag of candy clutched to his chest. He wasn't afraid of anything or anybody, Clara remembered. That was the part that made her sick, he would have trusted anyone who smiled at him.

"They found him a few months later," Clara said. "Hundreds of miles away. Dumped in a ravine." She stopped, heard the clatter of a dish in the kitchen, the faint trill of an owl through the double-paned glass. "He was eight. I was twelve."

It took her a moment to realize how much she'd said. In the careful, compartmentalized world she'd built for herself since the day of Alex's disappearance, any admission of guilt or grief was forbidden. She felt the old, familiar burn behind her eyelids, but she held it in check as she always had. It was crazy that she told him any of this but at the same time it was a relief.

Liam didn't speak. He sat with his hands folded, index fingers steepled, and regarded her not as an interrogator, not as a Harrington, but as a man who had lived too long in rooms like this one, surrounded by the cold stares of family and the echo of secrets. In that moment his age showed, not as a number but as an accumulation. Clara wondered how much of his life had been spent keeping watch over the pain of others.

"It drove you to the Bureau," Liam said, almost tenderly. "Didn't it?"

She nodded, not trusting herself to speak.

"And now you're here," Liam observed. "Why Cedar Hollow?"

Clara breathed. The answer was easy but saying it aloud felt like another act of desecration. "After the last case," she began, "I didn't have anywhere else to go. I needed…" She fumbled for the right word, then gave up. "I needed to disappear for a while."

He was quiet, letting the statement settle. Clara watched the flicker of recognition cross his face. Not sympathy, but identification. She realized he was telling her his own story in the pauses, that this was a negotiation of ghosts.

"My last case was a kidnapping," she said, the distance between them shrinking as her resolve grows. "It was supposed to give me some of the closure I needed, but I made a terrible mistake."

Liam waited, patient and intent.

"I wanted it so much," Clara continued. "I was careless with some of the evidence, broke the chain of custody. It wasn't admissible in court." She closes her eyes, the image of the suspect's acquittal burned there. "The whole thing fell apart. The family..." Her voice caught, a testament to the pain she still carried.

The admissions came easier after that first breach. She wasn't confessing so much as exorcising, the way a wound might need to be opened before it could heal. Clara saw, to her mild horror, that she was telling Liam the truth as she would have told a priest or a psychiatrist. The difference was that he didn't flinch from it. He let it in.

They sat in a static silence, the air refusing to move until Clara forced herself to breathe again. In the sideboard mirror, she noticed her cheeks were flushed, her chin set in a stubborn line. She'd wanted to appear impassive, but instead she looked animated, almost alive.

Liam's demeanor, always so calibrated, softened further. "My father used to say that the difference between a good Harrington and a mediocre one was whether you were willing to absorb pain for the family. Not just your own, but everyone else's." The smile he offered was bitter. "I thought he was wrong, but now I'm not so sure."

Clara stared at the table, at the veins in the wood running directionless beneath the glass. "What do you believe defines a good person?" she asked, surprised by her own question. "Is it about how much pain you can endure, or how much you can share with others?"

"Maybe it's about not turning away from it," Liam said quietly. "I don't know."

Clara thought of her brother, the way the neighborhood had turned inward after his disappearance. All the rules about curfews, about talking to strangers, about locking your doors, none of it had helped. People wanted to believe that if they could identify the evil, they could separate from it. But it always came from within. She shivered, this time not from cold.

The meal ended in silence, but it was a silence charged with mutual understanding, not fatigue or defeat. Clara pushed away from the table, the chair legs rasping across the expensive rug. She felt unburdened and heavy at the same time, like she'd swapped one set of chains for another.

Liam stood as she did, and for a moment, Clara thought he was going to offer her his hand, or an apology, or something else she couldn't accept. Instead, he just nodded, a gesture so small and matter of fact that it felt like a form of kinship.

They left the dining room together, the hush of the house resettling around them, all the spaces between things tighter than before.

She stepped outside, the air stinging her skin with cold clarity. In the thin light along the gravel driveway, the vandalism on the estate walls had already started to fade, the words less clear than they'd been at dusk. But the threat lingered: the sense of being watched, the sense of being marked.

She stood on the porch and looked up at the blur of stars behind the cloudbank. For the first time since coming to Cedar Hollow, she felt something give way inside—a fragment of acceptance, or maybe just the first breath after a long submersion.

Clara made her way to her car, the chill sharpening her focus. She didn't look back at the house, didn't let herself wonder if Liam was watching from the darkness of the window. Instead, she sat in the driver's seat, letting the engine idle as her thoughts raced ahead to the next step.

She didn't know if solving Lila's case would change anything about her past, or his, or anyone else's. But she knew she couldn't stop now. Not because she wanted to redeem herself, really, but because someone had to break the pattern. Someone had to be the one who didn't turn away.

She would keep going. And for the first time, she actually wanted to.

"You'll be back?" Liam's voice echoed in her memory as she pulled away from the house, gravel crunching beneath the tires.

Yes, she thought. The answer was simple and, for the first time, entirely true.

She drove into the night, the murk a little thinner, her heart a little lighter.

Chapter 12

Clara paused at the entrance, her knuckles lightly tapping the door that was as thin and weak as Cecilia's accusations. Inside, she could hear the soft patter of footsteps and sensed a wave of hesitation in the air. The moist tendrils curled around her shoulders, pushing her forward with the same relentless pressure as the unasked questions weighing on her mind. Her breath emerged in visible puffs, cold and empty. Fisher's theories looped around her thoughts, winding tighter and tighter, a constricting spiral of uncertainty.

She focused on the girl, her face pale and expectant as it emerged through the crack of the door. Clara had hoped for more, for the timidness to vanish outside the confines of the police station. But Cecilia's eyes were as hesitant as her last confession.

Cecilia held the door open, a signal of wary surrender. "You're here," she said. Her voice was thin, unsure if it was statement or accusation.

"Can we talk?" Clara kept her tone even. She watched Cecilia's reluctance like a slow-motion confession.

The girl stood there for a moment, a pause that felt like doubt.

"Sure," Cecilia finally relented, stepping aside.

The house was quiet, holding the same tentative breath as its occupants. Clara scanned the modest furnishings. She saw Cecilia's apprehension in the way the girl fidgeted, her fingers plucking at her sleeves.

"I need you to be straight with me," Clara said, her voice a mix of urgency and encouragement. "Are you sure about this affair with Liam Harrington?"

Cecilia's eyes darted away. "I don't know for sure," she mumbled.

"Then why say it?" Clara pressed, her patience a carefully held breath.

"I just heard it." Cecilia's words were evasive, the strain showing in her tone.

"Heard it where?" Clara kept the pressure steady, sensing that the slightest let-up would send Cecilia retreating.

"Church," Cecilia admitted. Her voice wavered, as if the confession held more weight than the accusation. "People there were saying..."

"That's a big leap," Clara interrupted, "from rumors to what you told me."

Cecilia's fingers tightened on her sleeves, the movement a small protest. "I thought it made sense. I didn't mean to..." She trailed off, her fear plain and fragile.

"Are you even sure she was seeing someone else, besides John?" Clara asked. "You mentioned gifts and disappearances."

Cecilia hesitated, a painful uncertainty in her expression. "She would have told me anything else." The words felt rehearsed, like she was convincing herself as much as Clara. "But..."

Clara leaned forward, her intensity pushing Cecilia deeper into her shell. "But what? If you're lying, this won't just hurt John."

"I'm not!" Cecilia's voice cracked, high with emotion. "I really thought..." She left the thought unfinished, hanging in the charged air between them.

Clara exhaled. "You need to tell me exactly what you know."

Cecilia was silent, the pause heavy with trepidation.

Clara insisted. "The rumors you heard, what did they say?"

Cecilia's response was slow, each word a struggle. "That she was seeing someone. Someone she shouldn't."

"Was the name Harrington ever mentioned?" Clara's question landed with precision, targeting Cecilia's evasions.

Cecilia flinched, then nodded. "Once or twice, I think."

Clara watched her carefully, probing the details with practiced skill. "And you never actually saw them together?"

"No," Cecilia admitted, her voice small and defeated. "But I was sure..." She didn't finish.

"You need to be certain," Clara said. "We can't just go on what you think."

"I am certain," Cecilia replied, the contradiction hanging in the air. "I think."

Clara saw the fear in Cecilia's eyes, the desperation to be right. It reminded her of her own need for certainty, the way it had undone her before.

"We haven't arrested anyone yet," Clara said, trying to coax more from the girl. "But this could change things."

Cecilia's expression shifted, a mix of hope and anxiety. "Really?"

"Yes," Clara replied. "If it's true." She let the implication linger.

Cecilia's voice dropped, barely more than a whisper. "I don't want to give anyone the wrong idea."

"Then help me understand," Clara urged. "Tell me what you know."

Cecilia's fingers fidgeted, her uncertainty a visible thing. "I heard he bought her stuff." Her words tumbled out, faster, more emotional. "That she'd sneak out and meet him when John was working." She looked almost panicked as she said it, as if releasing the words would make them more real.

Clara studied the girl, saw the tension that coiled in her slight frame. "You're sure it wasn't someone else?" Clara tried, shifting tactics. She wanted to be careful but precise.

"I don't know." Cecilia's frustration edged into her voice, a flicker of defiance. "Obviously she didn't tell me everything."

"Cecilia," Clara said, adopting a gentler tone, "do you have any idea who else it might possibly be? Someone I can look into, even if it's a long shot."

"No," Cecilia replied, her words clipped and defensive. "It has to be him." Her tone shifted, more uncertain than defiant. "Why else would they say it?"

"People talk," Clara said, trying to maintain patience, knowing how easily the town spins stories.

178

She'd seen it already, more than once. "But that only gets us so far."

Cecilia didn't respond, her silence a fragile barricade.

"Are you lying to get back at John?" Clara asked, probing one last time.

"I'm not lying!" Cecilia insisted. "Maybe I don't know everything. But I know something." Her desperation showed in her eyes, a raw sincerity that shook Clara more than she wanted to admit.

Clara heard the truth in Cecilia's doubt, in her need to be right. It worried her.

"If you know more," Clara said, "it could help us find who really did this."

Cecilia was quiet, her hands still for the first time. "I told you what I know," she said, a note of resignation in her voice. "I can't do more."

Clara exhaled, feeling her own frustration rise and struggle against the surface. She didn't want to show it, but it was difficult not to. "Okay," she said, giving Cecilia a long look. "I believe you." Her words felt like an admission of something else, of how tenuous this entire case was.

Cecilia watched her, an intensity in her gaze. "I just thought..." Her voice trailed off, unsure if Clara's belief was good or bad.

"You thought right to tell us," Clara said, trying to sound reassuring. But her uncertainty slipped through. "You're sure about what you heard?"

"Yes," Cecilia replied, her conviction returning with force.

"Thank you," Clara said, standing. The interview hadn't gone the way she wanted, but she couldn't let go of the possibility. "Really."

Cecilia seemed relieved, but her eyes stayed wide with concern. "I hope it helps," she said, her voice barely more than a murmur.

"So do I," Clara replied. She hesitated, seeing how much Cecilia believed in her own version of the truth. The fear and uncertainty were there, but so was something else, something fragile yet firm. Clara didn't know what to make of it, and it left her unsettled.

She walked to the door, her steps slow with doubt. She stopped and looked back, her mind turning over Cecilia's diffidence, unsure if it was the key to everything or nothing at all.

"Thanks again," Clara said, more to fill the silence than to add anything new.

The air outside was thick, pressing, and it clung to Clara like it was a part of her. Cecilia's words echoed in her mind, louder with each repetition, and Clara found herself caught in their orbit. She wanted to dismiss them, the contradictory statements of a confused teenage girl craving attention without even realizing it, but the weight of Cecilia's belief made it impossible.

Her path veered toward Father Callahan, toward another voice in the chorus of confusion, the locus from which all the rumors seem to originate. She didn't know if he'd be more help this time, but she couldn't leave it without trying. The priest had more to say; Clara was sure of it. Sure of something.

She picked up her pace, her determination cutting through the haze, her questions burning like bright spots in the gray.

————

Father Callahan's face betrayed his unease at seeing her again. Clara moved toward him, quick as the questions on her heels. Her mind churned with Cecilia's vague confession. She wanted more, more than the girl's evasion and fear. The priest seemed expectant, cautious, and it made her wonder how much he held back the first time. She stopped short of his shadow, her pulse sharp as the cold. He stood with authority and something else. Anxiety?

"Father." Clara's greeting was precise, the clipped edge of a scalpel. She watched his features writhe through stages of professional warmth, then priestly concern, then the brittle mask of self-preservation. His unease was barely contained, present in the way his hands worried at the sleeves of his ancient black jacket and in the sudden shallowing of his breath.

He blinked at her, recovering into a semblance of spiritual authority. "What brings you here, my child?" The greeting was smooth, but his gaze flicked over her shoulder as if expecting a parishioner or, more likely, an escape route.

Clara let the silence press in, the corners of her mouth set in perpetual gravity. "We need to talk," she said, her voice low and direct, flat as hospital lighting.

Father Callahan's fingers interlaced themselves, nerves running through the weathered joints. He tried to hold her eye for a moment, failed, and steadied himself with a gentle clearing of his throat. "Have you come," he asked, "to seek confession?" The line was a familiar one, a priest's defense mechanism, but it was clear even he didn't believe it.

Clara didn't smile, didn't allow even the subtlest curl of humor. She edged closer, narrowing the space so that every word would count. "There's more to the story," she said, each syllable measured for impact. "What rumors have you heard about Lila Hays? About Liam Harrington?" She waited, letting the names hover above their heads like the beginnings of a haunting.

Father Callahan made a vague, conciliatory gesture. "Rumors?" he repeated, the word caught as if on a fishhook. He seemed to be weighing the cost of each answer, balancing the scales of duty and survival. "People talk, Detective. It's a small town." The phrase was meant to be dismissive, but something in the way he said it revealed an undercurrent of dread.

Clara pressed. "I'm not a Detective. You know which people. You know when it started. Don't pretend otherwise."

Callahan exhaled, the breath loud in the hush of the rectory. "What are you accusing me of?" he asked, his tone part-wounded, part-warning. "Spreading idle talk?"

Clara ignored the question, instead continuing, "Did these rumors come from you? Or from Kane? Or from someone in your congregation?" She watched his lips, saw them quiver before regaining composure.

"Mr. Kane is a pillar of the community," Callahan said, the script dusted off and deployed. "He has nothing to gain from—" but Clara cut him off.

"You and Kane are very connected," she said, the words deliberate. "All this talk, it furthers his agenda." She let the charge drift, observed the tremor it awakened in Callahan's posture.

He hesitated. "The church relies on the goodwill of many benefactors. The lines between the

183

congregation and the rest of Cedar Hollow have always been… porous." He tried to smile, but it was a brittle thing. "But I assure you, whatever you think you're hearing—"

"I'm trying to find the truth," Clara interrupted, her tone calm but relentless. "But all I'm hearing out there is a lot of bullshit."

For a moment, Callahan studied her as if she were a particularly difficult passage from the Book of Lamentations. "Is it the truth you want, or the confession?" he asked. "Because they're not always the same."

She didn't dignify that with a reply. "You know the rumors about Lila and Liam Harrington. You believed them, or you wanted others to." She scrutinized him, hunted for the flicker of complicity.

He faltered then, the words ringing with more accuracy than comfort. Clara saw the blow land. She let it.

"Have you ever met Liam Harrington?" she asked, changing tack so quickly he nearly stumbled.

He blinked, surprised. "Of course," he replied, and the truth flashed in the sincerity. "The family has always been…well, you know what they are." He grimaced, the old village rivalries surfacing. "But I have never had cause to suspect him of anything like this. He was a… good boy. Proud. A little cold, but—

" He stopped himself, realizing the trap of saying too much.

Clara pounced. "So why accuse him now?" she asked. "Why repeat it, even hint at it from the pulpit?"

He was silent for a moment, wrestling with the answer. "Because I was asked to," he finally said, the words wrested from somewhere beneath his surface.

"Kane?" she asked, her voice cold and efficient.

He nodded. Clara leaned in. "And you? Do you believe it?"

The priest looked away, his eyes settling on the stained glass that decorated the rectory's inner office. "I believe in the power of stories, Detective," he said, the bitterness undisguised. "And in their danger."

Clara paced a slow, deliberate circle around him, every step a forensic examination of his guilt. "So, you told the story. And you let people believe it. Did you ever wonder what it would cost?"

Callahan's shoulders sagged. The collar at his throat looked suddenly too tight, pinching him at the edges. "I thought it would be enough. I thought...if we could rattle the Harringtons, maybe they'd leave. Maybe the darkness would follow them."

"And instead, a girl is dead. Your story got her killed." Clara's accusation was a blunt object, swung with purpose.

He recoiled at that, the words hitting like stones. "That isn't fair," he whispered. "You don't know the history here."

Clara stopped, folding her arms. "Then tell me. All of it. Not the church version."

He looked up, and for a moment the priestly mask dropped entirely, and she saw only the small, frightened man behind it. "Kane came to me last year," he said, the confession reluctant and queasy. "He said the old stories were resurfacing. The ruins, the night rituals, the marks on the stone. He wanted me to warn the town. To use the pulpit."

"Why did you agree to help him? Was it the condition for building the new church?" Clara finished, watching the priest closely.

The old man's shoulders sagged, an admission as clear as words. "I thought I was protecting people," he said. The desperation in his voice made Clara's skin prickle.

"What did you expect?" Clara asked, her patience stretched thin but her determination strong. "You talk about a cult, about danger, and someone gets killed. How did you think this would end?"

"The church is meant to be a sanctuary," Callahan insisted. "We only wanted..." He didn't finish, and Clara saw the turmoil in his expression.

"You only wanted to drive out the Harringtons," Clara said. "And you got more than you bargained for."

"We never meant for..." Callahan trailed off, his voice catching.

"That's what you keep saying," Clara replied. "But it's not enough."

Callahan's eyes met hers, the look in them a mix of desperation and defiance. "But it was him! Or his followers. You're forgetting that they are the true culprits."

"You still believe that? Don't you understand what really happened? Kane set up the whole thing, including the murder."

"No!" Callahan cried out. "You don't know him. He's ambitious, yes, but he cares most about this town. That...that is not in his heart!"

"Then why are there no cameras at the church site?"

"You don't need cameras at a house of God," Callahan stated with some smugness.

"It's not a house of God yet, it's a construction site. Kane had a plan for these rumors, he nudged John Mills to do it and he wanted to protect him afterward."

"That's preposterous! How do you explain the carvings on the tree? It was the cult."

"You really don't see the big picture," she sighed. "That's why you're such an easy tool for Kane to wield."

She left Callahan with his worries, left him standing in the shadow of the church he'd hoped to build. Let him think it out for himself. Her footsteps were quick and determined, cutting through the cold as her mind cut through the pieces she'd uncovered. It wasn't enough, but it was more than she'd had before. It pointed to Kane, but not as directly as Clara needed.

The drizzle closed around her, thick and clinging. Clara pushed through, a grim sense of vindication mingling with persistent uncertainty. If she was right, it would be exceedingly difficult to prove.

———

The mansion pulled Clara into its orbit. Her footsteps fell soft and hollow against the drive, a march of suspicion and uncertainty. She drew close, her mind awash with fragments of Callahan's admission. Her breath escaped in sharp bursts. She barely saw her hand as it moved to the door. Liam's shadow appeared, part watchful, part something else.

Clara wondered how much to tell him, how much to reveal. She measured his silhouette against the expectation she carried.

His greeting was calm, as composed as Clara wished she felt. "I knew you'd be back," Liam said, ushering her into the warmth of the house.

Clara gave a tight nod. "I talked to the priest again," she said. Her voice was sharper than she intended, but it felt good to get the words out. "He's been spreading rumors. About you. The family."

"Clara." Liam's expression was careful, but she sensed the edge of emotion he worked to conceal. "I told you the town was quick to believe."

She studied his face, saw the mix of certainty and vulnerability she'd now come to expect from him. It made her want to believe what she'd uncovered even more. "That's not all," Clara said. "Kane instructed him to do it."

Liam's reaction surprised her. It wasn't shock, not quite. He seemed...resigned. "And you're surprised?" he asked, as if he'd known all along. As if he'd been waiting for this revelation.

"I'm surprised you're not," Clara replied, her confidence shaken by his reply.

"He's been doing it off and on for years, it's the only real strategy he has," Liam said, an unsettling calm in his voice.

189

"Then why don't you do something about it?" Clara's question came out harsher than she intended.

"There were rumors before him and there'll be rumors after him," Liam answered. "They can't do me real harm."

Clara heard the certainty, the arrogance, and it rattled her. It made her doubt more than Liam.

"They did Lila real harm. That was the whole point."

"He's been trying to ruin us for years," Liam said. "But murder?" He shook his head. "Even he would be shocked."

Clara's pulse quickened with frustration. She wanted him to understand. Wanted him to see what she did. At the very least she wanted to see if she could prod a genuine reaction out of him. "Then you're being naive," she said.

"Am I?" Liam's eyes met hers with a steady challenge. "Or do you want to believe it's that simple?"

Clara felt the weight of his words, the weight of his insistence. "Kane got Callahan to do his dirty work," she said, pushing against the certainty Liam held like a shield. "He had at least an idea what would happen. He had the alibi ready, that's why there are no cameras at the church site."

Liam was silent, thoughtful. Clara couldn't tell if it was a defense mechanism or genuine belief. It was maddening.

"I've known Robert Kane a long time," Liam finally said. "He's ruthless, but not reckless."

Clara watched him, saw how measured and deliberate he was. "Then he's both," she replied. Her determination wrapped around her like armor.

Liam's expression shifted, a hint of doubt surfacing. "The alibi might be something. He'd take advantage of the situation," he conceded. "But not create it."

"That's not what it looks like," Clara countered. She felt the anger rise, not just at Kane but at Liam's refusal to see the connection.

"It's what I know," Liam said, his voice steady, the kind of steady that came from years of standing alone.

Clara was surprised at how much she cared, how much she wanted him to see it her way. "You're still playing his game," she said. "Even now."

Liam didn't flinch, but Clara saw something break in his expression. She felt the weight of his resistance, the strength of his resolve. She hadn't expected it to matter so much. She hadn't expected it to cut so deep.

"You really don't see it?" Clara asked, unsure of how far to push, unsure of how much this conversation meant to her.

"Clara." Her name was a pause, a thought, a softening of his gaze. "I know it's not what you want to hear."

Clara studied him, saw the vulnerability he tried to hide. She saw how much it mirrored her own. "What do you think it is?" Her voice was quieter, filled with uncertainty and a need to understand.

"Kane wants to ruin us," Liam said. "But a dead girl? He didn't plan that. Still, he knows an opportunity when he sees one. Protect John, keep the focus entirely on me. Yes, that I can see."

They sat in silence, the weight of their words hanging between them. Clara felt her determination fray, but there was something in Liam's response that pulled at her. The way he held his ground. The way he refused to let her shoulder this alone.

"You think he's just taking advantage. Then why does it feel like he's got all the control?" Clara asked, feeling the tension between them, the connection she hadn't expected.

"You're rushing to judgment, wanting to see something that isn't there. A rumor is nothing, you can't orchestrate a murder that way. Why should Kane expect John kill her because of it? More likely he'd ask her about it first and recognize the truth in her answer."

"Don't you wonder why he created a rumor about you and some random high school girl? Sure, it's technically a scandal, but not a juicy one, not compared to the other stuff already going around. He picked her because he knew John, knew what he was capable of, what he would do if he thought it was true."

"Maybe, but it still seems a stretch."

Was he right? The thought gnawed at her. Was she repeating the same mistakes, glossing over important details, and hastily shaping the case to fit her version of events? His suggestion infuriated her, yet some part of her couldn't dismiss it outright. As her anger simmered down, she found herself grudgingly appreciative of his candor. It stung, but it also pulled her back from the brink. She needed that, needed someone to hold her accountable, but the realization was a bitter pill to swallow. She was tangled in her emotions, knowing she wasn't thinking as clearly as she should be, putting too much pressure on herself.

Liam watched Clara, as if waiting for her to decide something important, something between them and beyond them.

She felt his anticipation and his hesitation, the push and pull of emotion she'd kept herself from for so long. Clara didn't want to admit what it meant, didn't want to think about it, but Liam made it hard not to.

"You think Kane wouldn't take it this far," she said. "Fine, but he's culpable for the rumors and if he's as principled as everyone seems to think then he must feel at least some guilt over the whole thing, even as he continues to use it to press his agenda. If he is protecting John, he may be doing so reluctantly. I can find a way to exploit that."

"I don't doubt that you can," he said with a smile.

Clara looked at him with gratitude. She made for the door, slowly, almost hesitating. But she left.

Chapter 13

The wind outside was surging in bursts again, rattling moss-clogged gutters and sending a low whistle through Clara's bedroom window. She sat cross-legged on her quilt, surrounded by concentric rings of case notes, each page and image an emissary from the silent world of the murdered girl.

Clara's hands stained slightly blue at the fingertips from her old highlighter. She'd been staring at the same three bullet points for an hour, her brain stopped cold at the problem of how everything connected. It had turned dark without her noticing.

The knock was so soft she ignored it. Then the door flung inward, bashing the laundry hamper, and Russ Hinton stumbled in. Cheeks ruddy and hair tousled, his entire body vibrated with the kind of reckless, inebriated energy that only emerges after several drinks and the temporary exile of marital responsibility.

"Clara!" he shouted. "You're not gonna believe—holy shit, listen—" He filled half the room with his presence, eyes wild with excitement, and then froze, as if just now registering Clara's chaos of documents. He grinned sheepishly, lowered his voice by two decibels, and repeated: "You're not gonna believe what just happened."

Clara's first instinct was annoyance. Russ was not subtle, and she didn't exactly want Emma's husband pawing through homicide evidence. But then she caught the urgency in his face, the way he fought for breath before speaking, and she realized he wouldn't have barged in unless it was important. She set her folders aside, spine straightening. "What is it, Russ?"

He closed the door behind him, an ill-fated attempt at discretion, and leaned in conspiratorially. "I was out for drinks at the Hickory," he began, gesturing excitedly. "You know, boys' night. A bunch of the Kane guys were there pounding them back."

Clara's mind immediately snapped to attention. "Go on," she said, voice suddenly taut.

"I was at the bar and I see Trevor Mills and Joe Mackenzie arguing. At first, it's just bitching about a card game, but then it gets real. Joe's face goes dark, like, scary dark. Starts pointing in Trevor's face and saying he's done waiting. He wants his money. Right now, no more excuses." Russ's hands mimed the aggression, stabbing the air for effect.

Clara's heartbeat thrummed a little faster. "Are you sure?" She pushed a printout of the Mills' bank records out of the way, scanning for any mention of gambling debts, payments, anything.

"Positive," Russ replied, clearly relishing his role as informant. "Joe got so loud, everyone at the

196

bar went quiet. Trevor tried to play it cool, but he was totally rattled. I swear, Clara, he looked like he was about to shit himself."

She scribbled a note and drew a hard underline. "Did you hear anything about what the money was for?"

Russ hesitated, suddenly aware that this wasn't just gossip. "No. Just that they had a deal, and Joe was sick of waiting. Kept saying, 'You think you can screw me over just because you're in with the boss?'" He dropped his voice, mimicking Joe's drunken snarl. "It got pretty bad."

Clara felt the tectonic plates of the investigation shifting. If Trevor and Joe were tied up in something private, it was probably nothing. But if it had anything to do with John's alibi...

"Did anyone else see them?" she pressed, unable to hide her rising adrenaline.

"Whole bar," Russ said, and then, after a beat: "Even the bartender tried to break it up. Clara, you think this is about the murder?"

It was almost too good, too convenient, too perfectly timed. Still, Clara couldn't help speculating. If Joe Mackenzie was getting paid off to lie about John working that shift, and getting frustrated with the payouts, they could get to him. They'd destroy the alibi and the whole thing would start to fit the way her brain kept insisting it should fit.

She glanced up at Russ, who now looked slightly sobered by the seriousness of her silence. "This is huge," she said, voice low. "You have no idea."

His face broke into a bashful smile. "Not bad for an old married guy, huh?"

She was already gathering her phone and recorder, adrenaline wiping away the exhaustion she'd felt all evening. "Not bad at all," she said, dialing the number she'd programmed to muscle memory over the past month.

Russ lingered, basking in the heat of his own heroism, before slipping back down the hall to his wife and leaving Clara alone with her storm of evidence.

The call connected within two rings.

"Fisher," he answered, his voice a low rumble on the line.

"I've got something," Clara said, the excitement electric. "Joe Mackenzie and Trevor Mills, they had a blowout at the bar."

She could feel Fisher's interest shift, sharp and quick. "Mackenzie?"

"Yeah, Kane guy. Threatening Trevor about getting his money. We have to talk to them." Clara's mind raced with possibilities, the missing pieces finally within reach. "Maybe this is the crack in the alibi."

"Not bad, Reynolds," he said. "I'll make some calls."

Clara hung up, her energy renewed. She felt the thrill she'd almost forgotten, the rush of something real and solid. It all lined up, all pointed back to what she knew, to where she almost lost herself. Clara sensed the break she needed, felt it carry her further than she dared hope.

———

The next morning Clara Reynolds stalked the edge of the Kane Construction site. The men gathered there were built from small-town resistance, their eyes full of the kind of suspicion reserved for outsiders and anyone who might threaten the world they'd built one pint and overtime check at a time.

She moved between the half-finished frames of a new subdivision, boots crunching over frost-stiff clay and littered Red Bull cans, while their glances trailed her with the wary patience of barn cats. They were grounded, solid, blue-collar to the bone; if you wanted to know where in Cedar Hollow the most dangerous rumors lived, you found the men who built its skeleton, then you found the one who'd been talking too loud after dark.

She located Joe Mackenzie behind a stack of insulation, eyes like hound dogs'—sleepy, drooping, but always waiting for the next reason to bolt. He wore a battered Carhartt hoodie and the kind of beard that grew to disguise rather than decorate. Joe was halfway through a twelve-inch meatball sub and looked as if he'd rather face a bandsaw than her. Clara saw his story in the set of his jaw, the nervous flick of his gaze. He'd chewed and recited the truth to himself, over and over, and it still stuck in his throat like a too-thick bite of gristle.

She didn't waste time. "Joe," she said, voice clipped, the only warning he'd get.

He set the sandwich down, wiped his hands along his thighs, and offered a smile as thin as the plastic on his hard hat. "Police lady. You lost, or just slumming it today?"

She ignored the bait and took the concrete block opposite him, letting the distance between them pronounce her intent. "You and Trevor Mills. You want to talk about what happened at the Hickory?"

Joe's face only flickered. "Just a misunderstanding."

Clara let silence grow, let it claw at him. "I heard you got loud enough to clear the whole bar. If you want to keep it simple, you'll need to do better than 'misunderstanding.'"

He tried a bigger shrug, as if the pain in his shoulders could outweigh what he owed. "Me and

Trevor, we got history. Sometimes we get into it a little. No big deal."

"I'm guessing," Clara said, leaning forward, "it was about money."

His fingers twitched. "Don't know what you heard, but it's just gambling. Cards, football pools, that kind of thing."

Clara's eyes swept him top to bottom, cataloging his tics, his tells. She saw the tremor in his pinky, the way he kept his left hand hidden beneath the table. "Gambling. So what, he owes you a few bucks and you're making a scene?"

Joe forced a hollow laugh. "I mean, that's how I get sometimes when I have a few too many. But it's cool. Sometimes he wins, sometimes I do. No big deal."

Clara stayed silent, let the weight of it settle. She saw the effect it had on him, how he shifted and squirmed. "If you want the truth," Joe said, his voice a strained whisper, "talk to Trevor."

"We're talking to everyone," Clara replied, letting him know she wasn't leaving without more. "You said you weren't going to wait for it to die down. What does that mean?"

Joe shifted, his resolve thinner than his excuses. "Trevor said it was a time of mourning. The kid isn't over losing his girl. Said he wasn't going to think about money right now." His words rushed and uncertain.

"But you think that's bullshit," Clara said, refusing to let him off the hook.

"Well," Joe said, less sure, less steady. "You know how it is. Beer don't buy itself." His gaze wouldn't meet hers, lingering on the ground instead.

Clara waited, let him sweat.

After a moment he said, "If Trevor told you different, he's lying to cover his own ass. Ask him about the debts, see what stories he tells you."

"I will," Clara said. "But here's what's got me hung up, Joe. Why were you so desperate to get paid that you'd risk a scene at the bar? Why now?"

Joe looked at his boots, the meatball sub, anywhere but her. He picked at a fleck of tomato sauce clinging to the corner of his mouth. "You ever been really strapped, Detective? Like, wake up and you don't know what you're gonna tell your wife when the gas gets shut off?" He barked a short laugh, softer now. "That's all it is. I wasn't thinking clear."

Clara let a second tick by before saying, "You were thinking clear enough to threaten to break his nose."

Now his eyes finally rose to hers, and for a moment she saw something that looked almost like pleading. "If I did, it was just talk. I'd never go that far. Cross my heart."

Their conversation was drawing notice; she could feel the gaze of the crew drifting over from the scaffolding, the hum of a power drill falling quiet. She pressed again. "Tell me about your shift the night of the murder. Did you see John Mills leave early?"

A pause, the kind that lasted just a breath but weighed a pound per second. "No, he was there the whole time," Joe said, but the words came out wooden. "Ask anyone."

Clara didn't nod, didn't even blink. She just let the pressure build a little longer, let the nervous energy in the space vibrate until Joe seemed ready to spill the rest. But he just gathered up his lunch and shuffled back toward the site office, shoulders hunched deeper than before, leaving a wake of uneasy silence.

———

Clara moved through the site, gathering the same answers, hearing the same denials. They stuck to the story with precision, with a precision that made her doubt.

Frustration tightened around Clara. She saw their loyalty, the fear that kept them from saying more. She pushed against it but got nothing, the story a closed loop, impenetrable.

Clara sighed, turning back to the trailer. She felt the heaviness of their silence, the weight of her need to break it. A figure moved in the corner of her vision, careful, deliberate. Mark Hogan. Clara stopped, saw him approach with caution.

"Can I help you?" she asked, knowing from his posture he didn't want the others to see.

"I need to talk," Mark said, his voice low. "Not here." He glanced around, nervous, making sure they were alone.

"What do you mean?" Clara felt the urgency in his words, knew they weren't part of the script.

"I need to speak with Liam Harrington," Mark said. "Privately."

"About?" Clara's curiosity sparked, sensing the opportunity.

"Can't say here." Mark looked at the other workers, the suspicion in their eyes. "Too risky."

Clara measured his expression, the desperation and determination that swam together. "Can you arrange it?" Mark asked, almost pleading.

"I'll try," Clara said, seeing a new possibility unfold.

Mark nodded, slipped away like a man with secrets. Clara watched him, her mind racing with what this meant. She felt the threads of the case

204

pulling tight, the rush of urgency and intrigue. It was more than she'd hoped, more than she expected. Clara knew she was onto something. It was more than they could hold back.

————

Clara stormed into headquarters, the sharp tang of desperation clinging to her in a way she barely concealed. She didn't remember the drive over, she only knew the case was moving again, that every ounce of intuition in her body pulsed with the feeling that John Mills was not working that shift and they'd soon have proof.

The front desk sergeant flinched at her entrance, and she ignored the startled hello, following the red pulse of her urgency down the hallway lined with decades-old wanted posters and the sad, faded Polaroids of missing children.

Fisher was already waiting for her, propped against the wall by the interview rooms, his badge a dull gleam in the hallway's yellowing light. He held a manila folder loose at his side, but his face was all business, the lines of fatigue etched tighter than usual. He barely nodded as she approached. "Trevor Mills is in." He jerked his chin at the closed door.

"You get him talking?" Clara asked, her pulse throbbed in her jaw.

Fisher shrugged, not dismissive, just honest. "He's like a fence post. Says he'll tell us whatever, nothing to hide." He passed her the folder, and as she took it, his thumb grazed her wrist—an accidental, human contact that made Clara realize how long she'd been running on fumes. "You want to go good cop, bad cop, or just… cop?"

She offered a ghost of a smile. "Let's see what he gives us."

Trevor Mills was already seated in Interview Two, his hands folded neatly on the tabletop, posture straight, the red of his work crew jacket a jarring splash against the institutional gray. Clara watched him through the glass a moment before entering, cataloguing every tick of his jaw, every flicker of the eyes. He looked different than the man described by Russ Hinton the night before: not shaken, not even particularly tired. If anything, he radiated a staid, resigned energy, the sort that comes from a lifetime of being overlooked and underappreciated and learning, over time, to weaponize it. Clara wondered how much of that was act.

Fisher started as soon as they were seated, not bothering with pleasantries. "Rough night?"

Trevor's eyes didn't linger, didn't squint. They simply landed softly on Fisher, then on Clara. "I've had worse," he said. The voice was soft, unhurried, flat. "Barroom arguments aren't uncommon after a long day."

206

"Joe Mackenzie doesn't strike me as the type to start a scene unless he's pushed," Fisher said.

Trevor shrugged, the movement just barely visible. "Joe likes to make things dramatic. Especially if there's an audience." He shifted his weight, and Clara noticed again the small marks on the back of his hands. Scrapes, maybe from work, maybe older. Trevor saw her notice and tucked his hands under his forearms.

Clara leaned in, elbows on the table, a posture of empathy she'd borrowed from training and made her own. "Trevor, we need to know if the argument had anything to do with the investigation. You understand the pressure we're under, right?"

Trevor's face softened a fraction. "You ever been in a town where someone got murdered and now no one trusts anyone?" he asked, and the question hung there, not rhetorical, not hostile. Just tired.

Clara nodded. "That's my job."

He smiled with just the left side of his mouth. "Feels like everyone's job now."

Fisher said, "We heard there was money involved. That Joe was asking about a debt."

Trevor didn't deny it. "He's owed, sure. That's not a crime."

"Depends who's getting paid by who," Clara said. "And why."

Trevor looked at her, really looked this time. His eyes were pale blue and full of something old and hard to name. "It's just gambling. Cards, football, March Madness. Joe exaggerates to make himself look tough. I pay my debts." He cleared his throat, and for the first time, Clara heard a tremor in his voice. "Eventually."

"So why did he get so heated last night?" Clara pressed, letting her investigator's mask slip just enough to show she wasn't convinced. "Why threaten you in the middle of a packed bar?"

Trevor hesitated. He ran his tongue along his bottom lip, found nothing there, and then said, "Joe's like that when he drinks."

Fisher, always the minimalist, said, "That all?"

Trevor's gaze flickered to the corner of the room, then back. "He overreacted."

Clara felt her own nerves edge in, felt the suspicion harden in her voice. "Just normal gambling debts. That why did you look so rattled?"

"I wasn't." Trevor kept his tone even, refusing to be shaken. "I just don't want issues back at home."

"Home," Clara repeated. "What does that mean?"

Trevor's composure slipped, a fraction of a second. But Clara saw it, caught the hesitation. "My

208

wife thinks I stopped gambling last year," he said. "It's been a rough time for us. Didn't want it getting back to her."

Clara thought back to Russ's story, how he said Trevor was frantic. Right now, in front of the police, he barely had a care in the world. "Joe thinks you're using this rough time to avoid paying."

"Like I said," Trevor answered, "he's overreacting." His eyes stayed on Clara's, a mix of defiance and certainty.

"What about John?" Clara asked, changing the angle. She watched Trevor's reaction.

His jaw tightened, but his voice didn't falter. "What about him?"

"How's he handling the suspicion?" Fisher asked, shifting the focus to John's state of mind.

"Not well," Trevor admitted. His tone held a trace of vulnerability, the first crack in his demeanor. Clara seized it.

"Worried he'll break?" she asked.

"Worried he'll lose it," Trevor said. "But he didn't kill anyone."

"Your alibi is a bit less solid," Fisher said, playing his own angle.

"Check it," Trevor shot back. "We have nothing to hide."

"He's a suspect," Clara insisted. "Maybe you are too."

"Then you're wasting time," Trevor replied. He leaned back, the chair creaking. His calm returned, unnerving in its confidence.

Clara let the silence press down, let it force a reaction. Trevor didn't waver. She felt her resolve tighten, but the doubt crept in too.

Fisher looked at Clara. She knew the expression, the calculation in his eyes. He was convinced. But Clara wasn't. Not yet.

"You can go," she said, frustration edging into her voice. "But this isn't over."

Trevor stood, his movements easy. "When you figure that out, call me."

Clara's suspicion lingered, but she watched him leave, the doubt growing stronger.

————

Clara and Fisher sat in the charged quiet, the air thick with unasked questions.

"What do you think?" Fisher asked. His tone was steady, confident.

"I think he's hiding something," Clara said, her voice firm. But her mind swam with uncertainty.

"You sure?" Fisher leaned back, studying her with careful eyes. "Because he didn't seem rattled to me."

"Too calm," Clara replied. "That's what makes me sure."

Fisher considered her words. Clara saw him weighing it, saw him wondering if she was too close, too eager.

"Then why did he come in?" Fisher asked. "Why talk if he's got so much to hide?"

"He thinks we've got nothing," Clara said. "Or he's trying to make sure it stays that way."

Fisher nodded, but Clara saw the doubt. It echoed her own.

"What do you make of him being so worried last night and so calm today?" Clara asked.

Fisher shrugged. "Makes sense what he said, he didn't want his wife knowing about the gambling."

"I think," Clara said, her mind racing, "he really was worried Joe was going to blow the whole thing in his drunken stupor. Now, with a ready-made excuse, he's not so concerned."

Fisher watched her, his expression careful. "Maybe you're seeing what you want to see, Clara."

Clara felt the tug of uncertainty, felt the worry creeping in with the damp air. "You think I'm jumping to conclusions," she said. It was more than the case. It was a fear she couldn't ignore.

"I think you want this too much," Fisher replied. His tone was gentle, but the impact was heavy.

"And you don't?" Clara asked. She didn't know if she meant the case or her need to prove herself.

"I do," Fisher said. "But it won't matter if we're wrong."

Clara nodded, a reluctant acknowledgment of his caution. She knew it was right, but the fear of failure pressed harder.

"I pushed too soon," Clara admitted, the frustration raw in her voice. "With the priest and Trevor. Kane will cover his tracks."

"Kane's only one possibility. Might not even be involved. You're getting worked up over nothing."

Clara wanted to believe it. But all she saw was the distance growing, the risk she might be wrong. The worry pressed in, suffocating as the gloom outside. Clara felt the momentum slipping, felt herself slipping with it. It wasn't over. But it might be soon if they didn't get something concrete.

Chapter 14

Clara had trouble reading Mark Hogan's face as she led him up the gravel drive toward the Harrington estate. He moved at a pace just short of urgent, hands jammed deep in the pockets of his work coat, gaze flicking between the main house and the ragged outlines of the outbuildings crowding the edge of the property. Clara kept a step behind, measuring each stride for signs he might break, bolt, or double back. The night was a living thing, the vapor dilating the glow of the porch lamp until it washed the whole façade in a sickly yellow. Gravel crackled beneath their boots, punctuating the silence Mark refused to fill.

The door opened with an indifferent sigh. The foyer was colder than she remembered, as if the house's grand old heating system had finally surrendered to the rot of the world outside. Mark paused, the bravado stalling out. He scanned the entryway, eyes snagging on the ancestral portrait that dominated the wall. Abner Harrington, founder, eternal patriarch, painted with the same feral, inward smile that Liam sometimes wore. The sight of it seemed to short-circuit Mark's forward momentum.

Clara broke the silence. "You good?"

Mark gave a brittle half-shrug, glanced at the two sets of boot tracks in the foyer mud. "I need to see him. Alone." The words fell out desperate, as if he'd been holding his breath for a week.

Clara tensed, jaw set. She'd been ready for Mark to call the whole thing off but somehow hadn't anticipated this abrupt declaration of terms. "That's not how this works."

He shook his head, eyes luminous with something like fear. "Sorry, Detective. I don't talk unless it's just me and Harrington. Non-negotiable." He started toward the closed, paneled doors at the end of the hall, the ones that led to the Harrington study.

Clara was so sick of everyone in this town calling her Detective. She felt herself losing control of the situation. Possibly the entire investigation. She could physically sense the loss of leverage, knew that every step Mark took down the corridor was one more degree of separation from whatever truth he meant to spill. Still, she followed, her own boots echoing sharp and accusatory in the hush of the house.

Liam was waiting in the study, perfectly composed. The man had a gift for arranging himself at the focus of any room, and tonight he looked like he'd been sculpted into place. He barely glanced at Clara as she arrived, his attention orbiting Mark as if he'd anticipated this intersection for weeks.

Mark hesitated at the doorway, then gestured at Clara, a flick of the chin more dismissive than respectful. "I said—"

She cut him off. "You really think I'm going to wait outside?"

Liam's gaze flicked toward her, gauging the threat. "Clara, if you'll give us five minutes, I promise you'll get what you want."

Two pairs of eyes were on her now, both quietly daring her to break formation. She gave a grunt, then slid back into the hall, spine rigid with mistrust.

The door closed between them with a weighted, final sound.

She stood motionless, fingers drumming the wallpaper as she tried to parse what she'd just surrendered. The house was a tomb, every clock tick amplified. Clara paced the corridor, scanning the generations of dour faces on the walls. Harringtons, all of them: judges, pioneers, politicians, each stamped from the same hard mold. She found herself lingering on a portrait of a matriarch, her eyes alive with suspicion and her mouth set in a line of perpetual disapproval. Clara wondered if the women had been distrusted as much as the men over the years.

Each generation looked as though it had never escaped the one before. Somehow it reminded her of her own family, of what she thought she'd left behind and the stories she never truly escaped. Even before Alex.

A minute passed, then another. The tension inside her was a living thing, gnawing at the careful scaffolding she'd built since the beginning of the case. She tried to distract herself with the architecture—the crown molding, the baroque sconces, the vein of a hairline crack running above the doorframe—but every detail only sharpened the sense of exclusion. She caught her reflection in the glass of a curio cabinet: tense, predatory, like a wolf denied a kill.

Muffled voices filtered out from the study, a modulation of tempo and pitch that told her whatever was being shared wasn't quick or painless. Mark's voice rose once, reedy and urgent, then dropped away. Liam's was lower, more controlled, a mezzo of reassurance and command.

She wrestled her impulse to crash the meeting, to reclaim ownership of the narrative. Rules were rules, and she was good at following them, but only when they didn't feel weaponized against her. She forced herself to count the seconds, slow and deliberate, as if the discipline might inoculate her against whatever came next.

Five minutes became ten and then twenty. Finally, she heard footsteps, saw the door open, and watched Mark leave. He gave her a quick glance, the look of a man unburdened. Clara felt the envy curl in her gut.

Liam found her in the hallway, standing over a battered tile like she hoped it might reveal a trapdoor out of the moment. He made no gesture, not even a polite cough; he simply waited, surveying her with the patience of a man who'd spent much of his life in rooms like this, on the receiving end of untidy news. His silhouette was carved sharp by the sconce light, blue and gold tracing the tension in his jaw.

"I know you expected to be there," he said, voice low, heavy with the certainty of someone who'd already measured out the consequences and found them wanting. "But this was the only way he would talk."

Clara scoffed, not at him but the universe's sense of timing. "You think so?"

He nodded, a single, deliberate motion. "He was going to walk if you stayed. Do you want to play things by the book, or get answers?"

She wanted both. She wanted every inch of leverage, every fragment of the equation of guilt and motive. But mostly she wanted to not feel like she was being played by the choreography of men who break all the rules and never think twice. She folded her arms, counted to three.

"What did he say?" The words came out clipped, almost professional. Clara's throat burned with the effort to keep it that way.

Liam glanced back toward the study doors, as if the residue of Mark's visit still lingered there, an echo in the wood grain with the faintest trace of a confession. "Kane bribed all the workers to say John was there," he began, each word placed with careful malice. "He's making them wait, the payoff is coming as a year-end bonus on the books. He wants to keep them on the hook, keep their stories aligned until it's all over and looks less suspicious."

Clara felt her jaw tighten. Her mind was already mapping out the cascading failure: the statements tainted, the collective memory rewritten, the incentive timed to perfection. "With Mark's statement the rest will follow one by one. Kane's house of cards is falling apart. He's too caught up in it not to go down himself, whatever his intention was at the beginning."

Liam's silence was deafening.

"There won't be a statement," he finally said. "The information was only for me; I had to pay for it."

Clara felt as if she were kicked in the stomach. "You idiot, you stupid idiot!"

"I know you're upset," Liam said. His tone was gentle, a quiet assurance. "But now you know what happened, you can prove it another way."

"How could I be so careless again? Jesus, Jesus…" she was bent over, hands on her knees, hyperventilating.

"Like I said, Mark wouldn't have talked to you," Liam insisted, ignoring the hurt in her voice. "He's a clever man, looking to secure his payday ahead of time in case Kane's doesn't pan out. This was the only play."

"So what are *you* going to do with *your* information then?" Clara shot back. Her control felt as fragile as ever, slipping through her hands like the smoke of every failed case.

Liam stood there, stung by the words.

Clara's anger melted into something else, a vulnerability she tried to hide. "I thought I was past making these mistakes," she said, more to herself than to him. "It's all slipping away."

She pressed her temples, trying to ward off the impending spiral. It was a familiar ache, equal parts rage and fatigue. You never think much about the cases you solve, but you never forget the ones that slip away.

Liam lingered a few steps behind, out of reach but not out of orbit. "I said I'd help you," he said. "I meant it."

"Oh, you're helping alright," she shot back. "Really doing a bang-up job of it, too."

He took a careful breath, and for a beat Clara thought he might say something conciliatory, or at least human. Instead, he locked his gaze onto hers, dark and impassive as a winter lake. In the distance, the grandfather clock in the sitting room sounded the hour, its chime a protracted dirge.

"So what now?" she finally asked.

"We wait until the next crack forms," Liam said. "And then we hit it. Together, this time, if you'll let me."

Clara wasn't sure whether to laugh or punch a hole in the wall. She compromised by digging her nails into the palm of her hand. "I don't need a partner," she said

"I know," he replied, voice nearly a whisper. "But maybe you need someone to believe in you."

She looked at him, really looked at the man who'd just played an end-run around her and still wanted to stay in the game. It was an audacious, infuriating kind of loyalty, and it was the first thing in weeks that felt real.

He smiled, not the politician's grin but something raw and true. "I can help you," he said. "If you trust me."

The line was so simple, so nakedly manipulative, that for a moment Clara almost recoiled. But then she felt the weight of the day—of too many days—press down on her, and realized how tired she was of everything, how desperate she was to trust in something.

"Let me at least make you a drink," Liam said.

She shook her head, but didn't protest when he led her toward the kitchen. The house seemed to thaw as they walked, the ancestral scowls on the walls fading into the periphery. Liam poured two glasses of rye, slid one her way without a word.

They stood there, side by side at the old butcher-block counter, nursing the whiskey in a silence that felt almost medicinal. Clara's body hummed with the aftershock of adrenaline and defeat, two beasts gnawing at opposite ends of the same bone.

They finished their drinks but neither of them was quite ready to leave the moment. Clara stared into her empty glass and watched the way the light fractured in the cut crystal. She found herself thinking of the first time a case faded away with no resolution, how Bryant had handed her a single malt and said, "Some days are just for losing. You start fresh tomorrow."

She looked at Liam. The sincerity in his eyes wrapped around her, drawing her close.

Clara felt the fear and uncertainty give way to something softer, something warm. She wondered if she should fight it or let it carry her. The relief in surrender was too much, and the risk of losing everything made her grip tighter.

———

Clara woke, the night still dark, the unfamiliar room slowly coming into focus. Her thoughts were scattered, tangled with the night and the blurred boundaries she'd never crossed before. She saw the edge of Liam's sleep-warm form, felt the pull of his promise, the danger of it.

She didn't want to be here, not really. Not in this bed, not in this house, not in this town. She didn't want to trace the outline of Liam's sleeping profile with her eyes, didn't want to remember how last night had felt inevitable and impossible at once. She didn't want to recognize that for all her training and discipline, she was, at her core, a creature of reflex and unfinished business.

I'm the stupid idiot, she thought, *how could I let this happen?*

She knew how it happened. Two lonely, broken people unexpectedly finding solace in each other. If it weren't for the case it would be no big deal, welcome even. But there was the case and only now did Clara realize how emotionally compromised she had been.

She'd already known she wasn't thinking entirely like herself due to the baggage she'd brought with her to Cedar Hollow, and it had been convenient

222

to attribute everything to that. While it looked like her theory about Kane was right, she knew that was plain luck. Her closeness with Liam could have blown the whole thing so colossally that the last case would have looked like child's play in comparison. She had no choice but to step away now.

She stared at the ceiling. She counted the cracks, mapped the shift of every shadow. She tried to find a version of herself that could stay in this bed for even one more minute, but it was no use. She needed distance or she'd risk suffocating under the weight of her own bad decisions.

Clara dressed quietly, each movement careful, deliberate. She felt the weight of her decision grow, solidify with every step toward the door. She couldn't stay, not now, not with the risk so high and the certainty so low.

"Clara." Liam's voice was a thread, tugging her back.

She paused, saw him watching her with a mix of knowing and vulnerability. Clara couldn't look away, but she couldn't stay. "I need to go," she said. The words tasted bitter and necessary.

"You're running," Liam said. There was no accusation in his tone, just the calm insistence of a man who thought he knew her too well.

"I'm being realistic," Clara replied. She felt the tension coil tight inside, felt the pull to him and to the case, felt how it could unravel her if she let it. "It's too close. I'm too close."

"We're just getting somewhere," Liam said. The intensity of his conviction cut through her hesitation. She didn't know if he was talking about the case or about them, but it didn't matter either way.

"I can't," Clara said, though it sounded more like a question. She looked into his eyes, searched for the certainty she couldn't find in herself.

Liam didn't let go. "You can," he said.

The truth in his words pressed close, suffocating and comforting all at once. Clara felt the old fear, the old worry, the familiar pull of her need to run, to escape.

"I have to," Clara said, her voice barely more than a whisper. "I can't lose myself again."

Clara drove, the road a blur beneath her, the vapor wrapping around the car like doubt. Most of her stuff was at Emma's but she couldn't afford to stop there. Her resolve was thin, brittle, and she didn't know where it would take her. She just knew she had to go, had to put distance between herself and Cedar Hollow.

It was only after she crossed the county line that she let herself cry. The tears came slow and hot, leaving streaks down her cheeks that stung in the cold air. She thought about Liam, about Lila, about the

224

case and the mistakes and the people who counted on her to get it right. She wondered if she'd ever be able to stop running, if she'd ever have the luxury of just staying still.

Chapter 15

She drove all morning, her entire body locked in that peculiar tension unique to running away. The car hummed beneath her, a battered rental that smelled like wet dog, chemical air freshener, and the faint, persistent undertone of panic sweat.

The further she tried to get from Cedar Hollow, the more she was reminded that escape was only ever an illusion. The town was a ring, a trap, every logging road a Möbius strip. The forest crowded the highway, moss-draped cedars leaning in as if to press their secrets against the glass, whispering their green accusations.

The pall thickened every half mile until there was only the tunnel of her high beams and the mirror, in which the same two pale, haunted eyes stared back.

She wasn't fleeing, she told herself, not exactly. The hum of the engine had a lulling rhythm, a metronome for obsessive thought, and with every mile the more insistent it became.

You're never getting away.

Over and over, the phrase clattered in her mind like a loose coin in a dryer. She watched the odometer spin and pretended it meant something.

The map was a joke, the distance meaningless; the real ground she can't cross is inside her own skull.

By the time the gas warning light flicked on, she hadn't eaten in nearly a day. She pulled off at a town so small it didn't even have a traffic light, just a three-pump station, a boarded-up bait shop, and a greasy spoon diner with a hand-painted sign.

She sat in the car for a full five minutes, watching her own breath cloud the windshield, before finally forcing herself out. Her legs nearly buckled, her hands trembled. She wasn't sure if it was hunger or adrenaline or both, but it felt like her body was being run off the fumes of her own panic.

Inside, the diner was strung with Christmas lights, though it wasn't yet the season, and the windows were fogged from the heat of the grill. The only other patrons were two logging contractors, all neon vests and beards and the particular reek of gasoline and sweat. They looked up at her like she was a ghost, or maybe like they half-expected her to be wearing a badge.

She took a booth near the back, the cushion hissing as she slid in. The waitress was in her sixties and wore her hair in a lacquered helmet. She brought coffee without asking, sloshing it half-over Clara's trembling hand, then waited, expectant, pencil poised.

"Menu?" Clara says.

227

"Eggs or pie," the waitress shrugged. "We're out of everything else."

Clara ordered both. She had no time or energy to perform the rituals of politeness. She just wanted to anchor herself in anything physical, anything not in her own head.

The coffee, once it cooled enough to drink, tasted like burnt sorrow. She tried to lace it with sugar, then gave up. She stared at her hands. At the reflection in the window. At the two loggers, who were now deep in muttered conversation, incomprehensible words drifting in her direction like cigarette smoke. She pulled her phone from her pocket and checks the signal. Two bars of nothing.

She wondered, for the thousandth time, what she was really doing. Not just here but anywhere.

The script she wrote for herself after Alex died was simple: become the kind of person who catches the people that took him. But even on her best days back in the Bureau she was never sure she was really that person. More often, she was a ghost haunting her own resume, moving evidence around on desks, drawing lines between photos, chasing patterns that never resolved into faces.

The eggs arrived, floating on a raft of congealed cheese, and the pie was half-frozen. She ate mechanically, chewing as if it was a dare. The waitress gave her the look reserved for women who come in alone and stayed too long. It's made up of part concern, part suspicion.

She nursed another coffee, the acid burn waking her up by degrees.

In the bathroom, she examined her face in the warped mirror. The dark circles under her eyes were less badge than bruise. She slapped her cheeks, cold water stinging, trying to jar herself into alertness. She wanted so badly to feel like the person she pretended to be. The agent, the protector, the survivor. But even here, away from Cedar Hollow, every surface reflected the same emptiness of her life since Alex's death.

She walked through the parking lot, the air cold and sharp. Behind the diner, a kid was spray-painting something onto the cinderblock wall. She watched him for a moment, long enough for him to notice. He dropped the can and bolted.

As she walked back to her car, she noticed the local paper in a battered vending box. MURDER AT THE HOLLOW: FBI CALLED IN, the headline read. Beneath it, a photo of her, grabbed from some public database, looking ten years younger and twice as sure of herself. The sight was so discordant it made her laugh, a single bark that rings loud in the deserted lot.

For a while she sat in the car, not starting it.

Alex, if she were to admit it to herself, wasn't a real person to her anymore. The uncomfortable truth was that he wasn't anything other than an idea, the reason for doing what she was doing. She could barely remember what he looked like, could barely conjure up a clear memory of him these days. Her childhood was like something she locked up in a corner of her mind and pretended wasn't there.

It wasn't a great one to begin with, filled with the kind of all-encompassing familial dysfunction that seeps into the young and is difficult to eradicate. Her father's parents had not wanted him to marry her mother. They never ceased telling her that to her face, even in front of Clara and Alex. Her two uncles, one each on her father's and mother's side, took it upon themselves to physically fight for the honor of their side of the family. Multiple times. Clara never really understood, had the feeling she barely knew the half of it, but that half was all it took to mess her up, to make her feel as if her physical existence was resented by almost everyone she knew.

Alex's horrible death, if it can be said to have any silver lining, eased much of the tension. At least for her parents. The tangled webs of conflicts and jealousies couldn't help but wither. It's hard to conjure up the same animosity against someone who lost their child in such a horrific way.

But nothing eased for Clara, everything was now a million times worse. As a girl just entering the awkward phase of childhood, Clara had in her brother her only source of strength and happiness. Having that torn away at such a crucial time was beyond devastating, it sucked her into a black hole that she still wasn't sure she really and truly escaped from. It had taken great effort for her to redirect her energies back in a constructive way.

The ache in her chest as she reminisced was familiar. Her oldest companion. She breathed, counted to ten, then twenty. By the time she sat up, the rain has turned to sleet.

She drove aimlessly for a while, not toward Cedar Hollow but not away from it either. The radio was static, a low white noise she finds comforting. At a railroad crossing, she waited for the train to pass, watched the graffiti blur by in blue and silver. She counted the cars, then lost track.

She wondered if anyone ever really figured it out, how to move forward. Or if all the books and lectures and therapy handouts are just ways of teaching you to walk in place with style.

She pulled over at a rest stop with a view of the river, though the gray blanket hides everything but the nearest dozen feet. She walked down to the edge of the water, pebbles crunching in silence. She wanted to let go of something, but she couldn't name what it was. She picked up a stone, weighed it in her palm, then tossed it in. The ripple was small, but it spread.

She joined the FBI to help catch the kind of people who killed Alex, that's always been the rationale. Really it was a selfish act, an attempt to fill an empty life with a noble sounding purpose.

It was no wonder she never truly felt like a real FBI agent when she was viewing all her cases through the lens of how it was going to give *her* meaning, give *her* closure.

She dropped to the ground, pressing her head against the sand, willing something, anything to take her away from herself. But she can't escape. She'd been trying so hard for so long that it wore through, leaving her vulnerable and afraid. That's why she wasn't as good as she wanted to be. She was so wrapped up in loss, in proving she was something more, that she couldn't see past herself to the case at hand. Her ego was too big, it overshadowed everything, made a mockery of her mission as an FBI agent.

Suddenly she realized that this was the insight she was looking for, what she came to Cedar Hollow to figure out. So simple but so hard to admit to herself. She'd tiptoed around it for years but retreated whenever she caught a glimpse, a hint of it. Now she felt it surge, hard and fast, forcing her to catch her breath. She closed her eyes and breathed. The truth is, she wanted to see this case through. Not for Alex. Not for herself. For Lila, the real victim.

The drive back was different. She took the long way, the side roads, the ones that wind through stands of fir so dense the sky disappears. She rolled down the window and let the cold in, let it sting her skin until she couldn't feel anything but the present moment. There was a clarity in the pain, a cleansing.

By the time she hit the edge of Cedar Hollow, the sun was going down, turning the sky to a rusty iron. She stopped at a bridge just outside town, the one that crosses the river near the ruins site. She got out, stood on the railing, and looked down. The water was dark and fast. She thought of Alex, and then she didn't.

She thought instead of the case file, of the symbols on the tree, of the way the town looked when she first arrived: closed, brittle, ready to break. She thought about the waitress at the diner, the graffiti on the wall, the boy running away. She thought about herself, and for the first time in a long time, she didn't flinch.

Chapter 16

The road was like wet black glass and the headlights of her rental car pierce each curve like surgical scalpels. She was back in Cedar Hollow. But there was nothing simple about it, nothing clean about retracing bruised memories and the residue they'd left.

She kept her eyes at the edge of the fog, searching for deer or ghosts or whatever it was that lay in wait on the empty roads.

She thought about the word "closure," how it was something you scraped together from what was left, not some gift provided at the end of a case, and certainly not after the kind of year she'd had. There was no closure for Clara Reynolds. There's only the persistent echo of unfinished conversations, especially the ones with Cecilia Day.

The girl's words echoed, confused and defensive. Her confused statements had sounded like lies, except Cecilia's lies always came wrapped in a thick layer of guilt and apology. She'd pointed the finger at John Mills right away and Clara was certain he had killed Lila.

She pressed harder on the gas now, as if acceleration might tear her out of her own mental spiral. The trees flashed by in alternating patterns: living wood, then dead, then living again.

She was aware, distantly, that she hadn't eaten much and that her left leg was vibrating with the beginning of a cramp. It didn't matter. What mattered was the way her memory replayed the last few seconds of her conversation with Cecilia, over and over, until it was all she could hear above the engine's monotone hum.

Clara could recall the stutter in her words, the eyes darting up, voice gaining a strange, steely composure. But Clara had shrugged it off with a lazy reassurance, the practiced detachment that can work on adults but never quite on kids. She realized now how wrong she'd been. Cecilia wasn't scared of being caught in a lie. She feared the truth landing on someone else's head, someone she loved, or hated, or both.

Clara wondered, briefly, if her entire career had been built on such near-misses, these half-glimpsed truths that she only fully understands days or months or years later. She'd always figured she was too direct, too unyielding, but the real flaw was the way she recoiled from emotional messes, the way she walled off her own uncertainty and pretended it was clarity.

Clara turned and headed up the winding road toward Cecilia's subdivision. She killed the headlights and glided the last block in darkness, careful not to spook the neighbors or herself. The houses here were mostly identical, ranch-style with neat lawns and tidy porches, a deliberate aesthetic meant to erase individuality and replace it with collective comfort. She parked beneath a sagging maple and let her eyes adjust. The Day residence was dark except for a faint blue glow in the upstairs window. A television, maybe, or a phone screen.

Clara sat for a moment, feeling the damp work its way through the car's firewall and into her jacket. She replayed her plan—knock, speak softly, let Cecilia set the pace. No pressure, no interrogation. Just an offer: If there's something you want to say, I'll listen. She'd spent years learning that secrets only surface when the water is still.

She approached the front door. Her hand hovered over the bell, then withdraws; she tapped gently instead, barely enough to be heard. She waited. Nothing. She tried again, this time three sharp knocks, which echo like rifle shots in the silent night.

She expected a parent, maybe Cecilia's mother, but it's Cecilia herself who answered. The girl was wearing the same denim jacket as before, face half-shadowed and expression unreadable. For a moment, they just stared at each other.

Cecilia seemed startled when Clara appeared. Her face is pale against the dawn, her eyes wider than Clara remembers. "What are you doing here?" Cecilia's voice barely rose above a whisper.

Clara nodded, uncertain whether to apologize for her return or defend it. "I needed to ask you something. But if this is a bad time…"

Cecilia shrugged, but opened the door wider and gestured her in. Inside, the house was warm and smelt of laundry detergent and something burnt. A single lamp cast a hard yellow light over the entryway. Cecilia's mouth twitched, as if she might smile but thought better of it.

They didn't sit. Cecilia leaned against the banister, arms folded, eyes tracing invisible shapes on the floor.

"I keep thinking about what you said," Clara began, voice softer than she meant it to be. "Not just today. Before. About that night. I think you saw more than you told me."

Cecilia's eyes flicked up, hard. "If I did?"

Clara felt the tension in her shoulders, the old habit of pressing an advantage and then pulling back before it breaks a witness. But this was not a witness. This was a kid with a wound older than the crime itself.

"I just want to know what's true. For you. Not for the report, not for the lawyers. For you."

Cecilia was silent for a long time. Then she managed to speak. "You ever feel like you're trapped in someone else's nightmare? Like no matter what you do, you're just making it worse?"

Clara nodded, because yes, that's exactly how she felt, and she was grateful for the honesty.

Cecilia licked her lips. "I followed them," she said. "Lila and John. I have this need to punish myself. I can't help it. I knew she was meeting him that night."

Clara held very still. "Punish yourself. Why exactly did you follow them?"

Cecilia's eyes were clouded with doubt, like she'd been chasing herself in circles too. She drew a breath, then released it in a flood of words. "Because. Because I had a crush on him," her cheeks flush with the confession. "Forever. Since we were kids."

Clara felt the relief of the confession. She gently pushed, urging the words to keep coming. "What about it?"

Cecilia twisted her fingers. She was small and defensive, trying to shield herself from the impact. "Lila was the only person I ever told," Cecilia continued. Her words were fast, climbing over each other in the rush to escape. "And then she..." Cecilia's voice caught, but she forced it out. "She told me John had asked her out."

Clara leaned in, each admission like a sliver of light. "And?"

"I didn't want to let her. But I couldn't say that." Cecilia's breath shuddered. "She wouldn't go with him unless I said it was okay." Clara heard the shame in Cecilia's tone.

Clara let the girl catch her breath. Cecilia glanced at her, uncertain, before the words came again.

"That night. I was hiding about twenty feet away." The memory pushed Cecilia forward, spilling more than she wanted to. "It was hard to hear because of the wind." Clara saw the struggle in Cecilia's expression, the desperation to be believed. "But I was there." She looked away. "It was so sudden, out of nowhere. She didn't see it coming. I saw him kill her."

The statement was raw, heavy. Clara felt its weight, felt it wrap around her. "And you went to the police." Clara was back on the edge of belief, but she was closer now, closer than before.

"Yes." Cecilia's admission was a wound reopening, spilling pain and vulnerability. "But I couldn't tell them everything."

"Why not?" Clara's question landed hard, cutting through the last of Cecilia's defenses.

The girl hesitated. Her eyes were full, as if the words might break her. "I didn't want them to know why I was there." Her voice was thin and fractured.

Clara watched the fear unravel, watched the truth unfurl with it.

"What were they doing?"

"Talking, nothing dramatic. John looked determined though, I think he knew he was going to do it. But I don't know! She looked to the side at one point, then he just grabbed her scarf. It was all so quick." She was sobbing now, uncontrollably. Tears she hadn't let herself cry until now.

———

Cecilia was silent. When the words finally came, they were nearly imperceptible at first, then delivered in a flat monotone that chilled the room further. "Later, I thought maybe he did the right thing." Her voice was dead, but the statement spiraled with so much unresolved grief that Clara could almost feel it on her own skin.

Clara studied her, saw the contours of a story she hadn't grasped. "Why?" Her voice was gentle but intent.

"Because..." Cecilia faltered, her courage almost spent. "Because of what she did. They said she was with Liam Harrington." She spat the name like venom. "John was justified."

Cecilia's face was a picture of conflict. Clara saw the tension in every line, every unsteady movement.

"So, you were quick to believe the rumors, even though you didn't know for certain," Clara challenged. Her urgency bled through every word.

"I thought it made sense." Cecilia was lost in a tangle of emotion. She was searching Clara's face for a sign, some signal that she was still sympathetic, but there was nothing to be found there but the mirror of her own confusion. "Why else would he do it?"

"You really think that justifies it?" Clara felt the room tighten around them.

The silence was the answer.

"I thought so," Cecilia whispered. "If she was cheating..."

Clara heard the resonance, the frequency of her own certainty and doubt. "Let's back up. What happened after you saw him do it?"

Cecilia's answer was shaky, almost breathless. "Nothing. I ran."

Clara tried to catch her gaze and hold it, knowing that if she lost Cecilia now, she lost the whole case. "You came to talk to us even though you didn't tell the whole story. Why?"

At this, Cecilia's whole body contracted. She folded inward, arms wrapping tight around herself, as if she could physically compress her guilt back into the hollow she'd made for it. "I thought I could point them in the right direction, and then they'd figure the rest out. That they'd find something, and it wouldn't matter what I said. I thought they'd arrest him and I wouldn't have to do anything." She laughed, a brittle sound. "That's how it works, right?"

Clara let the laugh die. "It never works like that. You saw him, Cecilia."

Cecilia flinched. Her fingers clenched, a final act of rebellion. "I won't testify."

"Why not?" Clara's pushed back.

Cecilia was still and small, a girl retreating from the weight of the world. "I just won't," she said. Her voice was a whisper, as if the admission might disappear if she spoke softly enough.

"You're letting him get away with it," Clara insisted. She reached for Cecilia's gaze, tried to pull the girl back to certainty.

"Maybe he should," Cecilia said.

"You can't do this," Clara said, her voice fierce with urgency. "Not now."

Cecilia seemed fearful. Clara watched the panic in her eyes, the belief and fear that circled like shadows. Clara waited, the tension taut between them. Cecilia dropped her head, and for a moment, all was silent.

"I won't testify," Cecilia said again. Her voice was weaker. "But..."

The pause was a lifeline, a fragile bridge. Clara's hope flickered.

"I'll think about it," Cecilia said finally. Her words quivered, the risk as real as the promise.

Clara released a breath she didn't know she had held. She saw the strain in Cecilia's face, in her own.

"I won't wait forever," Clara said.

Cecilia nodded, the motion tight with hesitation.

Clara left, her steps light with relief, heavy with doubt.

Chapter 17

The next morning Clara was at the police station before the sun came up. Her mind raced through the pieces, feeling the tangle unwind. Cecilia's voice replayed, raw honesty cracking through the static. Inside, the office was the usual tangle of rumors and restless energy. Clara went in, cutting through the noise and finding the sheriff in the thick of it.

"I got what we need," Clara said, trying to catch her breath. "Cecilia saw John kill Lila. She saw the whole thing. Not only that but a Kane employee, Mark Hogan, told Liam Harrington that Kane is bribing them all to give John the alibi."

Fisher looked up from his desk, a mixture of surprise and doubt in his eyes. "No shit?" His voice was wary.

"No shit. Neither is going to go on the record right now." Clara's words tumbled out, quick and eager. "But we know what happened. We've got the upper hand."

He absorbed her intensity, leaning back in his chair. Clara watched him, waited for his response, her own certainty bolstering her against his skepticism.

"Walk me through it," Fisher said. "Step by step."

"Alright," Clara let out a breath. "Kane is using Father Callahan to spread rumors about Harrington. He's been unable to buy land Harrington owns and he's trying to put pressure on him. One of these rumors is that Harrington is carrying on with Lila Hays, a high school student.

"I'm still trying to work out whether this specific rumor was designed to get the reaction it did. Kane knows John, knows what makes him tick. We'll give him the benefit of the doubt for now. So, John hears about the rumor, confronts Lila, and ends up killing her. The way Cecilia describes it he went to their rendezvous with this express purpose. In any event, it happened.

"Now we must speculate a little. John panics and contacts Kane for help. Or more likely, tells his father who contacts Kane. Maybe Kane is genuinely shocked at this point, but, ever the opportunist, he quickly sees exactly how this helps him. Give John an alibi, carve some symbols on the tree next to the dead girl, and get the whole town believing Harrington was behind it."

Clara couldn't help smiling that it all seemed to fit together logically. Fisher mulled it over.

"How exactly is he pulling off this alibi?" he asked. "He's got, what, seven or eight workers he's pulled into this?"

"He's paying them all a nice sum of course. The thing is, that would obviously look suspicious if word got out, so he has them waiting until it goes through at the end of the year as a bonus. Some of them are starting to get impatient."

Fisher stood up from his desk and paced around the office. He moved with a spark of energy, but his face was dour. The face of a man who knew that you could know everything and prove nothing.

"What are you thinking? Keep pressing the workers, get one of them to break?" he asked.

Clara shook her head. "We could do that, but by the time it worked John and Kane will know for sure we're on to them. We still need Cecilia to give her testimony, and we can't trust her an inch. Even if she does, she's liable to recant it at any time. The way I see it, we go hard at John right now. He thinks he's gotten away with it. We can get it out of him."

"And if we don't?" Fisher's question as sharp, a test of Clara's resolve.

"Then we miss our chance." Clara's determination surged. She sensed the weight of their last opportunity, and the urgency drove her.

"We don't have a shot without proof," Fisher countered. He held Clara's gaze, measuring her certainty against his caution.

"All the more reason to try now," Clara argued. Her voice rose with conviction. "Before he knows we're coming for him."

They sat in the charged air, the enormity of the decision stretching between them. Clara's mind reeled through the possibilities.

"He's a kid," Clara thought out loud. "He thinks he's protected. We make him think he's not and he'll crack. I know the type."

Fisher shook his head, half in disbelief, half in reluctant agreement. Clara saw him weighing the risk, the promise, the uncertainty.

"I thought you'd be the careful one," Fisher said, almost smiling.

Clara felt the tension give way to resolve. "So did I," she said.

Fisher studied her once more. "All right," he finally agreed. "Let's go after him."

Clara watched the last of his resistance melt away. "We have to be smart," she warned. "No slips, no hesitation."

"We have to hit him hard then," Fisher says, the plan was taking shape between them. "Make sure we break him the first time."

"He'll break," Clara insisted. The vision crystallized in her mind, a flash of success, a flash of possibility.

"We're counting on a lot," he cautioned. "What if we don't have it right?"

"Then we lose," Clara said, the thought stark, bare.

She stood, her movement quick, decisive. Fisher watched, and Clara feels his skepticism and support both pushing her forward.

Fisher stood too, and they gathered their things, their movements as quick as their decision, the energy pulling them, propelling them toward the risk, the possibility, the unknown.

————

They approached the Mills' house at a quick and deliberate pace, neither of them speaking, both knowing that the moment they crossed that threshold, everything changed. Clara's thoughts spiraled, each scenario bracing for confrontation: John red-eyed and stony with guilt, or Trevor shielding him with parental ferocity, perhaps even both gone rabid with denial.

She'd brought the file folder, filled with notes and printouts, more as psychological battering ram than evidence, but now, standing in the cold before the door, it felt inadequate. The looming silence of the split-level ranch pressed in; not a single curtain flickered, no shadow moved behind the frosted windows.

Clara raised her fist, knocked three times, then again. She was about to try again when Fisher reached past her, pounded once—louder, more insistent—then stepped back, scanning the street. The morning soup had only just begun to retreat, and Cedar Hollow's endless hush was broken only by their own breathing.

"We're not being subtle," Fisher muttered, mostly to himself.

"I want them to know," Clara said.

Fisher nodded but eyed the drawn shades with suspicion. Something about the place was wrong: the emptiness had a studied quality, the absence of life not accidental but purposeful, defensive, as though the house itself had been scrubbed of all activity.

They were turning to leave when a voice called out from the porch across the street. "Looking for the Mills family?" The speaker was an elderly woman wrapped in a pink cardigan, hair in tight blue-white curls, standing barely visible behind a waist-high hedge. Clara recognized her as the Mrs. Gunther type—tribal elder of the neighborhood, collector of grievances, endlessly vigilant in her observation.

"We are," Fisher said, showing his badge. "Did you see anything unusual?"

The woman, introducing herself only as Sarah, stepped out onto the walk, shivering with either cold or anticipation. "They left last night. Very late."

Clara tried to keep her tone professional, not pleading. "How late?"

Sarah beamed, relishing her own reliability. "After midnight. Close to two. I heard their garage. I always know when it's open, the spring squeaks a certain way. They were carrying bags, big ones, like luggage. The boy did most of the lifting."

"Did you see what they were driving?" Fisher asked, already scribbling in his notebook, looking up sharply between each question.

"That brown SUV. Subaru, I think. They didn't turn the porch light on, but I could tell by the sound. Left toward Main Street. Didn't see them come back." She paused, leaning in, voice pitched low with juicy implication. "This about the Hays girl?"

Fisher hesitated. Clara didn't. "We're following up," she said. "Thank you, Sarah. If you remember anything else—"

"Nonsense, nonsense," Sarah said. "I'll let you in."

Clara and Fisher exchanged looks, their unease mirrored. Before they could say anything the old lady pulled out a key and opened the front door.

Clara shrugged and followed her through the doorway.

Inside, the house was a study in forced normalcy. Warm, faintly scented with coffee and lemon cleanser. Clara and Fisher split the space, methodically moving through rooms. It took less than a minute to verify Sarah's story: most of the family photos were gone from the mantle, a fine white rectangle left behind on the wall where each had hung. In John's bedroom, the drawers sat open, half-full, as if someone had packed in a hurry but taken care not to leave a mess. The closet was stripped of jackets and shoes. In the bathroom, a toothbrush cup sat empty, toothpaste cap left ajar.

Fisher moved to the kitchen, rifled through the recycling bin. "Left the garbage out," he said, finding only two still-wet beer cans and a crumpled magazine. He squinted at the mail on the counter, then shook his head, tossing it aside.

Clara opened the fridge and saw all the usual food, but front and center, a six-pack of some regional IPA wasn't touched. She held it up. "Who leaves beer behind?"

"Someone leaving quickly," Fisher said.

Clara's pulse doubled. She suddenly felt foolish about how easily she'd assumed the kid would break under pressure. She shut the fridge, leaned on it for a moment, then started opening drawers, cupboards, anywhere a clue might be stashed.

They regrouped in the living room, their boots tracking faint puddles onto the hardwood. "So much for an ambush," Clara muttered.

Fisher shrugged. "We'll put out the APB now then."

Clara hesitated, eyes resting on a shelf above the TV, packed with soccer, karate, and football trophies. All for John. "Anything in his room?" she asked.

"Just clothes gone. No laptop, no phone, no chargers." Fisher wrinkled his nose. "Kid's smarter than we gave him credit for."

Clara's eyes moved over the disarray. She felt the sting of failure. "They knew we'd come," she said. Her voice was low, edged with resignation.

"Cecilia?" Fisher replied.

"I don't think so." Clara shook her head, the movement quick, as if denying the obvious.

She had a creeping suspicion that they'd underestimated someone. That while she'd pieced together the outline, the real game was happening in the negative space, in the things not said and the moves not made.

Fisher watched Clara carefully. "You think Kane moved them?"

Clara considered it, turning it over like a stone in her hand. "He's got the resources. He doesn't like loose ends. If he thought John would talk…" she broke off, the rest unspoken.

They stood in the foyer, the emptiness oppressive, until Fisher finally pulled out his phone and started dialing dispatch. His voice was clipped, urgent, as he relayed the necessary details. "White male, nineteen, about six feet, traveling with father. Possible mother as well. Brown Subaru Outback, plates… Hold on." He ducked out to the street, radio in hand, leaving Clara to wander the house one last time.

When Fisher came back in he jerked his head toward the open front door. "Let's go," he said. "They're already on the interstate. Best we can do now is ping the toll cameras."

The drive back to the station was a run of grim silence. Clara was angry at herself for misjudging, at Kane for the invisible hand, and at John Mills for evading her grasp. She didn't realize she was gripping the file folder so hard until she heard it crinkle in her hands. Clara felt the strain in every mile, knowing there was no choice but to go at Kane.

Chapter 18

She drifted through the final bend to the Harrington estate, headlights sweeping the stonework. Each crunch of gravel beneath her tires was at once an admission and a dare. It was almost fully dark now, the kind of darkness that dissuades visitors and buries intentions, and for a moment she considered parking at the end of the drive to gather herself, to smooth the edges of her resolve. But the engine's idle was loud in the hush, and she couldn't tell whether she was more afraid of postponing or proceeding.

At the door she hesitated, her hand lifted not just to knock but to steady herself against the old carved oak. She waited, listening to the distant hush of lawns and hedges and the unseen groundskeeper's cart puttering in the distance. The impulse to retreat was overwhelming, but before she can surrender to it, the door welcomed her in.

Liam's voice preceded him, the syllables of her name coiling around a practiced smile. "Clara," he said, not a greeting so much as a hypothesis. He's dressed with intent, casual enough to lower defenses, but precise enough to remind her who he is. The foyer behind him stretched with cavernous expectation, every polished surface reflecting her indecision.

She stood in the threshold with her hands in her pockets, knowing that the words she rehearsed were already fraying. "I'm sorry," she began, the phrase scraping past the lump in her throat. Her apology was a shape she tried to hold, but it leaked out as a confession, vulnerable and raw.

"For leaving or for coming back?" Liam's tone was respectful enough for dignity but edged with curiosity. Even now, he found a way to flip her discomfort to his advantage.

"Both," Clara said, aware of the unwelcome flush in her cheeks and the way her breath betrayed her. She let the moment stretch, because she'd never been good at lying or at small talk. "It was a lot. I couldn't deal," she said. "I'm sorry I left that way. I had to sort some things out."

He just nodded, neither forgiving nor judging, only accepting. He stood aside, an unspoken recognition that the power dynamic had shifted but not disappeared. Clara stepped forward, and the door glided shut behind her with an almost ceremonial finality.

Inside, the scent of the house—aged books, chilled stone, and a trace of lime from the polish—crushed her composure.

Neither of them spoke, not really, as they drift toward the study. And yet, everything was said in the cadence of their footfalls, in the way Liam's hand hovered near the small of her back without touching. In the study, a fire low in the hearth threw gold on the

Chesterfields and the old glass cabinets. Liam poured a drink, then poured her one, too, placing the glass at the far end of a small table. An offering.

"Are you staying?" he asked, and though it's a simple question, it's loaded.

Clara shrugged and sat on the edge of a leather chair, eyes tracing the seams in the carpet. "I'm not sure," she said.

Liam sat, gestured for her to join him. She felt the pressure of time, of her own indecision. She felt the room closing in with expectation.

"What have you sorted out?" he asked, the words curious, without accusation.

She met his gaze, willing to be open but having difficulty articulating an answer. "My motivations," she finally said, succinctly.

Silence stretched, but it's not as vast as before. "As they pertain to the other night?" Liam inquired, the softness of his tone betraying the vulnerability beneath his composed exterior.

"Well, as to that…professional boundaries, right?" Clara said. She tried to sound assured, but it wavered, even in her own ears. "Or the lack of them."

The fire crackled, filling the space where her confidence faltered. "You're not involved in this case in a professional capacity, technically speaking, as I understood it," Liam suggested, his voice steady, a lifeline to her doubts.

Clara absorbed the suggestion, feeling the texture of possibility.

"I wasn't being fair to either of us," she confessed, knowing she had more to reveal than just words. She saw him take it in, and felt his acceptance ripple out. It felt like it did that night, like the world has narrowed and grown larger all at once.

"It wasn't just you," Liam said, his voice rich with acknowledgment. Clara was struck by the sincerity, the depth of his words. "It's been a long time since I've met anyone I didn't know everything about."

She smiled, the tension easing. They'd come through it, whatever it was.

"You should get out of this town once in a while," she joked, feeling the closeness return.

Liam let the silence speak for them, let it knit a fragile understanding.

Clara straightened, feels the determination return. "I still need your help with this. I don't have a lot of time tonight. If I don't figure this out, I'm not sure how many more chances I'll get. Is that a problem?" she asked, the professional and personal intertwining.

Liam regarded her, the firelight tracing the outline of his confidence. "No," he answered. The surety in his tone kindled a new resolve in Clara.

She took a breath and centered herself. "Then I need to tell you where we are."

He nodded, and the distance between them felt manageable. Clara sensed the room shift, as if it, too, understands the precarious balance of her return.

————————

Clara settled into the leather chair, the tension softening but not dissolving as she brought him up to speed. She kept her eyes on the fire. The dancing light reflected the flux of her thoughts.

Liam walked to the liquor cabinet, unscrewed a bottle with the efficiency of ritual. He poured two fingers for himself, and then a bracing glass for Clara, which he carried over with a sort of rehearsed intimacy. It wasn't lost on her that their negotiations always circled back to the table, the glass, the memory of something sharper.

He handed her the drink. Their fingertips touched, and Clara wondered—briefly and unhelpfully—if Liam calculated that as well. Probably yes, she thought. Almost certainly yes.

"We're so close," she began, feeling the edges of frustration in her voice. "But the Mills family fled. We had John. I know we did."

Liam listened, his fingers steepled beneath his chin, his focus unwavering. Clara saw him absorbing each word, weighing it, calculating.

"They left late last night," she continued, pushing through the raw disappointment. "They must realize their story is about to crack."

Liam shifted slightly, a signal that he's following, that he's still with her despite the complications. Clara sensed the questions building in his silence.

"You're sure they're gone for good?" he asked, not doubting her but probing for what she might not see.

Clara nodded, the movement as clipped as her certainty. "They cleaned out most everything you can fit in a suitcase."

Liam leaned back. He was considering, assessing, recalibrating. Clara saw herself in his determination, in his refusal to concede.

"So, you need Kane," he concluded, his voice both a question and an answer.

Clara let out a breath she didn't realize she was holding. "We don't have a choice," she said. Her frustration mingled with the resurgence of their partnership. "Surprising John was our best chance and we lost it. That's why I need your help. I need anything you have on Kane. Anything that gives us an edge."

Liam rose, the fluidity of the movement surprised Clara. His certainty wrapped around them, pulled them close to a shared focus. "I might have something," he said, walking to his desk. His words were precise, giving Clara just enough to keep her with him.

"As you know he's financing the new church construction," Liam began.

"Yes, out of the kindness of his heart," Clara replied sarcastically, feeling the firelight reflect the edge in her tone.

"He's counting on a nice tax break for it," Liam continued. "I've been looking into it recently. He's misrepresenting his outlay."

Clara considered this, felt the angles and possibilities opening, the vulnerabilities she didn't expect. She felt the night opening too, the sense that this might be a way through. A path she could take.

"Ever the opportunist," she noted.

"Indeed," Liam said, "and it would ruin him if it came out he was taking advantage of the church to line his pockets." Clara heard the depth beneath his words, the knowledge he shared with her, the trust that went with it.

She downed the drink, the fire and whiskey a perfect match for her newfound determination. She stood, felt the momentum building, the fear and certainty that were driving her.

"To avoid that he'll make a deal and give up John," Clara said. "He can always spin that as misguided loyalty. It's bad but he might have a chance to come through it."

"My thoughts exactly," Liam said.

Liam moved with her to the door, the sound of their footsteps a shared rhythm. He caught her arm, his touch deliberate, lingering. "Be careful," he warned, his eyes steady on hers. "Don't let him rattle you."

"I know," Clara said, her voice stronger than she felt. She saw the worry in his expression, how it mirrored her own.

Liam let go, but the connection stayed. Clara felt the bond between them, felt it thicken with every step away.

She left, the night cold against her skin. Her silhouette faded into the darkening sky as she walked to her car, her thoughts already bending to Kane, to what she can do, what it might cost if she failed.

———

Clara moved into the house with the careful grace of an intruder. Each step was a test of secrecy, each breath a challenge to the silence. The dim light lends conspiracy to her movements, shadowed walls averted witnesses. She was trying to dodge the questions, trying to navigate the interrogation that waited for her. She didn't hear Emma at first and thought she was safe, that she'd slipped in unnoticed.

A rare miscalculation. Emma emerged quietly, the dark kitchen wrapped her like an ally. She regarded Clara with the silent expectation of an accusation. It cut deeper than words.

"Late night?" Emma's voice surprised Clara. She froze, the floor cold beneath her feet.

Clara tried to shrug it off, to regain the advantage. "Long day." Her reply was as thin as she intended it to be. As uncertain.

"I bet," Emma said, turning on the light. She looked at Clara with a mix of warmth and demand. "Didn't know if you were coming back."

"I didn't mean to worry you," Clara said. "I've been busy."

"I figured." Emma leaned in, her curiosity both gentle and piercing. "Busy with the case?"

Clara heard the doubt in Emma's tone, feels the subtle pressure. "Of course," she replies, defensive. "What else would it be?"

Emma didn't answer right away, let the pause draw Clara in. "People are saying you've been at the

262

Harrington house a lot," she said, the observation landing like an accusation.

"I'm not surprised." Clara tried to sound sure of herself, tries to sound in control. But Emma knew her, and Clara knew it.

"I am." Emma's voice was softer now, the challenge fading into concern. "I'm surprised you didn't call, left me worrying for two nights."

Clara saw the hurt, the worry, the expectation. She shifted, the weight of explanation hanging over her. "There's so much going on." Her words came slower, with difficulty. "The Mills family took off. It's a mess."

"What's that got to do with Harrington?" Emma pressed. Her familiarity cut deeper than her words.

Clara hesitated, the pause too long, too telling. "We need something on Kane," she said. "I was getting information."

"Is that what they're calling it now?" Emma's sly tone broke through the distance between them.

Clara met her gaze, an awkward dance of deflection and admission. "I didn't call because I didn't have time," she insisted. But Emma's expression said otherwise.

"So, it's true?" Emma asked, the persistence matched by a worried note in her voice.

"Depends on what you mean." Clara deflected, her defenses thin as tissue.

"All of it." Emma leaned back, watching Clara squirm. "How deep are you in, Clara?"

Clara wanted to hold the silence, to keep the doubt from creeping in. But Emma was relentless, and Clara felt the story unravel. "I don't know," she admitted, her voice catching. "Pretty deep."

Emma took a breath, her relief tempered with caution. "Be careful," she warned. Her words hung heavy with the stories she didn't tell. Clara saw the risk reflected in Emma's eyes.

"I will," Clara said. She tried to sound confident, but Emma's concern wrapped around her, thick as the air.

Emma let it settle, then moved closer. Her voice dropped to a near whisper. "If it was just Kane and the investigation, I'd get it." Clara heard the worry beneath Emma's conspiratorial tone. "But Liam..."

"He's not what you think," Clara cut in. But Emma's face was so pale that Clara doubts her own words.

"Really?" Emma challenged. "The town thinks otherwise."

Clara felt the tension tighten around her. "I'm sure they do," she said, her sarcasm shielding her uncertainty.

"Clara," Emma said, the name holding both concern and reproach. "I'm serious."

Clara absorbed the worry in Emma's voice, felt it echo her own. "It's not what you think," she repeated, softer. Less convinced.

"Good," Emma replied. She tried to sound reassuring, but the edge lingers. Clara sensed it, knew how easily it cuts.

"I don't understand why this is so important to you," Emma said. Her sincerity made Clara pause. "I know you were talking about redemption and all that, but you can find that back at the FBI. This town is nothing to you, it's not worth it."

"You know why this matters," Clara said, the statement as much to herself as to Emma. "Why it's personal."

"Because of the last case?" Emma pressed. She was close to Clara now, close to her intentions, close to her doubts.

"Because of the mess I've made of my life since Alex died," Clara replied, the confession unexpected even to herself. "I need to make this work, just not for the reasons I thought."

265

Emma saw the change in Clara, saw the vulnerability she didn't expect. "It's not your fault," Emma said. The reassurance came softly.

"Yes, it is," Clara insisted. "All of it." Her guilt threaded through her words.

Emma stayed quiet, let Clara's confession sink in. "And Harrington?" she asked, her voice gentle, pulling at the loose ends of Clara's story.

"What about him?" Clara said. She tried to sound dismissive, but the question lingered.

"Is he just the case?" Emma's inquiry was quiet but pointed.

"I don't know," Clara admitted, the honesty raw. "I thought so. Now I'm not sure."

Clara looked away. She didn't want Emma to see the doubt in her eyes, didn't want Emma to see what she couldn't.

"Clara," Emma said, her tone was more worried than before. "I don't know how he got you under his spell, but you don't know him. Be careful."

Clara looked away. She couldn't face the certainty in Emma's expression.

"Remember what I said," Emma told her. She stood, leaving Clara with the echoes of her concern.

Clara watched Emma go. She tried to absorb the distance between them, the difference between their realities.

"You don't understand," Clara whispered, but Emma was already out of earshot.

Chapter 19

Clara moved through the Kane Construction headquarters with a quiet tension, each step a small betrayal of composure. The building was all clean surfaces and whispered rumors. It breathed control, ambition, and Clara felt it press down, heavy and unwelcome.

She'd told Fisher over coffee this morning that she needed to do this solo. He'd looked incredulous but Clara convinced him: Kane would be more honest with her one-on-one, and Fisher's presence would only make the man nervous, defensive, closed off.

The walk through the glass divide to Kane's inner sanctum gave her time to count her breath and rehearse the story she would tell. The secretary greeted her by name, inviting her to "just walk in, Mr. Kane is expecting you." She did.

Kane was perched on the edge of his desk, a tableau of casual dominance with his arms crossed loose, like a king inviting a petitioner to kneel. His hair was brushed back a little too deliberately, and his suit, though flawless, was worn with the air of someone who saw such perfection as a birthright. When he looked up, the smile he gave Clara was all white teeth and opaque eyes, the kind that refract each emotion and hand back only what's useful.

"The rumors are true, then. We have the pleasure of another visit," Kane said, rising to greet her.

She took his offered hand for the briefest moment—that slick, quick business hand, skin as soft as cashmere and twice as practiced in the mechanisms of power. It was a handshake designed for false promises.

"There are a lot of rumors in Cedar Hollow," Clara said as she let go, matching his tone exactly, holding the rhythm of the exchange like a wire pulled taut.

Kane gestured her into the seat across from his, behind the desk now. The gesture was open, hospitable, but he kept a careful three feet between them. She sat; he did too, folding himself into his chair like a lizard into sunlight.

"How can I assist you this time?" Kane's voice was blankly polite, but Clara could sense the alertness, the sense of being sized up.

Clara responded without a smile. "I want to tell you a story," she said, "one that should be very familiar to you." She watched Kane's face the way a disappointed parent watches a child. She was looking for the twitch at the corner of the eye, the microsecond of vulnerability, anything that would crack the mask he wore for such occasions. "A young man named John Mills meets his girlfriend in the middle of the woods. He's incensed about rumors he's heard that she's involved with someone else. Being the hot head that he is, he loses control and strangles her with her own scarf."

Kane let the silence hang for a beat, then flickered up a polite smile again. "And is this a different John Mills than the one we've established was on my payroll during the time in question?" he said, laughing soft as though clarifying a point in a boardroom.

Clara leaned forward. "Now John panics. He doesn't know what to do except call his dad for help. Trevor Mills. Trevor doesn't know what to do either, but he's spent half his adult life working for you, so he calls you."

"Me," Kane states flatly, giving nothing.

"Sure. He knows you're the only one who could help him hush it up. He's worked for you a long time and is counting on your sympathy."

"My sympathy does not extend to such behavior," Kane said, the first edge of heat in his voice.

"Certainly not. It's a horrible thing, a girl's life taken so violently just as it's about to blossom. Nobody in their right mind would countenance such a thing." Clara made herself look directly at him.

"Then what's your point, Miss Reynolds?" Kane said.

"Not that you weren't upset to hear about what John had done, nor that you would extend your help in normal circumstances. But you're also a pragmatic man, and after your initial surprise you saw an opportunity you simply couldn't resist. After all, the girl is dead. What's done is done."

Kane started to protest, but Clara spoke over him. "The opportunity to finally get your rival out of the way. See, the rumor was that Lila Hays was seeing Liam Harrington. Naturally, he would be under as much suspicion as John. But that kind of suspicion isn't quite good enough, is it?"

She spoke the line like a punch and watched to see if he flinched. Instead, he simply cocked his head, owl-like, waiting to see if she could finish the story in a way that satisfied him.

"You, however, are in the unique position of taking suspicion away from John by providing him with an alibi. All you have to do is pay off everyone on shift that night to say that he was there the whole time, working."

Kane folded his hands, expression neutral. "An amusing tale. You really think something like that would work?"

Clara shrugged, letting the silence answer for her until the echo of his voice had faded. "No, I don't.

Because it's not working. Especially as you've left them twisting in the wind, waiting for payment, getting nervous the longer the case goes on that they won't ever see the money."

He tapped his finger on the desk, a small Morse code of irritation. "That's a lot to digest," he said, eyes sharpening. "If you had proof I paid my employees to lie, you wouldn't be here. So I don't see any reason to continue this farce."

"As it happens there's another way of telling the story," Clara said, her voice steady and stripped of any pretense now. "The rumor about Lila and Harrington was started by none other than Father Callahan. Who, for the sake of his eternal soul, admitted that he was put up to it by you in exchange for construction on the new church."

That stopped him. Kane's smile lingered, but Clara could see its anchor had slipped. He was weighing her, recalibrating.

"Nor was that the only rumor you told him to spread. Another was that an old cult, long associated with the Harringtons, with the murder of another teenage girl, was up to its old business again.

"It's always important to cover your bases, correct? That's why you also had those symbols carved on the tree. I mean, with everything pointing to Harrington, John's alibi shouldn't even undergo the kind of scrutiny that might break it. That's why it's not such a risk as it might seem on its own.

"The rumor of the cult, based as it is on something that did in fact happen, makes a lot of sense if you want to work people up even more about Harrington."

Clara pauses, watching Kane.

"The one about Lila is a little more perplexing, because everyone can see there's no basis for it. It doesn't seem to do much to forward your agenda against Harrington, but perhaps the point of it was Lila herself.

"Now this is especially interesting to ponder, and it's why I prefer to tell the story this way. Because, when I see someone has put out those two rumors intentionally, and they intersect in the murder of a young girl, I see intent. I see someone who isn't exactly surprised when he receives that phone call from Trevor Mills, someone who doesn't stumble into opportunity so much as he works hard to create it."

For a beat there was nothing, and Clara felt the cold glass of Kane's office press in around her.

He leaned back, letting the accusation hang between them. "You've made me out to be quite the mastermind," he said. "I'm almost flattered, but that version of the story is even more absurd."

"I don't think so." Clara remained firm as she saw the anger flash in Kane's eyes, knew he was ready to push back.

Kane let the silence stretch, sharpening the moment with a condescension that would have been more effective on someone who hadn't spent years listening to men like him talk for a living. His posture, at first relaxed, now subtly coiled. He was preparing to attack, but with words rather than fists. Clara waited, hands folded in her lap, letting him set his own trap.

"You have quite the imagination," Kane said at last, a smile flickering at the corners of his mouth, but not rising to his eyes. "Now, if you'll indulge me, I'll tell a story of my own. A fallen star, an agent of federal law who once commanded respect at the highest levels. Perhaps there was a time when she could trust her judgment, but somewhere along the way it slipped—subtly, then all at once. Now every case is a pretext, every victim's tragedy a stage for her private dramas to play out. She pushes herself into the lives of those around her, manufacturing crises where none exist, convincing herself she's the only thing standing between the town and something monstrous and unseen."

He paused, watching for effect. Clara let her gaze drift to the lacquered edge of his desk, refusing to give him the satisfaction of a reaction.

"In this story," Kane continued, "the agent becomes obsessed. She falls under the spell of the main suspect, one whose family history is riddled with rumor and innuendo. Together, they set about dismantling every institution that gives this town its meaning. They hound the pillars of the community— its spiritual leaders, its business owners—because they're bored, or wounded, or simply evil.

"She pushes too far and finds that she has no authority whatsoever to play these games with the lives of the good people of this town. While she can sucker the local idiots with her nonsense, she finds the state and federal authorities take a much dimmer view of her transgressions."

At this point Clara couldn't help but experience a quickening of her pulse. There was no doubt she was treading on thin ice. She didn't know for sure whether Fisher would find it prudent to back her up against the kind of pressure Kane was threatening, and it went without saying that Bryant wouldn't feel particularly inclined to back her up for numerous reasons, but especially because she was doing all of this without his knowledge.

"You must not think I'm unsympathetic," Kane continued. "I don't make it a point to assume the worst of people. I have no doubt you have meant well. The Harringtons make it their specialty to twist their evil tendrils around people who are in a vulnerable state. I've dedicated my entire life to trying to prevent them from destroying the lives of anyone else. That's why I'll give you the option of simply walking away right now before it's too late."

She calmed herself down. He'd just made a mistake, thinking she had something to lose. He thought her desperate, and she had to admit he was correct, but he misjudged the nature of her desperation, much in the same way she herself had done.

"I appreciate your concern for my well-being. The thing is, your little story is based on a set of assumptions that aren't quite as sound as you think they are. Why I'm here, my relation with my informant. It's not your fault, really, as they were manufactured to appear exactly as you have perceived them," she said, smiling slyly.

Kane's face went a shade paler. The surprise was brief but telling. It's not always easy to bullshit a bullshitter, but when it is, it's surprisingly easy.

"Why you're here," he repeated, almost absentmindedly, a hint of desperation behind his polished exterior.

"Yes, the books you've been cooking regarding the new church construction."

Kane's bewilderment mixed with the barest hint of guilt. She could see that he couldn't make out how she'd gotten her information, had been blindsided by the direction their conversation had taken.

"It would ruin you," Clara continued, knowing she had him. "If it came out, you'd lose everything."

She let the implication settle, watched Kane shift in his seat, the weight of his empire suddenly uncertain. He seemed to grasp for control, for the confidence that had always come so easily.

Clara leaned in, her voice a near whisper, cutting through the distance with intent. "But things changed when Lila was murdered. Your financial misdeeds are less interesting to me now. If you tell me where the Mills family is, if you admit to your part in the cover-up, we might be able to work out a deal. You're in trouble either way, but loyalty to John can possibly be construed as loyalty to the town, whereas corruption can only be seen as a betrayal of it."

She sat back, letting the offer hang between them like an uneasy truce.

Kane's expression tightened, then softened, then drew into a pensive line. Clara saw the thoughts move through him, saw his reluctance, saw his fear.

"What kind of deal?" Kane asked.

"Give me John and I'll tell the first version of my story. Construction on the church will terminate and we'll leave it at that for now. You'll be watched,

277

but if you're able to pick yourself back up again and stay on the level you'll be left alone."

She waited, watched him hesitate, watched him crumble. Kane's eyes narrowed, then widened. He was coming apart.

"I never wanted—" Kane began, but the admission caught in his throat.

"It doesn't matter what you wanted," she said.

"I don't know where they are," he said finally, his tone wavering with desperation.

"Of course you do," Clara replied, her gaze steady. "You warned them off. They don't have the means to go off on their own."

He looked at her, saw the inevitability of her conviction, saw the crumbling of his own.

"You're too smart for this," Clara continued, letting her confidence draw him in. "You must see you only have one real option here."

He slumped back into his chair, his last defense failing. "It was supposed to be easy," he said. The words were brittle, as fragile as the alibi he'd crafted.

Clara waited, felt the moment stretch, felt it tighten around them.

"It was much like you said," Kane said, his voice heavy with the admission. "Trevor called me,

278

asking for help. I almost hung up right there and called the sheriff."

"But?" Clara prompted.

"But it was too perfect an opportunity to pass up," Kane said. "There's no way to get rid of the Harringtons without getting your hands dirty, I'd already come to accept that. So, I told myself that the ends justified the means."

"Save it for someone who cares," Clara said, the skepticism sharp. "Where are they?"

"I really—" Kane hesitated, then continued, his words rushing to catch up with his uncertainty. "I really don't know."

"We'll see," Clara answered. She knew he was lying; knew she would prove it. "Don't go anywhere."

Kane's expression crumbled, his last resistance giving way to doubt, to the risk of losing it all. Clara saw fear in his eyes, saw it mirror the fear she'd carried with her, the fear she was leaving behind.

"You think I'm lying," Kane said, his voice breaking.

"No John, no deal," Clara replied, turning to leave.

She walked out, her movements quick, certain, leaving Kane to his collapsing world.

Chapter 20

Clara sat on the edge of her chair, watching the minute hand drag its way through eternity, the relentless tick of the wall clock digging fissures into her composure. Every muscle in her body vibrated with a taut, useless energy. The stale fluorescent light above her painted everything—case files, empty coffee mugs, unread messages on her phone—in a sickly, unreal palette.

Suddenly, a commotion built at the other end of the corridor. Clara recognized Fisher's heavy tread, the purposeful shuffle that meant he had news worth sharing. She stood before he even entered, heart stuttering as he swung into the doorway, his usual poker face broken by a wild, exhausted grin.

"We got him," Fisher blurted, barely catching his breath. "Kane confessed. He's going down for accessory to murder."

The words were a stone tossed through a still pond. Clara blinked, the tension in her chest uncoiling into a brief, incredulous relief. It should have been a victory but her mind immediately leapt ahead to the next, unfinished chapter. She steadied herself, voice flat.

"And John?"

Fisher shook his head, the smile dying on his lips as he gave her the rest. "Still claims he had no clue about them running. No idea where they are."

Clara clenched her fists, letting her nails bite into her palms. "It doesn't make sense. It does him no good at this point. Why doesn't he give him up?" She paced a tight circle, searching for a crack in the logic.

Fisher kept his distance, watching her with a mixture of admiration and caution. "We'll get it out of him. It's just a matter of time. The DA isn't letting Kane's lawyer cut any deals until we have hard evidence on John. He'll turn, trust me."

Clara stopped, shoulders bunched, as if trying to physically anchor herself against the uncertainty.

He softened, his tone shifting as he caught the doubt creeping into Clara's expression. "Listen, this is more than anyone expected. You broke the damn thing open. We wouldn't be here without you."

The gratitude in his voice startled her, but Clara refused to absorb it. "We're not there yet," she said. "Not until he's in a cell."

Fisher exhaled, conceding the point. "Just don't burn yourself out. We're close." He eyed the dark circles under her eyes, the battered knuckles on her right hand. "Seriously, Clara. Go get some rest. Shower. Eat. There's nothing else you can do right now. I'll call the second something breaks."

Clara relented and stepped out into the cold, the air thick with the questions she couldn't answer. She told herself she had to see it through. But as the mist closes around her, she wondered if she was lying.

———

The old church loomed out of the haze like a half-remembered dream, beams slicked with condensation, the stained-glass windows black and brackish from the outside. Clara hesitated at the foot of the steps, the pall of humidity and stone thick in her mouth, before mounting them one by one, each tread surrendering an exhausted creak. The front doors were already ajar, as if the building expected her, and from within seeped a chill that had nothing to do with the rain-swept evening.

She found Father Callahan in the nave, hunched over a pew in the half-dark, hands folded, and head bowed as if in prayer. He didn't move when she entered, not at first; the only sound was the drip of water from her coat and the distant scrape of wind stirring through the bell tower. When he did turn, it was suddenly, with the restless guilt of a man caught in a private act.

He gestured for her to sit, pushing aside his own fatigue to forcibly compose himself. "Thank you for coming," he said, the words barely carrying in the thick gloom. The emptiness of the church swallowed his voice. "I'm sorry for the summons. I just couldn't... I didn't want to see you in the station."

His face was a map of haunted lines and sleeplessness, eyes wild beneath the clerical black. For a moment, Clara felt a twinge of empathy; Callahan had aged a decade in a week. He looked less like a moral authority, more like a man who had been living under siege.

"I was blind," he said quietly, without the posture of self-pity. "I wanted the new parish so much, it's only right that I lose it." He squeezed his hands until the knuckles whitened. "I'm trying to make amends. Robert was still unsure, but I told him there was nothing left but to formally confess. He knows he was weak. He knows he failed the town and failed himself."

Clara studied him, measuring the edges of his defeat. The church around them was cold and abandoned, and it echoed with the ghosts of all the whispered secrets it had ever absorbed. When she spoke, her voice was softer than she intended. "He used you, Father."

Callahan cracked a smile that twisted into self-loathing. "Everyone is in thrall to some force or another," he said. "Even you, though you refuse to see it."

Clara bristled, but she let the comment pass. "I see the truth," she said evenly.

His gaze sharpened, and he shook his head with a weary finality. "You see your version of the truth. I'm not sure that's enough for this place."

She wasn't sure if this was a threat, warning, or simple regret. She had little patience for any of it.

"Well, Kane did what you wanted," she said. "He confessed. The story's over now."

Callahan looked at her as if she'd missed the point on purpose. "I wish it were that simple," he said. "After all this, you still don't see what you've done, do you?"

Something in his phrasing caught her off guard. Clara paused. "What are you talking about?"

He looked away, his hands trembling. "Robert told me of the conversation the two of you had. As right as you were, there was something important that you were very much wrong about. It's my fault, really. The last time we spoke I was still trying to keep things close to the vest, and I spoke in more generality than I should have. It's quite easy to see why you assumed what you did."

Clara arched an eyebrow, suddenly impatient. "About what?"

"The rumor," Father Callahan said, choosing his words with obvious care. "You said the rumor about Lila and Liam Harrington signified intent, that it was put out there to drive John to the murder." He looked up at her now, the force of his conviction shining through his exhaustion. "But that rumor was only started after the murder. Beforehand, it was only the stuff about the cult."

Clara went still, the words reshuffling all the logic she'd stacked against the crime. She realized she had assumed without thinking that both rumors originated at the same time. "It changes nothing," she said reflexively. "It doesn't save Kane."

Callahan's eyes flashed. "Not from his decision to protect John, no. But it does matter. Because the motive you believed in never existed. The real reason—the one you can't guess at, because you've never lived here—remains hidden. Not the crime, but the reason behind it."

Clara felt her skin prickle in the cold air. For the first time in days, she was unsure of herself. "His motive is irrelevant," she insisted. "He'll tell us when you bring him in."

"It may be irrelevant to you," Callahan said with an intensity that surprised her, "but it's not irrelevant to the people of this town. With what you've made public, with what you forced into the open, you've left us nothing to fight back with."

Clara paused, exasperated. She had a sense of what he was driving at, the same old story about the Harringtons and their deeds. But given what she knew, she only felt sorry for him.

They sat in silence for a few moments; each lost in their own thoughts.

"I knew Margaret Dooley quite well," Father Callahan eventually said, as if roused from old memories.

"The girl who was murdered forty years ago," Clara said.

He smiled, but there was no joy in it. "She was my cousin. We grew up together, ran through these woods as children. I left for seminary in Portland before it happened, but I never stopped thinking about her." He looked down, voice breaking. "She was the first ghost to follow me into this place. Cedar Hollow eats people alive, Ms. Reynolds. If you stay long enough, you start to believe it's normal."

Clara looked at the maze of pews, the looming crucifix above the altar, the splay of rain light across the stone floor. She felt the ache of inevitability in her bones. She began to say, "Father, the two things—"

"Don't," he cut her off abruptly. "I know what you're going to say. You have no understanding of what it's like living here." He sighed heavily. "That's not your fault, I know. That's what makes it so difficult for me to convey to you a sense of what you've done, when we were close to finally freeing ourselves…"

He trailed off, muttering incoherently.

"Father, I understand more than you think. What William did to Margaret was awful. It leaves a mark on everything it touches, even the family of the perpetrator. That can be its own burden to bear."

"My child," he said with great sadness, rising unsteadily from the pew. "What is it they say? History doesn't repeat itself, but it often rhymes. I will pray for you."

Callahan left her with his warning, with her doubts, with the weight of Cedar Hollow pressing down.

———

Clara returned to Emma's house, Callahan's words threading her thoughts, not quite catching but not quite falling away. The lights were dim, an uneasy hush wrapping the rooms.

"We need to talk," Emma said the moment she's through the door, the words gentle, unwilling.

Clara braced herself. This day was only getting more wearisome. Emma led her into the kitchen, each step measuring the strain between them.

"The town…" Emma began, then paused.

Clara saw Emma's concern shadowed with reluctance. The conversation stretched between them, already old, already tired.

"What about the town?" Clara asked, trying to feign ignorance, trying to deny what she knew was coming. Emma hesitated, as if choosing her words with great care. Or maybe trying to cushion the blow.

"People don't know what to make of all this. They're uneasy." The understatement stung Clara, leaving her raw and defensive.

She looked at Emma, sees the strain, sees the quiet desperation. "They'd rather have had the wrong guy?" Clara demanded, her voice brittle.

Emma shrugged, *maybe*, and Clara felt sick to her stomach.

"It's hard to articulate, but there are bad vibes going on," Emma said. "They know it's not your fault exactly, but you're easy to blame. Anyway, it would probably be best if you didn't stay here any longer." She tried to sound apologetic, but Clara heard the firmness behind the words.

"I thought you were different," Clara said, the accusation rising to her lips.

Emma flinched but doesn't back down. "We have to live here after you're gone," she said.

Clara recoiled at the words, saw the truth in them.

"I'm just doing what's right," she protested.

Emma looked at her, an unspoken question hanging between them, one Clara didn't have the answer to.

"I'll leave tomorrow," she said, defeated. Her voice carried the weight of decisions she hadn't yet made, the echo of uncertainty she couldn't silence.

"I wish it were different," Emma replied, but Clara couldn't look at her. She stepped into the night, the gloom closing in, and wondered if she was doomed to always be leaving.

Chapter 21

Clara's steps echoed off the marble floors, like those of an intruder, rebounding off the high ceilings and cavernous halls, each strike of heel and arch feeding a crescendo of unresolved emotions. The Harrington estate was a monstrous slab of architecture, but living inside its shell was something else, a sense of being both artifact and error at once, a fossil embedded in the stone of someone else's legacy.

She stepped into another hall, its windows wide, their drapes trembling. Cold air slipped through the cracks, slipping over her thoughts. The walls narrowed, tightened, then expanded. Endless rooms, their furniture cloaked in the white sheets of the forgotten. Each step wrapped around her doubt, drawing it closer, an embrace of uncertainty.

Her phone gave her nothing. No messages, no updates, nothing on John Mills. As the silence stretched on it made her increasingly anxious. The case had been the only tether she'd had to the world outside, but as days passed and the world refused to reach back, she felt her own reality begin to thin. She tried to picture John Mills hiding, but his face had already started to blur in her mind, replaced by the half-remembered features of every other suspect who had gotten away.

Pacing the halls again, she traced out the route to the study, then the conservatory, then back to the foyer, as if relentless movement could keep her from being dissolved by the house's inertia. She kept expecting to run into Liam, but he had become increasingly spectral, surfacing only for the most transactional sorts of communication. The household staff, meanwhile, moved like clockwork ghosts in their black uniforms, never pausing, never smiling, always knowing to avert their eyes at the exact moment her presence became intolerable. She caught them looking more than once and met their gaze with flat defiance, but the effect was always temporary—the next time, they would glance away even faster, as if to erase her from their world.

She sat in the library for hours, surrounded by tomes on law, history, and the doomed genealogies of the Pacific Northwest. She raked over the case files with trembling hands, mapping the timeline repeatedly. Lila Hays' murder. The symbols. The snap of Emma's voice when she recounted the past. Everything seemed to point to a resolution that had already occurred, and yet John Mills was still uncaught, still out there, somewhere in the murk and the pines. Clara's thoughts looped in endless ellipses, unable to break free.

Occasionally, she found herself conversing with the voices in her head—the old partners, Bryant, even her mother's brittle admonitions. Their reproaches stung less than her own. It didn't matter how many times she rehearsed the facts; the failure was always personal and unfixable.

On the fifth morning of her private exile, Clara sat at the edge of her bed, scrolling through the local message boards for rumors of John Mills. The top post was a grainy image, shot through a greasy pickup truck window, of someone who might have been Mills at a gas station in the next county. She forwarded it to Fisher but knew nothing would come of it.

She left her room midafternoon and drifted without plan through the east hallways. The air was cold and sharp, leeching the warmth from her arms. She touched the wall for balance, feeling the tiny hairline cracks spidering outward from every corner. The staff seemed to have multiplied since her last circuit; every alcove had a polished, silent presence in it, as if the house were being gradually fortified against her.

A table stood against the wall, a sentinel in the vast expanse. Clara picked up the newspaper, her fingers trembling against the thin, accusing paper. Kane's face filled the front page. His arrest sent ripples through the town, and the article spread the damage like ink on a pond. Words blurred and bled together. Local hero gone bad, local economy gone down the drain.

She dropped the paper, letting it float to the floor. Her presence seeped into Cedar Hollow like an ink stain, and she wondered if it would ever come out.

Clara felt the urge to pack her bags and leave. There was no sense in staying, she couldn't do anything to track John down. But as she stood in the middle of the corridor, the impulse ebbed. She couldn't quite put her finger on it, but something was keeping her here. She didn't think it was that dreaded word again, *closure*, but maybe she was just fooling herself.

She wandered to the solarium in a half-daze, the windows streaming gray daylight over a parade of dying ferns. She sat in the farthest corner, knees drawn up, and watched the clouds coil over the mountains. Time passed strangely in the house. The hours collapsed into minutes, the minutes stretched to fill the space of a day. She considered calling Emma again, but she already knew the conversation would be pointless, too full of things neither of them wanted to say.

Dusk arrived all at once, as if the sun had simply given up. The light in the hallway flickered on, and the house seemed to grow even larger, the shadows crawling along the edges of the ceiling. Clara made her way toward the main dining room, compelled more by habit than hunger. She stepped through the double doors and found the space already set—a single place setting at the head of a table long enough to seat a grand jury. The silverware gleamed. The napkin was a triangle of blinding white. She hesitated, then took her seat.

Moments later, a door whispered open, and one of the butlers entered carrying a covered plate. He set it in front of her with the precision of a croupier, then lifted the cloche. The food was perfectly arranged but as she cut and chewed and swallowed, she barely tasted a thing. The butler reappeared some minutes later with something vaguely resembling dessert. Clara set her utensils down and folded her hands, staring at the last course as if daring it to vanish.

Across the expanse, the windows reflected her image back at her, lone and diminished. Clara wondered what it would take to matter here, among these people and their rituals, among walls that had accumulated more history than she ever would. She wondered if it was too late to undo the feeling of being an impostor.

A grandfather clock began to chime in the hall. The sound was deep, slow, tolling just slightly off the note, as if the bell itself had lost interest in being correct. Clara rose from her chair, feeling the air thicken around her. She listened to the clock's echo until it faded, then moved to the window, staring out into the nothing between the estate and the black trees. She pressed her palm to the cold glass and left a perfect print. Proof, for once, that she had been here at all.

She gathered herself and walked back through the estate, past the muttering staff, past the closed doors. She paused in the entrance hall, studying the faces in the old portraits again. They seemed to watch her in judgment, but also with the boredom of those who had seen everything before.

———

The fire crackled, spitting sap and sparks as if in protest to the silence. Clara hunched over the table. Her eyes traced the tortured logic of her own handwriting, line after line of guesses, theories, and counterarguments that twisted into knots the harder she tried to follow them. In the end, it always came back to the same question: Why had the Mills family run?

The whiskey had begun to loosen the ache in her throat, but it did nothing for the heaviness in her chest. She toyed with the edge of a case file, flipping it open and skimming the familiar pages. Every detail had been pored over, every timeline cross-checked. The photos—Lila's body at the roots of the old oak, the carved symbols on the bark—seemed to leer at her from the manila folder, reminders of the triumph that wasn't.

She pressed her palm to the table, flattening the papers. She wanted to believe there was more to the story, that she was missing some crucial piece, but maybe there wasn't. Maybe they just panicked. But why? And what means did they have if no one helped them?

The room was stifling. The fire's warmth never made it past the brass rail, and the darkness beyond the windows pressed in like an accusation. She could see her own reflection in the glass—hair tousled, eyes too wide, a bruised half-shadow of herself. She hated the image, hated its vulnerability. She turned away and fixed her attention back on the open file.

A sound in the hall—a soft, measured footfall—drew her focus back to the present. She tensed, waiting. The staff had a way of making themselves invisible until the exact moment one needed to be reminded that they were always there. But this wasn't the staff. Liam's tread was distinct: heavier, deliberate, a little impatient.

He paused just outside the door, and for a moment Clara imagined he'd been standing there for some time, listening to the cadence of her failures as they unspooled across the desk. She didn't turn, letting him make the first move.

He cleared his throat. "You're at it late tonight."

She let the silence hang for a moment before answering. "Not much else to do."

He stepped inside, eyes flicking to the empty glass near her hand. "Did you eat?"

"I think so. I honestly don't remember," she said. "The food here is too... formal."

He studied her, as if weighing whether to challenge or accept the statement. "You're not sleeping, either."

Clara exhaled, the sound closer to a sigh than she intended. "If you're going to tell me I'm burning out, you might as well get in line."

He came to stand beside the fireplace, leaning on the stone with a practiced casualness. "It's just... You did it, Clara. You solved the case."

"Did I?" She glanced at the photos again, the tangled web of dates and locations. "If that were true, I wouldn't still be here."

He frowned, unaccustomed to being contradicted in his own house. "The evidence is clear. You're holding yourself hostage for no reason."

She pushed the file away, the gesture abrupt. "If we can't find them it means they have help. Kane has no reason to lie, and if it wasn't him then it means I'm missing a piece of the puzzle. A big piece."

Liam's brow furrowed. "Did you stop to wonder if you're overcomplicating things?"

"That's what Fisher thinks too." Clara bit her lip, barely holding in her anger. "I think everyone finds it more convenient to move on."

He took a careful breath, then crossed to the liquor cart. He poured himself a glass, offered her a refill. She shook her head. "If you don't mind me saying, you're not the most jovial guest these days," he said lightly, but his eyes were alert, watchful.

"You're not finding my stay here as enjoyable as you expected?" Clara asked snidely.

He grinned, and for a moment the formality fell away. "You're not as hard to read as you think, Clara."

She smiled then, but her attention drifted. Over his shoulder, through the dark of the window, she caught a flicker of movement on the lawn. A shape, a shadow, then nothing. She blinked. Just a trick of the night, or the clockwork ghosts of the staff making their rounds. Even so, a pulse of unease threaded through her. She wondered how many eyes were actually on her, here in this glass-and-stone diorama.

She tried to refocus. "If you want me gone, just say so."

Liam pursed his lips. "If I wanted you gone, you'd be gone." He snapped his fingers for emphasis.

The gesture stung. "I'm not a stray you can adopt or set loose at your convenience."

He didn't deny it. "The truth is, you're not happy here. You have a purpose elsewhere and you know it."

Clara absorbed his words, felt them bruise her certainty. She knew he believed this, but she was unsure if she did. Maybe she was just getting cold feet about going back to Omaha, having to explain to everybody why she'd be a better agent now.

He sipped his whiskey, considering. "I think you're holding yourself back."

Clara tensed, unwilling to concede. She wrapped her hands around her empty glass, and considered squeezing as hard as she could. "Something's nagging at me," she confessed, the struggle to articulate it a visible weight. "Somehow, something about the whole thing is off."

Liam's expression closed off, the way it always did when he was ready to end a conversation. He walked to the mantel and picked up the poker, stirring the embers. "Some mysteries just burn themselves out, Clara." He looked at her pointedly. "You should let them."

She wanted to argue, but exhaustion had hollowed her out. She watched him as he watched the fire, both lost in the conviction that they were right.

After a long minute, he set the poker aside and straightened his suit jacket. "If you find what you're looking for, let me know," he said, voice low. He left the room, his footsteps muffled by the thick carpet.

Clara sat very still, watching the embers until her eyes watered and the world blurred at the edges. She waited for the relief of certainty, but none came.

She gathered her files, stacking them with exaggerated care, and returned them to her bag. She left the library and followed the hallway, walking slower than before, as if savoring the friction of carpet beneath her feet. In the foyer, she paused at the window and peered out onto the lawn. The shape she'd glimpsed earlier had vanished, leaving only the wet shine of moonlight on the grass.

————

A bed, a suitcase, a life in transit. The room was exquisite, lonely. The temporary and the permanent squared off, warred against her indecision. Tall windows held the night at bay. The dark outside competed with the dark inside. Clara stood in the center, captive of both.

She let the door shut behind her, a gentle click that felt final and faintly accusatory. The suite was larger than her first apartment, and every surface gleamed as if waiting for a museum placard to be set beside it. It was designed for guests more important than herself, for visiting royalty or foreign investors, and even the air seemed reluctant to circulate without permission. The lamp on the dresser glared in a perfect circle, illuminating nothing but the ordered sterility. In here, the bed was a centerpiece, an island in a sea of neutral carpet. Clara hovered at its edge, suitcase in hand, evaluating the symmetry of her own displacement.

Her eyes swept the perimeter, cataloging the excess. Two sitting chairs by the window, upholstered in fabric so pale it might have been forbidden to touch. A cherry-wood writing desk with nothing but a single sheet of hotel stationery folded into a pristine triangle. On the far wall, a vanity table circled by bulbs, its surface bare except for a glass tray with tissue-thin monogrammed envelopes. The walls were hung with oil paintings of forests and rivers, always in the mist. Even here, the fog was inescapable, the trees forever caught between vanishing and emerging.

Clara set her suitcase on the stand and perched on the edge of the mattress. The fabric was taut, resisting her presence. She wondered who had slept here before her, if they'd left any trace of themselves or if the staff had erased it all. Part of her wanted to find a hidden hair, a forgotten button, any small evidence that she was not the only one to pass through. She ran her thumb along the bedspread, seeking a snag or loose stitch, finding none.

The sound of her own breathing unsettled her. The house had a way of swallowing everything, of pressing in with velvet gloves. Even the wind at the window seemed rehearsed. She stood again, restless, and paced the length of the room. Her reflection jumped from one polished surface to the next: a flicker in the mirror, a ghost behind the glass. She stopped at the window and looked out, past the careful landscaping, down the slope toward Cedar Hollow. The town was a smattering of yellow lights, flickering uncertainly in the shroud. She could almost convince herself it was a painting, too.

She pressed her forehead to the cold pane, hungry for sensation. The glass was so clean it felt imaginary. Below, the hedgerows cut geometric paths through the lawn, impossibly straight. There was no sign of the presence she'd glimpsed earlier, no movement at all on the grounds. It was as if the estate had decided, collectively, to hold its breath and wait for her to leave.

Cedar Hollow called to her, persistent, flickering lights beyond the glass. The bed waited, the case notes waited. The windows watched. Her resolve eroded and built, built and eroded. She moved like she thought, endlessly. A decision formed, fragile as the night.

She retreated from the glass and circled the bed, shoulders hunched, fingers tracing the seam where headboard met wall. The emptiness of the room was louder than any argument she could summon. She realized, with a sour smile, that even her own self-pity had started to bore her.

She drifted toward the vanity and caught her reflection, painted delicately in the gold-leaf frame. The face that stared back at her was washed out, hollowed by sleeplessness. The eyes were the only part left in high relief, sharp and blue and hungry. She tried smiling, then dropped the experiment. She didn't recognize herself, but at least the woman in the mirror looked like she wanted something.

On the desk, the folded sheet of stationery tempted her. Clara reached for it, ran her finger beneath the crease, then snapped it open. The paper was thick, almost pulpy, a weight that suggested importance. She half-expected to see a handwritten note—Welcome to your new home, or a veiled threat, or just a single word: Why? —but it was blank. The folded triangle mocked her, a shape with no message, just geometry.

She set it down, then opened the armoire. The scent of cedar spilled into the room, clean and sharp, but the hangers were empty. All the drawers had been left open, as if the staff wanted her to see the emptiness, to confirm that nothing was waiting for her inside. She closed them all, one by one, feeling the resistance of well-oiled hinges.

Her hands hovered over her suitcase. Open, closed, neither, both. It sat on the floor, a testimony to her vacillation.

She returned to the bed and stared at the suitcase. She couldn't remember what she'd packed anymore, only that it wasn't enough. She thought about the last time she'd packed a bag, how she'd done it in a rush, fighting a sense of unreality. She'd left half her belongings behind in that apartment—a favorite mug, a stack of paperbacks, a pair of shoes with the laces tied together—and had halfway expected to never go back for them.

The suitcase was battered, the handle scuffed to gray. She ran her palm along the zipper, then popped it open. Inside were the practicalities: two changes of clothes, a toiletries case, the folder of case notes. She touched each in turn, confirming their reality, as if she expected them to vanish while her back was turned.

Clara picked it up, held it, set it down. The gesture was uncommitted. She unpacked, the clothes spilling onto the floor, careless, defeated. She repacked, then stopped, breathed.

She pulled out a shirt, then tossed it across the bed. She did the same with the rest, until the suitcase was empty and the contents scattered, a forensic tableau of her own disarray. Then she gathered the clothes into a pile and stuffed them back in, not bothering to fold them. She zipped the case, then opened it again. For a minute she just sat, hands gripping the sides, staring at the heap of fabric as if waiting for it to rearrange itself into a solution.

The past, the case, the conversation with Liam. Everything circled. Everything pulled.

She could still feel the echo of his voice, the practiced sympathy, the gentle pressure to move on. To let the dead bury the dead, or at least to let other people grieve in peace. She closed the suitcase, but not completely. It stared back, half-open, a defiant mirror of her state of mind.

Clara's hand brushed against a familiar shape, cold metal, hard certainty. She pulled it from beneath the tangle of clothes and held it up. Her badge. The FBI emblem winked at her, a sly accusation. Clara remembered the impetus that drove her, that brought her, that almost took her away. She ran her fingers over its surface, tracing the truth and the lie.

Purpose. Ego. She saw them both, clearly, saw them flicker like the lights in the distance. She thought of her decision to stay. She thought of her need to leave.

It would be easy, now, to close the suitcase, throw it in the trunk of the rental car, and drive away while the town slept. She could move on, get back to her old life with the renewed purpose she'd thought she'd grasped. But somewhere between the impulse and the act, her hands always stopped. She couldn't abandon the question, couldn't leave the puzzle unfinished. Not even if it meant being haunted by it forever.

She put the badge on the nightstand, right at the edge, its reflective surface facing the bed. A small sentinel, a reminder. The restlessness in her legs wouldn't abate, so she circled the room again, arms folded tight to her chest. Every shadow seemed to twitch in the periphery, every silence interrupted by the creak of a board or the slow contraction of ancient pipes. The house was alive, and she imagined it listening, cataloging her movements, judging the rhythm of her uncertainty.

Her past pulled, her future pulled. They stretch her thin, stretch her tight. She wanted to snap, but she wouldn't allow it. She was stronger than this, she insisted. Clara spread the case notes across the bed. The pages trembled, uncertain, like her hands. The connections scattered and rebuilt. There was something she was missing. Something more than John Mills, more than the lack of gratitude from the town.

She unzipped the folder and poured its contents onto the coverlet. Photos, printouts, handwritten timelines kept on ruled notebook paper, marginalia from her own sessions staring at the board back at the station. She sorted them into piles, then ruined the piles, then aligned them again in a new topology. The tree, the body, the symbols. The search grids, the witness statements, the gaps in the logs. It was all there, but she'd looked at it so many times that the details had started to blur, become abstract.

She leafed through the scene photos, searching for a clue she'd missed, a vantage point she hadn't yet considered. Lila's face, frozen in that final moment, her eyes open, staring up at the canopy. The marks on the bark. The soil disturbed at the base of the trunk. Clara traced the grain of the photo with her thumb, wishing she could step inside the frame and see it herself, raw and unfiltered.

She looked up, senses prickling. Something moved outside, she was sure of it. A shape, a flutter, gone in an instant. She pressed closer to the glass, forehead leaving a smudge. Maybe it was a rabbit, or a branch, or the imagination that comes from too much caffeine and not enough sleep. But the feeling lingered, a certainty that she was being watched, evaluated, weighed. She wondered if Liam was spying, or if the house had its own agenda.

She heard the estate settle around her, the wind against the windows, the shutters tapping an uneasy rhythm. The sound wrapped her doubt, threading it into the dark. She heard her own thoughts, fragmented and raw.

She re-read her notes out loud, punctuating them with the sound of her own heartbeat. The words were meaningless individually, but as she strung them together, they built a structure, a temporary scaffolding to prop herself up against. She caught herself repeating the same phrase, "It doesn't add up," until it lost all sense and just became a mantra.

Clara considered the breadth of her dilemma. What would be left if she surrendered the question, if she retreated? Would her sense of failure be lessened, or would it just become another room inside her, another mausoleum to an unfinished case? She thought of the last meeting with Fisher, the way he'd looked at her as if she were a dog, refusing to give up a bone. Even then, she'd known she would never let go.

The decision formed, fragile as the night, fragile as her certainty.

She stared at the badge, at the photos, at her own hands, the skin stretched white over the knuckles. She wanted to make a move, any move, but every option seemed to trap her rather than release her. So, she did nothing. She sat down on the floor, knees pulled to her chest, and let the world go quiet for a minute. The silence was almost a balm, until the wind picked up and rattled the windowpanes, a sound like claws dragging across the surface of her mind.

She set her resolve like she set the pages, one careful corner at a time.

Stay, for now. Stop running, whether toward something or away from something. The same choice, a new direction. It feels as tenuous as it did the last time, as tenuous as she does.

She stacked the files and smoothed the edges, then placed them at the center of the bed. She turned off the lamp, letting the room fill with shadow, and sat on the edge of the mattress. For a while she just breathed in the darkness, letting it settle on her, folding her up tight.

The windows watched her, impassive, persistent. The room held her in its center, held her in its indecision.

Chapter 22

Clara wandered the main house late at night, its vast emptiness closing around her like a fist. The rooms spread out endlessly and she felt the weight of them, felt herself shrink. Her thoughts circled, and she followed, through corridor after corridor, chasing them down. Her own story, the town's story, the knot of stories she couldn't untangle. She wanted answers but the mansion only gave her silence. At this hour her existence seemed nothing but a flickering purgatory of indecision.

She found herself again in the library, the room dim and expectant. It was colder than the rest of the house and Clara drew her arms close as she walked through the shelves. Dust and memories filled the air, heavy with neglect. Her eyes moved over the rows of books, searching, not knowing what for. She pulled volumes from their places, the weight of them unexpected in her hands.

The photo album rested behind a fortress of thick, unread tomes. Its presence seemed quietly calculated, as if it waited for exactly this moment, her searching hand, an audience of one. Clara's fingers slipped into the gap and drew it free, surprised by its weight and the faint musk of its leather. She carried it to the desk beneath the window and opened it.

The first pages were a formal procession of black-and-white portraits: Harringtons posed in starched collars and lace, their gazes measured, defiant, none smiling. Liam was there, remarkably unchanged even at seven or eight: jaw set, eyes sharp, an old man's gravity housed in a child's body. In every shot, he held himself slightly apart—even family photos showed a sliver of space between him and the rest, as if a part of him always stood elsewhere, watching the scene unfold.

It was several turns in before another figure appeared beside Liam. A boy his age, lean and wild-eyed, hair perpetually mussed. The second boy's posture was the inverse of Liam's: reckless energy, arms flung around Liam's shoulder or caught mid-laugh, as if desperate to pull Liam into the orbit of normal childhood. The photos captured moments of rough play, mutual dare, a secret language between them on the margins of formal dinners and sun-bleached garden parties. Clara smiled at the humanizing glint it gave the otherwise glacial album.

She leaned closer, squinting past the faded gloss. The other boy's features were bright with youth, but there was something in the set of his mouth, the pattern of his hairline, that she'd seen before. She turned the page, and there it was: a snapshot of Liam and the boy, maybe ten or eleven by then, squatting at the banks of a river, their reflection a pair of smudged silhouettes. The image caught the

311

full force of the other boy's face, and Clara's stomach plummeted in recognition.

Trevor Mills.

She spoke the name aloud, as if saying it could chase away the chill crawling up her neck. There was no mistaking it. The eyes, the shape of the brow, the crooked tooth. The shock of it left Clara gripping the album with both hands, blood pounding in her ears. She stayed frozen for several long breaths, as if expecting the phantom of Trevor to step out of the page and demand an explanation.

Trevor and Liam. Raised together, practically blood brothers by the evidence splayed across the pages. Clara's mind rewound, shuffled through every statement, every memory, but couldn't recall any mention of a connection other than Liam saying he thought he'd met Trevor once or twice.

She fanned through the rest of the album, her hands trembling now. The boy reappeared in dozens of group shots: at the Harrington estate, on fishing trips, at birthday parties. There was a photo of Liam and Trevor perched atop the town's ancient stone ruins, both grinning, flanked by an older man who Clara guessed was Liam's father. That man's hand rested on Trevor's shoulder, not in affection, but in some grim, possessive grip. The message in the pose was clear: this one belongs to us.

The pages darkened as time advanced. Fewer photos, increasingly staged, the laughter sapped from the scenes. Clara noticed an odd pattern: in the last year the boys appeared together, Trevor's expression drifted from joy to an anxious wariness, while Liam's scowl deepened into something cold and practiced. The final image of them, taken on the day of high school graduation, showed the boys standing far apart, a chasm of unspoken resentment stretched between them. After that, Trevor vanished from the record. A neat, unnatural erasure.

Clara closed the album gently, as if worried she might disturb the ghosts shut inside. The significance of what she'd uncovered pressed against her, trembling at the edge of clarity. The Mills family wasn't merely entangled with the Harringtons by circumstance; they were bound by history, by secrets, by something rotten that spanned generations. She sensed the awful truth it suggested, though she couldn't quite grasp how the pieces fit together.

She pushed back from the desk, heart hammering, mind reeling. Her night had been sliced open and she needed air, needed to move, needed to find some new vantage from which to view the puzzle. She had to confront him.

———

She didn't knock. She entered Liam's bedroom at a full stride, transforming the air as abruptly as a burst of cold through a cracked window.

The room was all shadow and amber firelight, the hearth painting orange bands across the heavy curtains and the foot of the bed. Liam sat upright, sheets tangled at his waist, the weight of his presence somehow undiminished by the hour or the intimacy of the setting. He blinked once—registering, recalibrating—then composed himself with an economy of motion that told Clara how little she'd surprised him, even now.

His face was still and expectant, the faintest smile playing at the corner of his mouth. He looked like a king receiving a delegation, rather than a man presented with the evidence of his own past. Clara loathed him for that, and herself for the flicker of admiration it brought out in her.

She stood at the foot of the bed, breathing hard, and held the album at her side like a cudgel. Liam regarded it with a sardonic arch of the brow.

"Couldn't sleep?" he said, the words sanded down to the smoothest edges.

"Don't," Clara warned, voice raw. "I'm not here to talk in circles." She tossed the album onto the covers. It landed with a thud, disgorging a handful of loose photographs that fluttered toward his legs.

Liam looked down at them, then back at her. His composure was so complete it bordered on insolence.

"I haven't seen this in years. My mother was always a bit sentimental, strangely enough," he said. His tone was measured, unhurried. "May I get up?" He gestured to the fireplace, where the warmth invited a false sense of comfort. Clara shook her head.

Clara stepped closer. She could feel the thrum of her own pulse in her jaw and fingertips. "You've known all along," she said, acid in every syllable.

He didn't flinch. "Known what?"

"Don't play dumb." She snatched one of the loose photographs from the bedspread and held it up to the firelight. The image—Liam and Trevor, arm in arm, maybe twelve or thirteen, standing atop the mossy parapet of the old ruins—seemed to glow with an accusation all its own.

Liam watched her, and if the sight of Trevor Mills' younger self affected him, he gave no outward sign. Clara tossed the photo at his chest. It bounced and slid to the edge of the mattress.

She pressed forward. "You lied to me. About Trevor. About the Mills family. About everything."

He nodded, almost approvingly. "I admit, I wasn't as forthcoming as I might have been. But in my experience, directness is a privilege one rarely gets to enjoy in this life."

Clara laughed, a brittle sound. "That's rich, coming from you."

He shrugged. "It's in my blood."

"Is that what you tell yourself?" Clara asked. "That all the old secrets and power games are hereditary, so you get to wash your hands of responsibility?"

He considered that. "Not exactly. I would say, rather, that having a legacy means never being allowed to pretend that your choices are entirely your own. We're all haunted, Clara. Some of us by the past, others by what comes next."

She paced, staring at the fire, trying to rein in her urge to throw every question and accusation at him at once. The evidence of the album, the certainty in her gut that everything she'd uncovered so far was only the shallowest part of the truth—they pressed at her temples like a migraine poised to burst.

She wanted to scream, wanted to force the answers out of him. Her heart pounded a violent rhythm as she waited for him to fill the silence.

"It's really difficult to converse lying down like this, with you glowering over me. I'm getting…"

"Don't fucking move!" Clara yelled.

He shifted up a little, leaning his back against the headboard. The firelight caught the steel in his eyes. Clara watched him closely, alert to any sudden movement.

"Trevor Mills," she said.

316

"We Harringtons have quite an interesting history," Liam spoke casually, seeming to ignore her. "You've never asked much about it, almost as if you preferred not to know."

"Tell me about Trevor," she repeated.

He sighed. "Where would you like me to begin?"

"The truth. All of it. Why you acted like you barely knew Trevor. Why none of this showed up in the records I could find. Why you helped them disappear."

Liam smiled, but it was a tired, private gesture. "You already have most of your answers, Clara. I can't determine whether you want me to confess, or to simply confirm what you've already decided is true."

"Try me," she said.

He ran a hand through his hair, slow and deliberate. For a moment, Clara saw a flash of the boy from the photographs. A Liam before the mask of adulthood, before the layers of calculation. It was gone in an instant.

"When I was young, there were very few people in this town who treated me as an equal," he said. "Most kids just wanted things from me. The cache of a Harrington friend, or the security it someday might offer to their parents. Trevor was

317

different. He was clever in a way that scared even the teachers, and he never let me forget my place. He was always pushing, always challenging. It made me respect him, even when I wanted to strangle him for it."

Clara interrupted. "You don't respect anyone, Liam. You use them."

He gave a noncommittal shrug. "The two aren't mutually exclusive. But you're right that I used Trevor. I used his ambition, his need for belonging. I used all the ways he was different from the rest of this town. And he knew it. That was the real bond between us, not friendship. Mutual exploitation, dressed up as camaraderie."

"You used him to spy on Kane," Clara stated.

"Yes, that's where he was most useful. I could tell almost immediately that Kane would be an annoyance, someone who would need to be swatted away if and when he threatened to become something more."

It was evident to Clara that Liam was warming to his story now, was relishing the opportunity to demonstrate to her the depths of his intellect. He'd tell her everything, but he'd be even more dangerous once he did. She carefully eyed the poker by the fireplace. She might need to get to it fast.

"So you had him cozy up to Kane, and reporting back to you all the while."

"Correct. The town hates me and loves him, slaves to his empty oratory. I'd have to bide my time and tread carefully, which is what I always do. The long game, you see, is the Harrington specialty, from the moment my great-great-…"

"Where are they now?" she demanded, feeling the need to keep him on track.

"Oh, you won't find them," he smiled. "They're on the other side of the world, enjoying the fruits of their labor. A bit earlier than expected, I must say, thanks to you."

She had to take deep breaths, fighting the urge to despair. If it was true then John was beyond her grasp. She needed time to think.

"Your plan. The murder. I want you to walk me through it, from the beginning."

Liam leaned forward, the fire casting long shadows across his face. "The plan was simple. To use Kane's hatred of me against him. He's an impulsive man, quick to take advantage of an opportunity after only thinking it through once. His fatal flaw, you might say, is that his ambitions outpace his caution. A man like that, under the right circumstances, can be manipulated into doing something he wouldn't believe himself capable, something that will bring about his downfall."

He cast a knowing glance at Clara as he spoke. As if to say, *yes, I'm talking about you as well.*

It took her breath away. She tried to speak, but the words caught in her throat. Liam watched her, waited, let her process.

"Manipulated into doing something," Clara repeated. "You put John up to the murder."

"John's a brute. He'd be more a liability than an asset to me, unlike his father. So I offered him an opportunity, an initiation into the Harrington fold, as I believe I put it, after which I'd reward the family richly for their service. A ride off into the sunset, if you will, away from this forsaken place. The sad part, for the girl I mean, is that he didn't need any convincing at all."

The casual cruelty of it made her sick. How had she so badly misjudged him?

"You had most of it right," he continued, unaffected by the look she was giving him. "Except the hand guiding it all. But how could you? Kane himself couldn't see it."

"I wasn't part of the plan," Clara stated.

"Of course not. I didn't know quite what to make of you at first, I had to improvise a bit."

"So how was Kane supposed to be exposed?" she asked.

"You already saw the beginnings of it. Joe Mackenzie, that awful drunk, and the easiest of the workers to manipulate. To be honest he probably would have made the same scene of his own volition anyway. This is what I mean when I say Kane doesn't think things through enough. Trevor played his part during the confrontation to perfection. Fisher would have connected the dots eventually."

"And Mark Hogan?"

"Another bit of surprise!" Liam was practically gleeful. "I must say, I was quite proud of how deftly I handled that, using it to drive you out of town like that. It was perfect. Until your little revelation or whatever you said it was that brought you back. At that point I decided not to take any chances and ushered the Mills' out earlier than I originally intended."

"So that's it," Clara said.

"That's it," Liam repeated. "Other than you showing up at my doorstep and refusing to leave. Not that I fully minded, however. At first."

She saw the gleam in his eye and felt sick all over again. Sick beyond anything she'd felt before in a life that had more than its fair share of sickness. *Steady*, she told herself, *or you won't get through this.*

He seemed almost amused by her silence, as if savoring the tension that strung the air tight between them. "You are, of course, still free to go," Liam said, his voice unexpectedly gentle. "I understand you may not believe it at this moment, but I am—truly—quite fond of you, Clara."

She nearly spat at his feet. "Lies. Everything you've ever said to me is a lie."

He offered a ghost of a smile. "Not entirely true. The manipulation part, yes, I'll grant you that. What choice did I have, given who I am, who you are? But it's not all a game. I shared with you feelings I've never told another person. Things about my past, about this family, that I never intended to speak aloud. I see now that was foolish." He glanced at the photo album, the edge of it just visible from where Clara had thrown it aside. "What I didn't tell you, and probably never would have, is that as I grew older, as I grew further from the boy you saw in those pictures, I realized my feelings had to change. I had to become something bigger than my own life. Do you see? I had to—"

He hesitated, searching for words, then looked up at her with something almost like vulnerability. "I had to be a Harrington."

She felt a wave of revulsion. "You can just do whatever you want, to anyone, so long as it serves your 'legacy?' You think that excuses all of this?"

That seemed to get under his skin. "Don't be reductionist. You're smarter than that." He resettled on the mattress, his hands clasped. "You developed feelings for me when you recognized how similar we are, how we've been molded by our experiences and shaped into things we didn't expect to be. You're not so far from sharing my worldview as you think."

322

She tried to ignore the almost hypnotic cadence of his speech. Measured and deliberate, like a man building a case in court. "You murdered a girl. You orchestrated all of this. You terrorized and manipulated half the people in this town. Is that what you want me to respect?"

He set his jaw. "You have your own body count, Agent Reynolds. Not in Cedar Hollow, maybe, but you live with the things you've done. I can see it in you. We both know how it is to be haunted."

She forced a deep breath. "Don't you dare—"

He silenced her with a raised hand. "Let's not waste time with moral high ground. You're here because you want answers. I'm giving them to you. I could have lied. I could have played dumb. But I want you to understand the truth before you make your choice."

She shivered, the fire's warmth now only a memory. "What choice?"

A look of genuine regret passed across his face. "As I said, I'm fond of you. As a matter of fact, I was prepared to make you an offer of marriage had things gone a little differently for you here, had you not pieced yourself together a bit and made a success of things."

It was so absurd she almost laughed. "You'd make me your queen? Stand me up next to you as you keep killing for your sacred family line?"

He smirked at her, almost fondly. "I think you could have been the ideal wife for me."

She nearly saw red. "You're delusional."

He shrugged, the motion casual but his gaze never leaving hers. "There's no need for melodrama. Go back to the Bureau, I'll be quite happy for you. Leave Cedar Hollow, and that's the end of it."

"Do you think I can just walk away?" she breathed. "A girl is dead because of you. You tore apart her family and this whole town—"

"You won't be able to prove anything," he interrupted, his tone gentle but final. "You'll humiliate yourself if you try. Unless you intend to provoke a violent confrontation right now—" and here he paused, letting the threat shimmer between them—"there is no other option. That's not a threat, Clara. It's inevitability."

The air in the bedroom seemed to shrink, thickening until she could barely breathe. For a full minute neither of them moved, the fire snapping quietly in the hearth. Finally, Liam exhaled and stood, the movement slow, deliberate, as if he were defusing a bomb that might go off if he stepped wrong.

He padded to the fireplace, stoking the flames, then set aside the poker. He nodded to the two low chairs at the foot of the bed, but she stayed on her feet, every muscle in her body ready to snap. He didn't push; instead, he retreated to the liquor cabinet and poured two glasses of whiskey, sliding one toward her on the small table. "Suit yourself," he said when she ignored it.

She almost wished he would attack her, anything to break the deadlock. He leaned back against the mantle, with folded arms, expression utterly at ease.

"It's a shame, really," he said after a while, voice barely above a whisper. "If you'd accepted my proposal, you could have saved us both a great deal of trouble. Whatever you think of me, the other Harrington branch is infinitely worse. I've kept them at arm's length for years, but without an heir, I'll have very little leverage. I really did think it was fate, the two of us. A clever woman, ambitious, with the right instincts—" He trailed off, eyes glazing with some private nostalgia.

"I don't care about any of it. Shut up and let me think," she said, voice ragged.

His words made her sick, but Clara recognized the ploy: keep her agitated, keep her unbalanced. She struggled to keep focus, her mind running possibilities. She was armed with nothing but her own rage and the fire poker, and she doubted she could reach it first if it came to that. She regretted confronting him in the open, but she could not bear to withdraw now, even when every instinct screamed at her to run, regroup, return with backup.

He was circling her now, not quite predatory, not quite affectionate, just gradually forcing her toward the window, the fire's warmth at her back. She kept her stance, watching for any flicker of intent.

"I was being honest, earlier. Youth is a rebellion, but my father showed me what it means to truly be a Harrington. The responsibility. The horror. It's a sentence, not a privilege." He looked away, almost ashamed, before recovering his poise. "Everything I've done, every miserable thing, was for a reason."

"And what's the reason for murder?" she asked, trembling now.

He exhaled, calm returning. "Sometimes violence is the only way, when you're defending something greater. You know this. I can see it in your eyes."

He stepped past her to the bookshelf, knelt, and withdrew a slim, leather-bound volume. On the cover was a symbol she recognized from the ruins: a spiral locked inside an angular cross. He set it on the table between them.

"It goes back farther than you can imagine. The symbols are a code, instructions for us to carry out. The legacy isn't in the name, or even the bloodline. It's in the obligation." He traced the sigil with one delicate finger. "We're custodians. The things we've done, the things we must do, all have a purpose. A purpose higher than ourselves."

My god, he's insane, she thought, *or he's trying to drive me insane.* It was working too. Her whole body was shaking now, swallowed up in rage, confusion, and fear to the point where she could barely control it.

The knife sprouted from her left thigh, no warning, no sense of motion or even intent from Liam, just a white-hot steel flower blooming in her flesh. The pain was so immediate and total it seemed to erase all time before it. Clara dropped to one knee, her leg refusing to hold her, and as her hand instinctively went to the hilt, a second blade zipped past—so close above her head she felt the parting of her hair in its wake.

She didn't remember seeing him grab the knives; she didn't remember him moving at all. In that split second she feared he must have hidden blades all over the room, that he'd been preparing for this confrontation since the moment she arrived, perhaps for weeks, months, years. Panic rattled up her spine.

The room shattered, fragments of sense and sound spinning in a kaleidoscopic blur. She tasted copper and ozone and the sharp mineral tang of her own sweat. She saw the fire flicker, the shadows crawl along the spines of old law books, portraits of dead Harringtons leering from their eternal frames, and the library itself spinning violently as she tried to stagger to her feet. Instinct—some ugly, primitive survival code—kicked her body into gear. She rolled left, crashing through the lacquered side table and knocking loose the lamp, which tumbled, fracturing on the hardwood. The room went dark. Only the fireplace threw light, pulsing orange and furious, turning everything else into a theater of jagged silhouettes.

She landed hard and used the momentum to slide her back along the rug toward the hearth. Liam's slippers squeaked as he circled, the drag-sound of silk on wood. She heard him rummage, maybe at the bar, maybe in the closet. Somewhere she couldn't see, which was what mattered. She made for the fireplace tools. Her left hand, sticky with blood, closed around the poker, blessedly heavy and well-balanced, the comfortingly mundane weight of it at war with the utter derangement of the moment. She hefted it, pivoted onto her uninjured leg, and scanned the room.

She pressed her thigh tight with her palm, trying to slow the flow, and staggered to the corner of the room. One wall at her back, poker in both hands, she braced herself for his reappearance, half-expecting him to bide his time, let her bleed out, savoring the inevitability of it. Instead, he walked into her line of sight, unarmed, arms out like a supplicant, the face he wore eerily unchanged from the man who'd been calmly reciting family history five minutes earlier.

He launched himself at her, his speed astonishing. He was on her before she could ready the poker for a full swing: she clubbed at his shoulder and he ducked under it, grappling with her arms, twisting her around. She felt the hot lines of his breath on her ear as they crashed together into the wall. She jabbed with the poker but missed and struck the window frame, planting a desperate spiderweb of cracks in the old glass.

Her left leg buckled and she nearly toppled, but in the maelstrom of pain her senses had gone razor-edged, able to instinctively sense his next moves. He switched tactics, shoving her to the ground, and only then did she see the glint of the second blade in his hand—a paring knife, butcher-bright, which he must have grabbed from the bar. He slashed at her face and she jerked back, the blade skidding off her cheekbone with a cold, almost polite sting. She jammed the fire poker into his ribs and heard—not a crunch, not a crack, but a deep, instinctual sound, an animal gasp. He let go of her hair and staggered back, and for a second she thought he'd retreat, but some perverse inertia kept him coming, face twisted with something between regret and disbelief.

He flicked the knife at her belly; she dodged, the blade just grazing her shirt. She whirled, grabbed a whiskey bottle from the sideboard, and flung it at his head. It missed, smashing against a column by the fireplace, sending up a volatile cloud. Clara, dizzy with loss of blood, swayed sideways, caught herself on the mantel, and swung the poker again, clipping his forearm. The smell of burning flesh hit her—the poker had picked up heat from the fire, and where it struck him it sizzled, just for a moment.

"You were supposed to leave, Clara," he said, panting. "Why couldn't you just leave?" He sounded—she couldn't believe it—hurt.

She didn't answer, only advanced, limping, brandishing the poker. The pain in her thigh was multiplying, bright nodes of heat radiating out to her calf and hip. She could feel the blood pooling in her boot, sticky and warm, and every step required a new, superhuman act of will.

He feinted to her right and tried to get behind her; this time she anticipated and swung, narrowly missing his temple. He dropped low, sweeping her bad leg, and she crumpled, but brought the poker down on his back, eliciting a coarse yelp. They rolled together, crashing into the bookshelf. Tomes rained down on them, dust and old paper and the scent of mold. Her fist closed over the knife still in her thigh—she screamed as she pulled it free, the world going completely white for an instant. Using the momentum, she thrust it upward—not at him, not at anything, just, out, away from herself, and by dumb animal luck the blade caught the inside of his bicep, severing something deep. Blood, his now, splattered her face.

He howled and reeled away. She rolled to her side, the poker still clamped in her right hand, and forced herself up, using the window ledge for leverage. In the glass she saw her own ruin: hair wild, face slick with sweat and blood, eyes doubled or tripled by the cracks. She blinked, trying to steady herself. The room was a gallery of violence, liquor pooling beneath the broken glass, the floor littered with books and shattered family relics.

He was behind her, silent but not stealthy. She could feel the displacement of air, the tremor in the floorboards. She spun, put every ounce of what was left into the swing, and caught him square in the jaw with the poker. It was an awful sound, akin to stepping through mud. He stumbled backward, crashing into the armchair. For a moment he looked so strange, so dazed and lost, she might have pitied him.

But as she watched, he recovered, got up, and came for her again. His eyes were glassy, his right arm half-useless, but the rest of him was pure engine. He pulled another knife from somewhere—pocket, maybe, or sleeve, or hidden in the armchair's cushions—and this one he held with absolute calm, point down. Almost gentle.

She braced herself against the window. "Don't," she said, and her voice was hoarse, nearly gone. Her vision tunneled; the world shrank to just that knife, just the blue-white shimmer of its edge.

He didn't hesitate. He lunged.

Time did not slow. There was no cinematic pause to weigh consequences or regrets. There was only impact, the collision of bodies, and the force of his mass knocking her backwards into the fractured glass. She felt the icepick cold of the new knife entering her left shoulder. She choked, coughed once, and brought the poker around, stabbing it through his neck.

For a second nothing happened. Then he made a noise and let go of the knife, staggering back. She looked down and saw the poker jutting from the side of his throat, blood spilling down his pajamas in a roaring, surreal flood. He clamped a hand to the wound, looked at her with perfect clarity, and then collapsed face-forward onto the rug.

She waited, breathless, watching for any twitch or sign of life. Her own vision was fading around the edges, the world shrinking to a funnel aimed directly at Liam's corpse. The fire in the hearth hissed, wood collapsing, scattering embers onto the flagstones.

She closed her eyes, opened them again. He hadn't moved. Still, she made herself wait. Give it another minute, two, ten. She could last. She was nothing if not stubborn.

Her blood smeared on the floor. The pain had become secondary, a background radiation. Her hands didn't shake anymore. Maybe she was in shock, maybe she was dying, but the only thing she felt was a dull, exhausted certainty.

When she was finally sure Liam wasn't getting up, she used the window ledge to force herself upright, wobbled across the room, and out into the hallway. Every step felt like walking on glass. Her phone was in her jacket on a chair by the front door; she fumbled it free with numb fingers.

She dialed 911, but when she tried to speak, nothing came out but a wet rattle. Maybe she managed "Harrington house," maybe not. A rattling hush poured into her head, louder and louder. She felt herself slide to the floor again, the world softening under her. The last thing she saw before her vision went black was a streak of blood on the banister, red as memory.

Chapter 23

She came to in a haze of white light, the hospital's ceiling tiles over her head like dots on a test card. There was no sound for a long time except the distant squall of machines. Every part of her body ached as if she were filled with battery acid, but at least the pain was less of a knife, more of a dull, sullen pressure. Her right wrist was bound to the side rail and she was afraid, for a moment, that she was under arrest. Then she realized it was only to keep the IV in place.

A nurse noticed she was awake and called for someone. Clara's mouth was so dry it hurt to swallow.

The doctor was a small, jumpy man with a fading accent she couldn't place. He checked her pupils, nodded, then left her alone. The nurse administered something through the IV and said, "You're all right, Agent Reynolds. We've got you." Coincidentally: not the first time Clara Reynolds had heard that exact phrase. She wanted to laugh, but she was afraid it would hurt too much.

They'd patched the wounds—her thigh, her shoulder, even the superficial slash on her cheek. She was stitched and bandaged and, if the nurse was to be believed, in "stable but serious" condition. The room was private, with a single chair in the corner and a whiteboard listing the date and nurse's names. Clara stared at the board until her eyes crossed.

She drifted in and out for what felt like hours, then days. When she finally opened her eyes again it was dark outside, and a familiar figure sat next to her bed.

Sheriff Fisher looked worse than she felt. His right hand was wrapped in a brace, and the bags under his eyes made him look twenty years older. He regarded her with a complex mix of awe, relief, and something else. Maybe suspicion, or maybe sorrow.

"It's over, you know," he said quietly.

She nodded. Or tried to. "Liam?"

"Dead," Fisher said, with no joy. "House was a mess. We had to call in the state troopers just to process the scene. You're lucky you survived."

She wanted to say so much. She only croaked, "What day is it?"

"Thursday," he said. "You've been out two days."

She let that sink in, the numbness of the word Thursday, the fact that days had passed and the world was still stubbornly here, holding itself together by inertia.

"You'll have to make a statement," Fisher added, but it didn't sound like a threat.

The effort to smile felt like a journey of its own. Clara's voice cracked through a dry throat, echoing with disbelief. "I killed him."

"That much I figured. Are you able to tell me what happened?"

Her memories were shards, fragments, and she pieced them together slowly. The house, the fight, the blood. She saw Liam's face in the blur, the anger and shock. She spoke slowly, carefully, as if one wrong word might shatter everything.

"Damn," he said. "You're lucky that second knife missed. Don't worry, there won't be any charges."

"The family. Have you heard from them?" she asked.

"A few of them are coming to settle affairs." He paused. "I was instructed through their lawyer to pass on a message to you."

"What?" she asked, gasping.

"'Thank you,'", he replied. "That's it."

The words were absurd, shocking, a spark in the numbness. Clara tried to absorb them, tried to let them in, but they slipped past like everything else.

"What does that mean?"

"I don't want to speculate, but it seems you don't have anything to worry about from them."

Clara lay still, thoughtful. "He said they were worse than he was."

He laughed. "That'll be tough. Sounds like he was just throwing crazy stuff out there, trying to distract you enough to pounce."

"Maybe." She believed it, mostly. "But you can't trust them."

"No worries on that count. I'll keep an eye on them."

"You sure you can handle it?" she asked.

"Fairly sure. For a satanic cult they're a bunch of amateurs, really. A few hundred years and all they've managed to accomplish is torment a small town."

She laughed uncontrollably. The stress of the past few weeks seemed to vanish along with it.

"I take it you've decided to finally hightail it out of here?" he asked.

"Yes," she said, turning serious again. "I think it's time."

"Good, because I have another message for you. From Director Bryant. Your boss I take it?"

"Oh boy, let me have it," she said.

"He said if this is what you're going to get up to on your damn vacation you might as well get back to work. He some kind of hard ass?"

"He's not too bad," she said with a grin.

"Guess they do want you back," he said, then paused. "It really was a pleasure."

"I can still help track down the Mills'. It may take a while, but I won't give up."

"They'll turn up. They don't have their protector anymore and don't have the discipline to lie low forever. I wouldn't worry about it. Now get some rest, I'll be back when they're ready to discharge you."

She watched the sheriff leave and, in the dark, turned over the image of Liam on the rug, his life seeping out onto the expensive wool. She wondered if the other Harrington branch really was worse, whether someone would now step in to fill his place, whether the legacy could ever be drowned, even in blood.

Sleep came slow and heavy. When it finally took her, she dreamed not of the past, nor of the fight, nor even of Liam's last breath, but of the forest outside Cedar Hollow, thick with fog and whispering voices, the ruins shining with morning dew and the hidden promise of winter.

She woke to a nurse adjusting her IV and sunlight filling the room like a silent blessing. The pain was present but manageable, like an old scar. The nurse told her that Emma had been by when she was asleep. Clara knew she'd have to stop by to let her know there were no hard feelings before she left town.

That night, Clara lay awake, listening to the subtle machinery of the hospital, the comings and goings of staff, the shifting of her own blood through the narrow passageways of her battered body. She wondered what it would be like back in Omaha, if any city would feel real after the haunted claustrophobia of Cedar Hollow. Behind her eyelids, the images replayed—the knives, the rage, the sick intimacy of killing a man who she'd felt something for. She saw the Harrington crest in miniature, burned into the flesh of her memory.

The Harrington legacy was a wound, and some wounds never really heal. They scar and ache and, sometimes, bleed anew. But in the end, she decided, you could survive them.

She had plenty of shame and regret about how a lot of it went down, yet there was no denying that she was leaving the town with a renewed sense of purpose and confidence. It was hard fought, she realized now these things must be, but it felt earned, unshakable. For the first time, in perhaps her whole life, she felt a true sense of who she was and what she

339

could accomplish. Now it was time to get back to work.

Acknowledgments

Thanks to Pete and Rosemary for the editing and other helpful suggestions.

What's Next for Clara Reynolds

Clara's story doesn't end here. Her next case is already in progress — darker, more dangerous, and closer to home than she ever imagined.

Stay tuned for the next installment in the **Clara Reynolds Thriller** series, coming soon.

About the Author

Colin Anthony has written several books in his head over the years before finally putting one down on paper. After years of imagining stories and characters, he took the leap to share his work with readers. He lives in New Jersey with his wife and two sons, where the daily rhythms of family life continue to inspire his writing journey.

Thank You

If you enjoyed NOTHING CLEAR REMAINS, please consider leaving a review on Amazon.

Printed in Dunstable, United Kingdom